"This is dangerous, Lorabeth."

It felt right to raise her hand to his face and rest her fingertips against his cheek. It was an intimate touch. Foreign. Forbidden. Exciting.

"Because you want to kiss me?"

He nodded without speaking.

"I want you to."

He turned and took her head in both hands, pulling her to him for a meeting of lips. The kiss detonated, setting off a robust clamor in her heart and a throbbing rush of heat to her limbs.

Lorabeth's senses reeled. Nothing had prepared her for this rush of desire, for the desperate craving she had for this man. She wanted to belong to him, possess him, crush him to her and never let go.

* * *

The Preacher's Daughter
Harlequin® Historical #851—June 2007

Praise for Cheryl St.John

His Secondhand Wife

Nominated for a RITA® Award

"A beautifully crafted and involving story about the transforming power of love, this is recommended reading."

—*Romantic Times BOOKreviews*

Prairie Wife

Nominated for a *Romantic Times BOOKreviews* Reviewers' Choice Award

"*Prairie Wife* is a very special book, courageously executed by the author and her publisher. Her considerable skill brings the common theme of the romance novel—love conquers all—to the level of genuine catharsis."

—*Romantic Times BOOKreviews* [4½ stars]

The Tenderfoot Bride

"Cheryl St.John once again touches the hearts of readers. Not many readers will be able to hold back their tears as they reach the conclusion."

—*Romance Reviews Today*

The Preacher's Daughter

CHERYL ST. JOHN

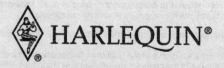

HARLEQUIN®

TORONTO • NEW YORK • LONDON
AMSTERDAM • PARIS • SYDNEY • HAMBURG
STOCKHOLM • ATHENS • TOKYO • MILAN • MADRID
PRAGUE • WARSAW • BUDAPEST • AUCKLAND

ISBN-13: 978-0-373-29451-0
ISBN-10:   0-373-29451-4

THE PREACHER'S DAUGHTER

Copyright © 2007 by Cheryl Ludwigs

This edition published by arrangement with Harlequin Books S.A.

® and TM are trademarks of the publisher. Trademarks indicated with ® are registered in the United States Patent and Trademark Office, the Canadian Trade Marks Office and in other countries.

www.eHarlequin.com

Printed in U.S.A.

Author Note

So many readers asked for more stories set in Newton, Kansas, and were especially eager for a story about Benjamin Chaney. It took me a while to come up with a story and a woman I felt was deserving of him. If you've read THE DOCTOR'S WIFE or THE LAWMAN'S BRIDE, then you're aware that Benjamin is a special guy. He required the perfect woman—or the most interesting one I could give him, anyway. So I listed three different types of young ladies and under each I tallied up why this person would create the most conflict. The preacher's daughter won, hands down. I hope you enjoy reading Ben and Lorabeth's story as much as I enjoyed creating it for you.

Prologue

Florence, Kansas, 1878

Sounds woke him. A shoe scraping against the floor. Muttered conversation. The clink of a bottle. Familiar sounds. The smelly fire had gone out hours ago, and the tiny cabin was cold.

Ben buried his head beneath his arm, adjusted his bony hip against the inadequate padding between him and the floorboards, and slid closer to his younger brother for warmth. Flynn's belly growled in his sleep. They hadn't had a meal since early that morning, and it had consisted of eggs and milk his sister had stolen.

"Wake up." A man's voice. Gruff in the silence of the room.

Ben peered through the darkness to see the man touch his sister's shoulder. Several feet away, she jerked and sat up. A light shone from behind the threadbare blanket that served as a divider between this sleeping area and their mother's, enough light to see that the figure leaning over her was one of Della Foster's nighttime callers.

"What do you want?" Ben's sister whispered, shrugging the man's hand from her shoulder.

"Come quickly. Your mother has taken a fall and I need your help to get her back inside."

Ben sat up. "I'll help."

Ellianna pulled on her moth-eaten sweater over her underwear. "No, you stay here with Flynn," she whispered and tiptoed around their younger brother where he lay. "It's just Mama needing help to get to bed again. I can do it."

She followed the man around the blanket curtain.

Ben sat up and looked at Flynn. Getting to his feet, he peeked to see that his mother truly wasn't in the cabin. Sometimes she had trouble walking right. And she could be really heavy when she was like that. After tiptoeing to the door in stockinged feet, he stepped outside.

From a little farther on Ellianna asked, "Where is she?"

"Here," the man replied. "Over here."

"I don't see her," she answered.

"In here."

Ben followed behind quietly. A horse and carriage sat a hundred yards from the shack. Mama was in that buggy? She never went anywhere.

Ellianna was peering into the carriage.

Ben had a bad feeling. Was Mama dead? Had something really bad happened to her?

"I don't see anything," Ellianna said.

Winston Parker grabbed her around the back of the neck. "Get inside."

"No! No, I—"

"It wasn't a question." He shoved her into the carriage and she fell. "Get in!"

"Stop!" Ben scrambled forward, reaching them just as Winston pushed Ellianna all the way inside and tried to climb in behind her and shut the door.

"Let her out of there! Where's Mama?" Ben grabbed the man's arm, and Parker flung him away. He pushed Ellianna flat on her stomach and she cried out.

Parker clamped a hand over her mouth and she clawed at him, blindly reaching for his eyes, his throat. His hand slipped and she managed a scream.

Terrified now, Ben beat at the man's back and head with all his might. A fist met with his jaw and he fell back on the hard earth, seeing stars, momentarily stunned.

The carriage door slammed shut.

Ellie's muffled cries shot terror through him. "Mama!"

Ben turned and ran for the house. "Mama! Help Ellie! You have to help Ellie! That man's hurting her!"

Ben had to help her. But how? His eight-year-old brain thought over the meager contents of the room and settled on an iron skillet. He grabbed it and ran out the door.

His mother came stumbling onto the porch at that moment, a bag in the crook of her arm.

"Mama! Help Ellie! Hurry!"

She pushed him away and yanked the squeaky door open.

Ben grabbed her arm. "You gotta help her! He's hurtin' her!"

She pulled away and carried her bag inside.

Ben stared after his mother for a moment, then

shook himself into action and tore back to the carriage. There was no one but him to help Ellianna. No one but him who cared.

He pounded the carriage door with the skillet, beat the handle until it fell to the ground, but still the door didn't budge. Inside he heard muffled crying, and it wasn't long until his own wail drowned out his sister's.

He wasn't big enough or strong enough to help her.

Chapter One

Her mother had died of boredom. Tedium. Monotony. Lorabeth Holdridge looked up from the worn Bible on her lap to her father, sitting with his eyes closed in prayer. She was convinced that no one could spend every night of their life in this manner without a little piece of their dreams drying up and dying week by week, month by month, until finally there was nothing left alive and their spirit simply left their body.

Beneath her backside, the hard wooden chair deliberately kept her from being too comfortable or allowing her mind to wander. Her father would consider it sinful, but her imagination had been her escape to alluring places ever since she'd been old enough to know there was more to life than this.

She glanced at her seventeen-year-old brother. She'd been waiting to make waves until she was sure he could take care of himself without her here. Until she knew he'd be okay. Simon stifled a yawn behind his hand and raised dark eyes, dull from boredom, to hers.

She crossed her eyes.

The corner of his mouth twitched in an effort to keep a smile from forming.

Ambrose Holdridge reached over and thumped Simon on the knee. He gave Lorabeth a stern look that told her he knew she was the instigator of this disruption.

A knock sounded on the back door. It wasn't unusual for a caller to arrive of an evening, a parishioner needing prayer or a bit of advice.

"Continue in my absence," their father said, and left the room.

As soon as Lorabeth heard voices in the kitchen, she whispered, "I'm dying here, Simon."

"You'll meet a man," he began.

"Where? Where will I meet a man when I stay at the Chaneys' all week, then obey Father's demands and come home on Friday evening so I can clean, do laundry and tend the garden all weekend? Sundays I play the piano for church, prepare your dinner, bake and iron. Monday morning I head back to the Chaneys' until the next Friday night. My only moments to myself are late at night after the Chaney children are asleep."

"You convinced Father to let you take that job," he said.

"And I love it. I do," she said earnestly. "I'm not complaining about the work. It takes me away from… from this." But she'd been functioning at this frantic pace for nearly two years. Now that she'd seen how other people lived and the freedom they enjoyed, she could no longer wait.

Only three chairs remained around the hearth. Her older sister Ruthann had married and now lived in Florence with her husband and new son. Her younger brother Jubal had married and was farming a few miles away.

"I've prayed *hard* for that husband, Simon." She curled one hand into a frustrated fist. Though Lorabeth slept very little, when she did, she often dreamed of a man with a wild untamed spirit like hers. Someone handsome, Lord, she constantly entreated, but not taken with himself. Someone filled with life and vitality who would slash open new horizons and show her the world she craved.

"I know how badly you wanted to attend university," Simon said with regret in his eyes.

Her father had staunchly refused. University was too worldly for a pure young woman, held too many risks and offered far too much exposure to unseemly conduct. She had responsibilities to the family and to the work of the church.

"I'd be happy for you if you got to go," she assured him. She'd always gone through the motions and done what was expected, but she'd never really felt alive or content until she'd worked in the Chaneys' home, until she'd lived in the midst of their family. But glimpses weren't enough. Hearing their laughter and watching her employers with their children exposed the aching emptiness that had existed hidden inside Lorabeth her entire life. The memory of her mother, thin and pale on her sick bed, begging Lorabeth not to settle for less than her dreams had been nagging at her every waking moment.

For months she'd been thinking that perhaps there

was an answer besides the elusive husband she'd been praying for. Perhaps there was a way to take those last few steps away from her father's suffocating control.

"I have a plan," she said, keeping her voice low. "You'll be left on your own for now, but before long you will leave, too. You'll find someone special. All the young ladies in church are taken with you."

He grinned. "What's your plan?"

The back door closed and footsteps sounded on the wooden floor in the hallway. Promptly, brother and sister sat back and composed themselves.

Lorabeth closed her eyes and waited with her heart pounding.

Her father's chair creaked. "Mrs. Jenkins brought eggs," he said.

"I need to speak with you, Father," she said. Carefully, Lorabeth worked out the correct words in her head.

He fastened his stern gaze on her. "Can it not wait, daughter?"

"I have waited," she told him. *A lifetime.* Her memory dredged up images of her mother, more weary, more downtrodden as each year passed and hope steadily ebbed away. "This is the only chance I have that I'm not baking or doing laundry or sitting in church."

He raised a censuring eyebrow. "A virtuous woman looketh well to the ways of her household and eateth not the bread of idleness."

That same Proverbs Thirty-one woman had a husband who praised her and children who rose up and called her blessed, but Lorabeth bit her tongue instead of pointing out that this was not her own household. Arguing that she was quite inconveniently the last Holdridge female left would only be hurtful, and she would never hurt him. "It's just that this is my only opportunity to speak with you," she said as respectfully as she knew how.

"Very well. What's on your heart?"

Ellie Chaney hadn't asked Lorabeth to work any more days than she already did, but Lorabeth's future depended on her belief that the woman would be glad to have her living with them full-time. She chose her words and said, "Mrs. Chaney is expecting another child soon."

Her father lifted the same dark eyebrow.

"She could use more help on weekends."

"What about your duties at home?" her father predictably asked. "It's well and good that you are able to help the doctor's wife with her children, but not at the cost of your own family."

"I'm twenty-one years old, Father," she pointed out. "Ruthann was living away from home when she was nineteen."

"She had a husband of her own to care for. You do not."

As if she needed that pointed out. Her neck and cheeks warmed at his reminder. She composed her thoughts before speaking aloud. "I believe I'm old enough to make important decisions for myself."

His fingers twitched on the Bible he held on his knees. With her heart racing, she anticipated his objections.

Simon darted a look at his father. He seemed to be waiting as breathlessly as Lorabeth.

"I do want your approval and your blessing, of course," she added. "And I don't wish to leave you without help. I'm sure I could arrange to come over one or two mornings a week to do laundry. Perhaps I could mention to the Widow Hinz that though the pies she brings you are welcome, bread would be more practical."

The woman who had taken over as proprietress of the bakery after her husband's death five years ago supplied the Holdridge men with pastries each week.

"And of course I'll still be in church on Sunday mornings." She was proud of herself that her voice hadn't been pleading or begging, though her heart was on callused knees in supplication.

Simon studied his father for another minute, but clamped his eyelids shut when Ambrose glanced in his direction.

"As you say, Lorabeth, you are a grown woman," Ambrose began. "I can see that you've given this matter much thought."

She nodded. "Yes, sir."

"I've trained you up in the way you should go. Now that you are older, I must trust that you will not depart from those ways."

Her relief was like a weightlessness that started at her feet and worked its way upward. His consent was all she'd hoped for. "I won't, Father."

"I will talk with Dr. Chaney to remind him of the enormity of his responsibility while you are living under his roof."

"He's a wonderful man, Father. And Mrs. Chaney is a remarkable woman. I'm completely safe in their home."

"I would be more confident if he attended services on a more regular basis."

"He's a doctor. He's often called away to help people.

Mrs. Chaney is always in church with her children and her brothers."

Her father nodded. "Very well, Lorabeth. You have my blessing to live in the Chaneys' home."

She wanted to jump up and hug him, skip and dance around the parlor, shout her joy to the rafters—sing, even! But she held it all inside, a warm tingling expectation that buoyed her young woman's heart and sang hallelujahs through her veins until her limbs quivered.

"Now we shall continue with our prayer time," Ambrose directed.

Lorabeth felt like a butterfly that had emerged from its cocoon inside a glass jar and the lid was finally being unscrewed.

Oh, thank You, Lord! Thank You that by next week I will be free! Thank You I can buy some pretty things for my room at the Chaneys'. Help me find time to stop at the library. Oh, and please help Simon find a good wife.

Lorabeth closed her eyes and smiled with her heart.

Lorabeth could hardly contain her excitement the following morning. She hummed a cheerful tune as she snipped flowers from the tidy garden and arranged them in a vase to place before the pulpit, then picked up her pocketbook and Bible. Simon held open the back door and she met his eyes as she passed him.

"I've seen the doctor's home," he whispered. "It's big. Do you have your own room?"

"I do. The quilt on the bed was one of Mrs. Chaney's wedding gifts. It's red and blue, Simon. She wears colorful dresses and she laughs and plays with the children. The doctor reads them bedtime stories from books of fables written by a man named Aesop. I wish you could see it all. I wish I could take you with me."

She took her place beside her brother as they walked the width of their yard behind their father to the United Congregational Church next door.

"They truly are good people?"

"Truly," she assured him.

He gave a nod and touched the back of her hand. "Don't worry about me, Lorabeth. This is my last year of school and then I plan to apprentice to one of the tradesmen in town."

He was a thoughtful young man, and she appreciated his effort to set her mind at ease regarding his welfare.

This morning she didn't mind arriving an hour before service or straightening the hymnals on the backs of the pews or dusting the organ and the windowsills.

Her father handed her a sheet of paper listing the hymns they would be singing that morning, so she took a seat at the organ and practiced the chords and notes she could play without music. She turned to the pages anyway, because her father thought it looked prideful and careless to have the music memorized.

When the people began filtering into the building, she watched for the Chaneys. Eighteen-year-old Flynn, Ellie's younger brother was the first family member she saw, and he was carrying three-year-old Anna on his arm. Her red-blond hair had been threaded with blue ribbon and fashioned into two braids.

Lorabeth noted that her father was occupied in a conversation before hurrying to the aisle where the Chaney family had begun to settle. Five-year-old Lillith greeted her with a hug, so Anna leaned from her uncle's arms to do the same. Nate and David, ten and eight, had their heads together as though they were concocting a scheme, but David looked up to notice her and both boys grinned ear to ear. Nate was the spitting image of his brown-haired father while David had Ellie's violet eyes and delicate chin.

Finally she reached Ellie. Caleb was holding his wife's elbow to guide her into their row. Lorabeth had to hurry to the pew ahead and lean over the back to speak to her employer. "Ellie! No, don't get up."

"Good morning, Lorabeth." Ellie stood for a hug anyway, a challenging task because of the girth she carried out front. Her friends were predicting twins. Her lilac-colored dress made her eyes look almost purple. Her delicate appearance belied a strength of character Lorabeth had grown to appreciate. "You're positively glowing this morning."

"I have exciting news," she explained. "My father has given his blessing for me to stay with you *permanently*. I can be there with you even on Saturdays and Sundays from now on."

Ellie's smiled dimmed slightly.

Lorabeth's breath hitched in her chest.

"This is such a surprise," Ellie said. "I don't know what to think."

Lorabeth had placed all her hopes on Ellie accepting her. She'd faced her father and won his approval. If Ellie didn't want her full-time, her dream would be dashed. She'd been so sure. She'd been so…impulsive.

"Are you sure you want to do that?" Ellie asked, concern creasing her brow. "You're a young woman, Lorabeth. You deserve time for yourself. I don't expect you to work seven days a week. You do so much for me now, and I can't afford to pay you what you're worth."

"My pay is sufficient, that's not a problem. And I won't work seven days. If it's all right with you, I'll take a couple of mornings off during the week." Lorabeth's heart pounded in apprehension.

"But of course it's all right." Ellie grasped Lorabeth's hand. "I don't know what I would do without you. You're the best present I ever got."

Relief lifted the cloak of concern from Lorabeth and she could breathe again. Tears smarted behind her eyes.

"No more than you deserve, my dear." Caleb Chaney had overheard and now wrapped his arm protectively around his wife's shoulders.

"If you're certain this is what you want, then I'm delighted," Ellie told her, still clinging to her hand.

There was no doubt in her mind. She had promised her mother she wouldn't abandon her dreams, and this was an important step toward keeping that promise. "I'm certain."

The room had grown quiet. Lorabeth turned to find people settled in their pews and her father casting her a stern look from his place behind the pulpit. She gave Ellie a last appreciative smile, then squeezed her hand before releasing it and hurrying to her seat at the organ. She played the introduction to the first hymn, and the people stood.

A tall, broad-shouldered latecomer entered, casting

a long shadow in the patch of sunlight on the smooth wooden floor before closing the door behind him. He removed his hat, revealing sandy-colored hair, and moved forward along the outside aisle to join his family.

Benjamin Chaney, Newton's young veterinarian, took a seat beside his brother, Flynn, at the end of the Chaney pew, and little Anna immediately reached for him. He and Flynn weren't actually Chaneys, from what Lorabeth understood. Shortly after Caleb and Ellie were married, the doctor had adopted her two brothers.

Benjamin had his own place and was still somewhat of a mystery to Lorabeth. Though he'd established his practice the better part of a year ago, all she knew of him was what she observed on Sundays and the occasional brief times he stopped by the house, and that was that he was part of a close-knit family unlike anything she'd ever experienced in her own household.

Lorabeth didn't know much about Ellie's life before she'd married Caleb. No relatives other than Caleb's ever visited or were mentioned. From all she'd observed, the Chaneys were a tight-knit, loving family.

And they were the key to liberation she'd always wanted and yearned for. Lorabeth played with new determination, glancing up often to appreciate the family into which she had ingratiated herself. Becoming a permanent part of their household would be a dream come true. The past two years had been the best of her life, but to truly fulfill her wishes she would have to work doubly hard and prove herself. She prayed she was up to the task.

Chapter Two

"Benjamin, you should sell the house in town and live in the other one," his sister Ellie said as she placed a bowl of steaming mashed potatoes on the table. "How can you keep up both places when you're so busy?"

It was a customary Sunday dinner at his sister's. Ben still wasn't used to this house. He hadn't been living with them when they'd moved here. He'd gone to university only a few years after Caleb and Ellie had married, and during that time more children had been born to them. As their family had grown, Caleb and Ellie had needed more space. The seven-bedroom dwelling had belonged to a railroad tycoon and had sat empty for a year before Caleb bought it.

"It's just a house," his sister was saying. "Be practical. Sell it."

The house she referred to was the one they'd all lived in together. Ben was buying it from Caleb on monthly payments, but he'd also purchased property and buildings on the outskirts of town for his veterinary practice.

He had needed stables and a place to do surgery. The new place had been a necessity, but he couldn't let the old one go. There were too many memories in those rooms.

"You might as well be talking into a bucket," Caleb said to his wife.

Ellie looked at Benjamin. "You're not listening to me, are you?"

He shook his head with a grin.

"Sit down, Ellie." Caleb pulled out a chair and insisted that his wife take a seat. "I'll bring the rest of the food from the kitchen. Flynn will help."

Ben's brother jumped up to assist. Caleb was more like a father to him than a brother-in-law. Flynn would walk over hot coals to please Caleb.

Though Flynn was eighteen, he was still finishing school. He'd only attended one or two years before coming to live with Caleb and Ellie. He hadn't caught up as quickly as Ben, though he'd accomplished a significant achievement and would earn his diploma this year.

Ben discussed school with Nate and David until the food was all set and bowls passed.

Caleb paused behind Ellie, his hand on her shoulder, and leaned down to speak near her ear. She turned to look at her husband with such tenderness in her expression that an ache expanded in Benjamin's chest. She cupped Caleb's jaw, and their lips touched briefly.

None of the children had noticed the typical display of affection. Ben looked away, spooned up some potatoes and placed them on Lillith's plate.

Ellie was the mother every child deserved. If Ben

ever had children he would want them as content and safe as Ellie's. On occasion he'd thought about having his own family, but always dismissed the idea in a hurry. He wouldn't want to mess them up.

"You're a good cook, Mama," Nate said.

Ellie cast him a grateful smile. "Why, thank you."

It had never made a lick of difference to his sister that Nate had been born of Caleb's first wife, Ben thought. The children had always been treated equally and fairly. Just like it had never made a difference to Caleb that his wife and her brothers didn't even know who their fathers were. You were who you were in this family, no matter where you came from.

"Do horses hafta eat nasty ol' green beans, Uncle Ben?" Lillith asked.

"No, horses eat oats and hay and sorghum with a little molasses added. They crop grass, too. Have to watch they don't get into weeds though, 'cause they'll twist their insides."

Lillith's eyes widened. "What if green beans do that to my innards?"

"They won't," Ellie replied. "You're a little girl, not a horse. Little girls need vegetables to grow strong."

While his sister was helping Anna with her meat, Ben leaned over and stabbed a heaping forkful of beans from Lillith's plate and popped them into his mouth. She looked from him to her mother and grinned.

"I saw that," Ellie said.

Everyone at the table laughed, but a knock at the door interrupted their humor.

"I'll get it." Ben pushed back his chair and gestured

for Ellie to stay seated. "If it's a patient, I'll come get you," he told Caleb.

His boots echoed across the floor of the huge wood-paneled foyer before Ben reached the door and opened it.

"Hi."

Ellie's helper, Lorabeth, stood on the porch, her arms filled with an overflowing crate. The drawstrings of a lumpy cloth bag hung from her elbow. Another stack of packed items stood on the painted floor behind her. Her presence here on a Sunday was surprising, as was the sight of the preacher behind her, still in his dark suit and starched white shirt. He stood holding his hat by the brim.

"Miss Holdridge. Reverend. Come on in."

She moved past him and glanced toward the dining room. "Did we interrupt dinner? Perhaps I was in too much of a rush."

Ben reached for the preacher's hat, but the man held on. "I won't be staying."

"We were just startin' to eat. You're welcome to join us." He gestured toward the other room.

"We've already eaten," Reverend Holdridge said.

"Well, come have a seat, anyway. I can see Lorabeth is achin' to talk to Ellie." He took the crate from her arms and set it on the floor at the foot of the stairs. "Movin' in?"

Her bright, tawny eyes sparkled. "Yes."

He'd been kidding, so her reply took him by surprise. She set down the bags and removed her bonnet. Shiny curls the color of honey fell to her shoulders. During the week she wore her hair in a more practical braided fashion.

She hadn't changed out of the high-necked spring-green dress that she'd worn while playing the organ that morning. He glanced at the stern-faced man waiting just inside the door. He was watching Ben like a hawk, and Ben appreciated the man's protectiveness toward his daughter. "Inspiring message this morning, Reverend."

"Thank you, Benjamin. Which part did you especially appreciate?"

Ben knew he was being tested to see if he'd paid attention. "I liked what you said about pressing toward the goal with singular determination. Looking at the circumstance on the left or the right can get mighty confusin'."

Reverend Holdridge's eyebrows rose in appreciation. "It blesses a preacher's heart to see a young man such as yourself in church every Sunday. Unmarried young men of your age are often feeling unwell on Sunday mornings."

Ben couldn't help grinning at his elusion to the men occupying the saloons till the wee hours of the morning. "I'm not a drinkin' man, sir."

"Admirable," the reverend replied. He glanced around at the furnishings and decor. "Please tell Dr. Chaney that I require a moment of his time."

"Sure."

"I'll join the others in the dining room," Lorabeth said.

Ben nodded and gestured for her to move ahead of him. She usually smelled more like bread and babies than the soft floral scent floating behind her now, and he wasn't sure why the difference disturbed him. Lorabeth made Ellie's life easier, and anything that made Ellie happy was fine by Ben.

She reached the wide doorway ahead of him, but paused as if unsure of her welcome.

"Lorabeth is here," he announced from beside her.

The picture of the Chaneys seated around the table made Lorabeth feel like an outsider for mere seconds until she reminded herself she was here to join them. Heads turned, and they greeted her with smiles.

Lillith jumped down from her chair and Lorabeth knelt for a hug. At the warm welcome, her heart swelled.

"Reverend Holdridge would like a word with you," Ben told Caleb.

Lorabeth glanced over from where she knelt and noticed Caleb and Ellie exchange a glance. Caleb laid down his napkin and stood. "Excuse me."

"Uncle Ben ate my green beans," Lillith whispered in her ear.

Lorabeth glanced up at Benjamin who waited with her chair pulled out. She gave Lillith a gentle hug and stood so she could be seated.

"Ben, will you get Lorabeth a plate?" Ellie asked, as Lorabeth got settled.

"I had a quick bite at home—I mean at my father's," she corrected herself. *This* was home now. "I could get a plate myself though. I'm not company, you know."

"No, you're not. Stay seated, anyway," Ellie insisted and smiled at Ben.

He headed into the kitchen and returned with a plate and silverware. She'd never had a man wait on her in this manner, and she noticed his long thumb and fingers as he set down the rose-patterned china in front of her.

"Where are the napkins?" he asked, his voice near her shoulder.

He stood closer to her than any man except her father

or brothers had ever stood, and his nearness unnerved her. Without thinking, Lorabeth gestured toward the built-in sideboard. "In the second drawer there."

He got one and shook out the folds before handing it to her.

"Thank you," she said softly, and he resumed his seat on the opposite side of the table, but several chairs away.

"Lorabeth is going to be living here," Ellie announced.

"Even Saturdays and Sundays," Lorabeth added unnecessarily.

"But you will take your two mornings off," Ellie insisted. "And you'll have minimal responsibilities over the weekend. You need time for yourself and your own interests. Seeing friends and the like."

"Yes, ma'am," Lorabeth answered, a wee bit troubled over misleading Ellie about her intentions for her mornings off. Promising to handle her father's household on those days had been the only way she could make this work, but she wanted to be here so badly that she would have made any sacrifice.

She helped herself to small portions of food as Benjamin and Ellie passed the dishes. She picked up her fork while conversation ebbed around her. She'd eaten many meals with this family over the past two years, and she never lost her appreciation for their easy chatter and the relaxed atmosphere. Growing up in her father's home, she and her siblings had been required to sit straight and eat quietly.

"I've purchased a piano for the parlor," Ellie announced. "It should arrive sometime next week."

"Who plays the piano?" Flynn asked.

"Aunt Patricia plays the piano at Nana's house!" Lillith replied.

"You children will play once you've had lessons," Ellie told them.

"I don't wanna play no piano," Nate declared with a frown.

"I'm certainly not going to force you." Ellie dabbed her lip with her napkin. "But I do ask you to try before you say no."

In his father's temporary absence, Nate looked to Benjamin as though he might get some support from the only man at the table.

Lorabeth couldn't help wondering how Ellie's handsome brother was going to respond.

Benjamin didn't hesitate before saying, "If you try playing and don't like it—or you can't get the hang of it—there's no shame in making the effort and decidin' it's not for you."

Lorabeth smiled at that reasoning.

"I bet it's hard," David said. "Is it hard, Miss Lorrie?"

Benjamin turned his distracting gaze to Lorabeth. His eyes were piercingly blue and expectant and the direct look made her stomach quiver.

She had to look away and gather her thoughts to answer David's question. "Not that difficult, dear. You'll learn to read the notes. You're all bright children, so it won't be a problem. Then you'll learn where to place your fingers on the keys, and after that it simply takes a lot of practice."

"Maybe Miss Lorrie can give us our lessons," Lillith suggested with a hopeful smile.

"Miss Lorrie does enough already without adding more to her list of duties," Ellie told her daughter.

"But she can play for us, can't she?"

"If she wants to."

"Will you, Mith Lorrie?" Anna asked. "Will you play for uth? We can thing!"

"I like 'My Bonnie Lies Over the Ocean,' don't you, Mama?" Lillith asked.

Uncomfortable warmth flooded Lorabeth's neck and face. "I'm afraid I don't know that one."

"Then, 'Turkey in the Thtraw!'" Anna shouted.

She regretted disappointing the children, and more than that she was embarrassed at her incompetence. Lorabeth's knowledge and experience was so narrow she'd never known anyone who owned a piano for a purpose other than worship. "I don't know that one, either."

Lillith got that charmingly inquisitive crease between her pale eyebrows. "But you play music every Sunday."

"I only know hymns," she explained. "But I could learn to play those songs you like if I had the sheets of music."

"Can we help you put your dresses an' stuff away, Miss Lorrie?" Lillith asked in a typically abrupt change of subject.

"Miss Lorrie is capable of putting away her own clothing," Ellie told the girls. "Ben will carry her things up the stairs. Do you have much more to bring?"

Lorabeth shook her head. "It's all in the foyer."

She glanced at Benjamin and their eyes met for an uncomfortable moment while she wondered what he was thinking. The Chaneys weren't ostentatious by any means, but they were well off, living with fine furnishings and wearing fashionable clothing. All of her modest belongings were in those few crates and bags. She lowered her gaze and looked away. It was a big wide world, and she only knew a tiny fraction of it.

She remembered her father's visit and strained to hear any snippets of conversation coming from another room, but the house was large, and Caleb had most likely taken him into the parlor and closed the doors. Her father had agreed to her plan, and she prayed there would be no reason for him to change his mind or add any more ultimatums. She could only imagine what he was thinking of Dr. Chaney after seeing his lavish home.

They had finished eating by the time Caleb returned to the dining room alone.

Lorabeth's heart fluttered nervously, waiting to hear what he had to say, praying her father wouldn't change his mind.

Chapter Three

Lorabeth clutched her hands in her lap, compelled to explain. "My father has very rigid ideas about propriety, Dr. Chaney."

"He's concerned for the welfare of his unmarried young daughter," Caleb replied, his voice as kind as she'd always heard it. "Which I can appreciate."

Lorabeth stood. "Let me reheat your dinner for you."

Caleb raised a palm to stop her. "My food is fine." He placed his napkin in his lap and picked up his fork.

Smoothing her dress beneath her, Lorabeth eased back down, her attention focused on Caleb. "Was he…did he say anything to discourage you from wanting me here?"

"I assured him I had your best interests in mind and that I'll look after you as a member of my family."

Relief washed over her, then pleasure at his reference to treating her as part of the family. A grateful ache blossomed in her chest. "Thank you, Dr. Chaney."

"We've come to rely on you. Living with us now, you'll be an even bigger help when the new baby comes."

Ellie smiled at her husband and then at Lorabeth.

Lorabeth flicked her gaze from one child to the next, finally reaching Benjamin. She'd always had the nagging feeling that he didn't like or approve of her, not because he'd ever been unkind, but because she sensed his reserve where she was concerned. Her joy dimmed a fraction, but she caught herself and offered him a smile.

Benjamin returned it hesitantly, then seemed to notice Ellie's glance. He got up to get the pies from the sideboard and set them in front of his sister to cut. Lorabeth's mouth watered at the dark red cherries and juice visible through the lattice crusts. She watched Ellie slice thick wedges.

"There's a horse auction this week," Flynn said. "Did you know about it, Caleb?"

"Seems I did hear something. Don't need any more horses, though."

Ellie's younger brother wore a hopeful expression. Flynn talked a lot about horses.

"I heard mention that a fella from Arkansas is selling a couple of Missouri Fox Trotters," Benjamin commented.

Flynn sat forward. "Ever seen one of 'em?"

"Never have. Maybe we should go have a look."

Benjamin promised they'd attend the auction together. Flynn's pleasure shone in his smile.

"I saw Martha Wick the other day." Caleb directed the comment to Benjamin.

Benjamin glanced up from his pie. "Who?"

"You went to school with Martha," Ellie reminded him. "She married that Pratt fellow who farms to the west."

"They live with her father-in-law, Milo Pratt," Caleb said. "Milo's been laid up with a leg injury."

Their discussions fascinated Lorabeth. She studied each family member with keen interest.

"Lillith and Anna, will you help me set up for croquet?" Caleb asked, pushing his empty plate away. Anna was barely more than a baby and would require his supervision, but Lorabeth had noticed that he always included her. "Nana and Papa will be arriving soon."

The two girls jumped up and down with excitement and Ellie helped Anna from her seat.

Ellie turned to Lorabeth. "You remember Caleb's parents. They attend the Presbyterian church in Florence with his sister Patricia's family, but every other Sunday they come to Newton for the afternoon."

Lorabeth nodded. She had seen them several times when they'd stopped by the house during the week. "My sister and her family live in Florence, too."

"You must take pleasure in their visits," Ellie said.

"They don't visit much," she answered. She hadn't seen Ruthann or her brother, Jubal, for over a year.

Caleb glanced at his sons. "You two young men clear the table, and be mindful of the good china."

Nate and David looked at each other before obediently rising to scrape plates. Lorabeth had never before heard their father ask a kitchen chore of them.

"I can clear the table," she offered.

"No," Ellie replied. "The boys will handle it while you see to your things." She glanced across the table. "Ben?"

Benjamin placed his napkin beside his plate and stood. "I'm not sure which room is yours," he said to Lorabeth.

Without hesitation she stood. "I'll show you."

He followed her to the foyer and bent to pick up a substantial stack. "Lead the way."

She gathered one of the remaining drawstring bags and climbed the stairs ahead of him.

Ben watched her hand on the banister so he wouldn't be tempted to study her curvaceous backside swaying beneath the green dress.

Lily of the valley, that was the delicate scent that floated behind her. Her skirts rustled as she walked, the fabric whispering secrets he couldn't quite make out. He didn't pay much attention to women's apparel, but he knew that it wasn't a fancy dress she wore. In fact, now that he really noticed, the garment was rather plain, without lace or trim or ornamentation of any kind. She didn't need any; she was as pretty as a spring day.

He caught himself and worked determinedly to arrest those unacceptable thoughts.

She stopped in the hallway and gestured to a room, indicating where he should take her things.

He stepped into the square interior. He'd seen all of the bedrooms at one time or another, knew there were one or two extras at this end of the hall, but he hadn't been upstairs much since she'd been staying here during the week.

A wide window overlooked the side lawn and gauzy white curtains were draped to each side, revealing the branches of a cedar tree. A cushioned rocking chair sat beside the window. He wouldn't have guessed she used this room if he'd gone looking on his own. There were no personal items in sight.

The metal bed frame was plain, and a red-and-blue

quilt neatly covered the mattress. He pictured her sleeping here, and discomfort scratched at his self-possession. He wished Ellie hadn't assigned this task to him.

He set the stack of crates on the floor.

She moved farther into the room and placed the bag she'd carried on the bed.

"I'll get the rest." He had the remainder of her belongings carried up in two more trips.

He set each individual crate down on the floor so she wouldn't have to lift them from a stack. It appeared the contents were mostly clothing. He averted his gaze and spotted what looked like a sewing box.

"Thank you," she said.

"Can I help with anything else?"

"It's only clothes I need to hang or put in the drawers."

To distract himself from thoughts of her clothing, he glanced at the papered walls. "You should have a picture or two."

She drew her brows into two slashes of concern. "I realized when I was packing that I don't own much."

He hadn't meant to point that out. He'd been making conversation to distract himself.

"My father is opposed to storing up treasure on earth where moth and rust can corrupt," she said.

He didn't know what to say to that. "Didn't mean any offense."

"None taken." She glanced at the bare walls. "Ellie said they'd never used this room."

"I have a few framed pictures at the house that Ellie left behind," he said, sorry to be the one to chase the cheer from her voice. "I could bring one for you."

"That's so thoughtful!"

Her smile would have lit a dark night, and it almost embarrassed him because he hadn't done anything extraordinary to earn her delight.

"You bought their old house, didn't you?" she asked.

He nodded. "Don't stay there often, though. My office and examining rooms are out at my other place. Horses, too, of course. And I almost always have a few ailing animals to look after."

"So you have two homes?"

"Ellie nags me about it every week," he replied with a nod. "I keep the house in town in case I need to stay over." He glanced around. "I'm glad you're here for Ellie."

She gave him a half smile. "I'm glad to be here, too. There's so much more I can accomplish now."

He'd never noticed before that her eyes were a rich caramel color. Expectancy made them sparkle. Her statements intrigued him. "What do you want to accomplish?"

She folded her hands over her heart as though searching for a way to explain. His attention followed her hands and rested on her breasts beneath her dress a moment too long before he tore it away. Never in the last couple of years had he given her as much consideration as he had in the past hour, and noticing her this way made him uncomfortable.

"I want to meet people and learn all I can." The yearning in her voice surprised him. "I want to read every book in the public library and walk through all of the shops in town. I'd like to take a walk at night. Maybe even go somewhere on the train."

Her aspirations didn't sound very high to Ben, but her

desire to do ordinary things told him quite a bit. She'd been living under her father's guidelines, and now she apparently had an agenda of her own. Maybe she hadn't appreciated a parent who cared about her.

A frown creased her features and her gaze fell to the top of the bureau as though she was thinking.

Ben couldn't stop himself from asking, "What's the matter?"

She glanced up. "Oh. Nothing, really. I was just thinking I still wouldn't have much time for all of that."

"Ellie gave you two mornings off each week," he reminded her.

She nodded. "Yes." Her smile seemed a trifle forced. "She did."

"You can go to the library and visit the shops on those days, can't you?"

She'd never voiced her dreams before, and after revealing an aching piece of her heart to a near stranger, Lorabeth experienced a twinge of embarrassment. Benjamin didn't look particularly surprised or judgmental, in fact, his ice-blue eyes showed a flattering measure of interest.

She nodded, bent to pick up one of the bags and placed it on the foot of the bed. "Yes, of course."

She'd had her fill of holding back and living up to expectations. She was curious about the opposite sex, fascinated by the relationship her employers shared and eager to spread her wings and experience life to its fullest.

He could never know how glad she was to experience a taste of the life she'd missed out on. For the first time she felt as though she could actually take a deep breath.

The air smelled cleaner. The sun shone brighter. Even this room looked bigger than it had when she'd left it late Friday evening.

Life was ripe with possibilities. She wanted to pick and taste every last one of them.

Benjamin took several steps toward the door. "This shouldn't take you long. You can join us for croquet when you're finished."

His suggestion caught Lorabeth by surprise. Of course she'd heard them talk about playing, but she hadn't imagined... "I'd be welcome, do you suppose?"

A line formed between his sandy-colored eyebrows, but his expression quickly smoothed into a teasing smile. "Of course you're welcome. In fact, the girls will plead for you to be on their team since Ellie will be sitting out. The first game is always boys against girls. Not sure why. See you in a few minutes."

He left, closing the door and leaving her alone in the room.

Lorabeth turned in a wide circle, reveling in the buoyant sense of freedom. She still had just as much work to do, in less time actually, but for some reason just the fact that she was here for good made the weight of it all seem so much lighter.

The sound of childish voices reached her, and she hurried to slide open the window. The cedar tree blocked much of her view of the yard, but through lower branches she could make out the girls' colorful dresses. Caleb was helping them do something in the grass.

The sound of a team and buggy at the front of the house arrested her attention. She couldn't see the front from her room, but it wasn't long until the girls squealed and greeted the newcomers. Lorabeth recognized Caleb's parents, but she'd never seen the other couple.

Eager to discover what the family was doing, she quickly unpacked only the things she would need this evening, leaving the rest for later. After taking a few minutes to check her hair and dress in the mirror, she hurried down the stairs.

No one remained in the house. She replaced the crocheted tablecloth Ellie kept on the mahogany dining table, then dried and put away the pans that had been left on the drain board.

Making her way out the back door, she paused on the shaded porch to familiarize herself with those gathered on the lawn. Her attention was so focused, Ellie's voice from behind startled her.

"Did you get settled?"

Lorabeth turned and found her employer and Caleb's mother seated in two of the comfortable wicker chairs. Ellie had her feet resting on one of the footstools from the parlor. In the shade behind her chair, David's cat, Buddy Lee, lay with all four paws tucked neatly beneath him. He spared Lorabeth a blink before closing his eyes.

"Yes," Lorabeth answered with a nod.

"You remember Caleb's mother," Ellie said.

"Yes, of course. Pleasure to see you, ma'am."

"And you, dear. I hear we'll be seeing more of you from now on." The handsome woman wore her faded red hair in an elegant upsweep.

Lorabeth smiled. "I hope so."

Ellie rested a hand on her rounded belly and sighed.

"Can I get you anything?" Lorabeth asked.

She shook her head. "This baby is either a dancer or a runner like Ben."

"Benjamin's a runner?"

"A fast one," Ellie replied. "Wins all the local competitions. He won footraces at the university, too."

. "I'll remember not to try to beat him to the dinner table."

Ellie laughed, then called, "Patricia! Denzil, come meet Lorabeth."

The couple strolled arm-in-arm across the lawn and stood in the grass below the porch rail.

"This is Lorabeth," Ellie told them. "For the last couple of years she's helped with the children during the week, but now she's moving in with us." To Lorabeth, she explained, "Patricia is Caleb's sister, and this is her husband, Denzil. Their daughter, Lucy, is out there by Flynn."

"It's a pleasure to meet you," Lorabeth said. "The girls have told me you play the piano when you're all together at Mrs. Chaney's home."

The fair-haired woman offered her a kind smile. "I've heard all about you, too."

Anna bounded up the stairs as fast as her short little legs allowed. "Nana! Nana! It'th time for the girlth to beat the boyth. Weddy to pway?"

Mrs. Chaney lifted the child onto her lap and kissed her pink cheek. "Nana's going to sit here and visit with your mama today, darling."

"You're not gonna pway?"

"Not today. Next time."

Anna scooted from her lap and ran to take Lorabeth's hand. "You're gonna help uth win, right, Mith Lorrie?"

Lorabeth glanced from Anna's hopeful expression to the yard where the family was gathered. "I've never played croquet before, Anna. You'll have to teach me."

Anna's eyes widened big as saucers, and she turned to her mother. "Mama! I'm gonna teach Mith Lorrie!"

Ellie laughed at her daughter's delighted expression.

Anna grasped Lorabeth's hand and led her down the stairs where they followed Patricia and Denzil into the side yard. "We're the black-and-blue team!"

"Goodness! Is the game dangerous?"

"Only if you stand too close to another player who's swinging his mallet," Benjamin replied, walking forward with a crooked grin. "Or you hit your own foot, of course."

"That's where the black-and-blue part comes in?" she asked.

Lorabeth liked the sound of his laughter, though she wasn't entirely comfortable that it was at her expense. He explained, "The girls will be hitting the black and blue balls, the boys the red and yellow."

She took note of the curved wires protruding from the ground in two diamond shapes with double wires and stakes at each end.

"Do you know the point of the game?" he asked.

She shook her head. "But I want to learn."

"Okay, well, there's a pattern here," he told her. "The object is to get your ball through all the wickets in this double-diamond pattern. You want to try to hit the other team's balls. If you do, you get an extra turn, and you get to hit their ball in the wrong direction."

"You get an extra strike for scoring a wicket or hitting the turning stake, too," Flynn added. "Watch out for Ben, 'cause he likes to send another person's ball flying."

"It sounds rather complicated," Lorabeth said, voicing her concern.

"Nah, it's easy," Flynn replied.

"You'll get the hang of it as we go," Benjamin assured her.

"I'm apposed to be teaching Mith Lorrie," Anna admonished her adopted siblings.

"So you are," Dr. Chaney agreed, setting a coin on the bent knuckle of his thumb. "Heads or tails?" he asked Anna.

"Heads!" she answered immediately.

With a flick of his thumb, Dr. Chaney sent the nickel soaring into the air and caught it. He slapped it onto the back of his hand with an impressive flourish, then raised his hand away. "Heads it is."

"Hurray! We getta go firtht!"

Listening to garbled instruction from a three-year-old made learning a challenge, but every so often, Caleb or Benjamin would explain Anna's meaning or supply a rule the toddler wasn't aware of.

Lorabeth's heart pounded as she prepared to take her first swing. She felt everyone's attention, but was most concerned over Benjamin's. She glanced up and found him watching.

"You should have let her practice!" Ellie called from the porch.

Benjamin waved away her comment and pointed to the

black wooden ball in the short-cropped grass. "Go ahead," he told Lorabeth. "You want the ball to land over here."

Lorabeth swung her mallet and sent the ball in the wrong direction. She covered her mouth with her hand. "Oh, my."

"That's okay," Caleb called. "It's just takes a little practice."

She discovered she wasn't the only one with a wild swing. The balls the girls struck rarely landed where they were intended. She caught Benjamin subtly rolling Anna's blue ball closer to a wicket with the toe of his brown polished boot, and when he looked up to discover her watching him, he shrugged sheepishly.

He strolled closer. "We'd never get the game over this afternoon if we didn't make a little magic happen," he said in a low conspiratory tone.

On her second round through the wickets, Lorabeth accidentally hit one of the other team member's balls. She grimaced. She really didn't want to send one of the Chaney men's game pieces in the wrong direction.

Groans escaped the men. Ellie cheered her on from the porch. "Whose was it?"

"Ben's," the elder Mr. Chaney replied.

"Whack it a good one, Lorabeth!" Ellie called.

"Yeah!" the little girls chorused.

"Oh, I don't think I can." Lorabeth gripped her mallet in hesitation.

"Sure you can," Patricia said, good-naturedly. "He won't hesitate to send yours flying, trust me."

Lorabeth exchanged a look with Benjamin. There was an element of daring in his eyes.

Patricia demonstrated the technique Lorabeth had seen the others use. She placed Lorabeth's ball against Benjamin's and touched Lorabeth's with the toe of her dainty leather shoe to hold it in place, then drew back the mallet as though she would swing to hit it. "Hold it lightly, just like that so you don't hit your foot or trap his ball."

Lorabeth glanced at Benjamin, assuring herself his expression was one of amusement.

Lorabeth did as Patricia had instructed, feeling self-conscious and inept as she placed her left foot on her ball and visualized striking it with enough controlled force to send Benjamin's across the yard.

She didn't do so well for her first attempt, only managing to send the ball about four feet, but the girls on her team cheered for her, anyway.

Their team won, though Lorabeth couldn't for the life of her figure out how. The only players with any accuracy had been Patricia and fourteen-year-old Lucy. She suspected either Benjamin or Dr. Chaney had nudged a good many more blue and black balls with the toes of their boots than she'd actually observed.

"Nana and Ellie have set out cookies and lemonade." Patricia rested her mallet in the wooden rack and gestured for the others to join her. She shooed Buddy Lee from the banister, and the cat sprang over the side into the yard.

The Chaney family laughed and teased each other as they picked up sweating glasses of lemonade, helped themselves to cookies and spread out in chairs and on the wide stairs of the enormous porch.

Comparisons slipped into her thinking, memories of Sunday afternoons spent reading their Bibles under her father's watchful eye while the rest of the world shared meals and played games. On the very rare occasion that her father accepted an invitation for dinner, she and her siblings were instructed to sit silently throughout the meal and to decline offers of amusements with other children. Even her mother was expected to sit silently and show no interest in their hostesses' furnishings or nonsensical chatter. But Lorabeth had seen it in her eyes. The yearning. The disappointment. And eventually, the hopelessness.

The Chaneys' interaction and gaiety was all so natural, so informal and unlike anything Lorabeth had ever participated in that she was numb from taking it all in.

"We're gettin' a piano," Lillith told her aunt. "Then you can play for us when you're here, just like at Nana's. Miss Lorrie's going to learn to play songs we like, too."

"Won't that be grand?" Patricia said as though impressed. She gestured for Lorabeth to join her on a wicker settee. "Where did you learn to play?"

Lorabeth settled on the other end and rested her napkin and cookies in her lap. "My mother taught me."

"Do I know your mother, dear?" the elder Mrs. Chaney asked.

"She died when I was twelve. You may have known her, but I doubt it," she answered. Lorabeth's mother had been hardworking and devoted to her family and the church. Socializing had never been a part of their life. If it didn't relate to the church, they didn't participate.

"I'm sorry, dear," Mrs. Chaney said. "It must have been difficult for you to grow up without a mother."

Lorabeth nodded. At her father's decree, she'd taken

over all the household chores and the church duties that her mother had performed. "I've played the organ every Sunday morning for the past seven years...except once when the roof was damaged during a storm and we were forced to hold service at city hall. There was no piano."

"I remember that," Caleb said thoughtfully.

"Do you have brothers and sisters?" Patricia asked, and Lorabeth told her about her siblings.

"Lucy is our only child," she said with a smile for her daughter. "She's fourteen already."

Lorabeth had had trouble taking her eyes from the lovely young woman with the dark hair and flawless fair skin. Dressed in a pale yellow dress with ruffled hem and bodice, she carried herself with incredible poise for one of such a tender age. The girl couldn't know how fortunate she was to have this family in which she could flourish and be herself.

Not once today had any of the young people been asked to keep their voices down or hang back from the others so as not to appear forward or coarse. Outbursts of laughter appeared as natural as breathing air. And there was plenty to laugh about. Lorabeth felt as though she'd been transported to a bright new land where people interacted with one another and enjoyed life.

For a split second she thought of Simon left at home to sit through solemn meals and hours of evening prayer. But she'd made her own way, as had Ruthann and Jubal, and her younger brother would be fine. One more year and he'd be working in town. She turned her thoughts back to where she was.

Benjamin observed the pretty young woman who

seemed to have become a part of the family today. She'd lost her mother, and her father had done his best to guide and protect her. Lorabeth Holdridge was unlike any of the girls he'd known while attending school. She was less worldly and more disciplined than the girls he'd seen at the university. She'd been sheltered her entire life.

A young woman's main goal was usually to land a husband to care for her and give her children. Lorabeth probably wanted those same things, but she didn't seem the kind to care about social standing or monetary things.

He glanced at his sister to find her observing him with a question sparkling in her eyes. "How do the cookies suit you today, Benjamin?" she asked.

Coconut macaroons were his favorite as she well knew. "Nobody makes better," he replied with a grin.

She returned a smile as fond as those she gave her own children.

"Are we going to change teams for the next game?" Flynn asked. "I want Miss Lorrie on my team this time."

"Ask Miss Lorrie if she wants to play again," Ellie suggested. "She may have had enough of your tomfoolery."

The children turned hopeful gazes toward her.

"I'd be happy to play again." She lent enough enthusiasm to her reply to assure them she meant what she said.

"You'll have to do without Papa this time," Ellie said, referring to her husband. "I'd like him to join me for a while."

Caleb gave his wife a look with a measure of concern attached. When they divided into teams, Mrs. Chaney joined them, giving her son and his wife privacy on the porch.

They weren't far into the match in which Lorabeth seemed completely absorbed, when Ben noticed that his sister and Caleb had gone inside. She'd looked tired all day, and he'd read the concern on his brother-in-law's face. Benjamin lost interest in the game.

A twinge of something like fear stabbed his chest. Ellie held his world together. If anything ever happened to her, he wouldn't know what to do. He glanced at his younger brother, laughingly engaged in a battle of boasts with their pretty cousin, Lucy.

Caleb's father stood in the shade beside Ben. A tall handsome man with gray shot through his thick hair, he ran a ranch and his family with a stern but fair hand.

"Something botherin' you, son?"

Matthew often called Benjamin "son," and Ben didn't take any offense to it. He held the man in high regard.

"Ellie's looking a mite tired, don't you think?"

"Probably no more than any woman ready to birth a new life," Matthew replied. "Can you imagine the world if that chore had been left up to us men?"

Ben gauged his expression. "No, sir, I can't."

Matthew chuckled. He scratched his chin with a thumb. "I wanted my son to ranch with me, did you know that?"

"Probably seemed like the natural course," Ben answered.

"He had a mind to be a doctor. Wanted it so bad he sold off a share of inherited land to pay for his first year of education. After I saw how much his dream meant to him, how bad he wanted it, I kicked in the next year."

Ben nodded to show he was paying attention.

"He's a damned good doctor. There's nothing more important to him than your sister and this family. He'll take care of her, you don't worry yourself."

Matthew was right. Ben had learned to trust his brother-in-law to do the best by all of them, and Caleb had never let them down.

Ben gave Matthew a nod and they strolled back to referee a disagreement between Nate and Lucy regarding a ball that had glanced off a wicket.

The sun was an orange sphere heading for the lavender-streaked horizon when Matthew and Denzil gathered their families. Ben had unhitched Matthew's horses and tethered them in the shade, so he gave them water and hooked them up to the traces. Caleb's father headed the black buggy toward Florence.

"Where's Mama?" Lillith called as they entered the house.

Caleb loped down the staircase. "Did they head home?"

Ben nodded. "Just a few minutes ago."

"Where's Mama?" Lillith asked again.

"Mama's tired and her ankles are swollen," Caleb replied, including the entire gathering. "I've told her to stay off her feet. You'll all have to mind me and help with chores."

"Tomorrow is a school day," Lorabeth said to the boys immediately. "Go lay out your clothing and books for morning. I'll do the evening preparation for lunches."

"Ellie told me earlier that there's a ham to be sliced," Flynn told her. "I'll get it from the cellar."

"That's thoughtful," she told Flynn, and he hurried off to his task.

"You'll read us a story before bed like Mama always does, Miss Lorrie?" Lillith asked.

"Of course, dear." She ushered the children up the stairs.

Ben gave his brother-in-law a direct look. "She's all right?"

"She's perfectly all right. She just needs some rest."

Ben trusted him to know what was best. "Tell her I'll stop by tomorrow."

"You can go tell her."

He shook his head. "No. Tomorrow will be good. I'll clean up the yard and carry in the dishes before I go."

Ben counted wickets and balls and carried the croquet set to the shed behind the house. His attention was drawn to the mallet with the green rings and he remembered Lorabeth holding it as though it might break or vanish in her grasp. She'd seemed happier than a pup with a new bone to join them today.

He thought back to the first times he'd participated in family dinners and activities with the Chaneys and how out of place he'd felt. Lorabeth's hesitation hadn't seemed to be because she didn't feel like she belonged, but more as though she was tiptoeing to make sure she didn't wake herself up.

That was an odd thought, but it fit his observations. Her presence here was going to make the difference for Ellie getting the rest she needed. The fact that Lorabeth triggered his interest and piqued his curiosity was a distraction he could ignore. And intended to.

Chapter Four

Later that week, Benjamin stood on his back porch in the yawning silence of the evening and studied the last fading streaks of orange in the darkening sky. A battalion of fireflies had flickered to life to dot the alfalfa field behind the barn. It was the last day of September and, while the crisp air felt good on his face, it reminded him that a long winter was in store.

The wide wooden stairs creaked beneath his weight, and he headed for the rows of stacked boxlike cages with chicken-wire doors that lined the side of the barn. A three-legged cat meowed, and he opened the door to scratch her ear. "Don't be gettin' used to chicken livers and cream," he told the accident-prone feline called Lazarus by his owners. "Few more days and you'll be back to catchin' mice at the Fredericks's place."

The cat meowed a reply, and he hooked the door shut.

He stopped at the end of the row of cages where he'd been keeping an owl isolated and peeled a gunnysack curtain away.

"Well, Hoot, it's your big night. Time for you to go back to your kin and your favorite knothole."

The enormous bird blinked at him and waddled sideways away from his touch.

Ben urged the heavy bird onto his forearm and lifted him out. Three weeks ago, the Stoker kids had told him about the injured owl, and Ben found the creature on the bank of a creek, its wing broken. It appeared to have been there for some time, exposed to the elements and hungry, and Ben hadn't been sure if the animal would live.

Carrying the owl to the front of the barn, he raised his arm. "Go on. Go home."

The bird didn't need any encouragement. It flapped its wings, slapping Ben in the face as it pushed away from his arm. The owl perched on the corner of the barn roof for a full minute, head swiveling as though getting its bearings. A moment later it flew into the darkened sky and soared overhead before disappearing into the night.

Closing his eyes, Ben listened and imagined he could hear the sound of wings in the distance. The heartfelt sense of satisfaction and fulfillment that always accompanied an animal's healing and recovery cleansed Benjamin's soul and set his world to right. He got too close, too attached, took it too personally when, in that occasional instance, an animal died in his care. He valued the life of all creatures. He lived to heal and care for them.

He'd killed a man.

Whenever the night was heavy with stars and loneliness rolled over him like a dark wave, Ben pondered loopholes in that "thou shalt not kill" commandment.

The incident had been years ago. He'd been young, and the law had deemed it a defensive act.

That commandment was pretty cut-and-dried, but if God was Who the Missionary Baptists and the First Episcopals and the United Congregationalists said He was, then He'd known what kind of man Winston Parker was anyhow.

If he closed his eyes he could see that night all over again, just as vividly as if it had been yesterday. He'd been seventeen and had only recently come to live with Caleb and Ellie. Caleb had been called away that night and Ben had been attacked when he'd gone down to the darkened kitchen.

He'd recognized the man. Knew he was the same man who'd haunted his nightmares since childhood.

Ellie had struck a match, lighting a lantern and defining three people in its glow. Her face had blanched with shock. Ben sat tied to a chair with a rope. Winston Parker stood beside him, a gun pointed at Ben's head. Ellie took a step forward. "Let him go."

"I'll let him go. Just as soon as you step outside with me."

Ben struggled against the bindings, fear clawing at his heart. "If you hurt my sister, I'll kill you, you son of a bitch!"

"I'm *real* scared," Winston said with a smirk. "Now come on, Ellie. Out the door. I'm tired of waiting."

"Where to?" she asked.

"My carriage," he replied. "You remember my lovely carriage."

She grabbed her stomach in revulsion.

Winston slowly pulled back the hammer of the gun until it clicked. He pressed the barrel directly against Ben's perspiring temple. Strangely enough Ben was more afraid for Ellie than for himself. Death was certainly less painful than the life he'd endured until now.

"All right," she said. "Put away the gun."

"Don't go," Ben pleaded. "Let him shoot me! The noise will bring someone to help."

She looked at him with tender appreciation. "Move the gun away," she said calmly.

"No!" Benjamin howled in anguish.

Winston pulled the gun away from Benjamin's head and backhanded him across the face. Ben's lip caught fire and his head throbbed.

Ellie moved toward him, but Winston moved the barrel to point at Benjamin's heart.

She halted, then walked stiffly to the door.

"Ellie, no!" Ben screamed. It was all happening just like before. Just like the last time when he'd been eight and unable to help her. He wouldn't let this happen again. With every ounce of his strength, he strained against the bonds, rocked the chair sideways and turned it over, banging his head against the stove in the process.

He shook his head to clear the flash of dizzying white, ignored the pain shooting through his arm and shoulder where he'd hit the floor, and swung his legs so that the chair crashed against the stove. He did it again. And again. That man was taking his sister farther and farther away with each passing moment.

Finally the wood splintered and his ankles came free. He kicked out of the rope and stood, banging the back of the chair against the doorway until the pieces fell and he was loose. Without pause, he shot into the cool foggy night.

With dread clawing at his chest, he ran through the bushes and gardens in neighboring yards to the adjacent street. There, looming out of the enveloping darkness was the black carriage.

Winston was trying to shove Ellie inside, but she was putting up a good fight. Ben caught the man off guard, lighting into him with years of pent-up helplessness adding strength to his seventeen years.

He spun Winston toward him and pummeled his face with a fist. Winston returned the punch and lights flashed behind Ben's eyes. He tasted blood.

Winston turned, raised the gun to Ellie's head and shoved her back against the side of the carriage. "Get inside," he hissed.

She clamped her teeth and said through them, "Shoot me."

He glared.

She reached up, locked her fingers into Winston's hair and yanked for all she was worth. He yelped and his head jerked back, dislodging the gun from her temple.

Ben regained his footing and barreled into Winston with all he was worth. With a grunt, Winston released Ellie. She grabbed the man's hand and bashed it against the edge of the coach door. He howled and shoved her, the gun falling from his grip.

Ben struck him again and Winston toppled onto him, arms and leg flailing. Ellie beat at Winston's head with both fists. Winston pressed Ben's face into the ground until Ben thought his jaw would break. Moonlight glimmering from the barrel of the gun lying in the dirt caught his attention. He stretched out his arm, flexed his fingers and closed them around the barrel. This time he could help her. This time he could keep his sister safe.

In the next second a blast echoed in his ears.

The horses reared and whinnied and harnesses jingled; the carriage rocked. The smell of gunpowder burned his nose.

"Ben!" Ellie screamed.

On top of him, Winston's body lay still and heavy. Ben rolled him off and staggered to his feet.

Ellie stared at the unmoving body. Looked at the gun in Ben's hand.

"I didn't mean to," Ben said on a released breath.

A light came on in one of the nearby houses, then another. She knelt over Winston's prone body and she pressed her fingers to his throat, then looked up at her brother. "He's dead."

When the truth about Winston Parker had been exposed, Ben had been pardoned. Sometimes the truth still haunted him. But he wouldn't change what he'd done.

He'd do it again today if he had to.

Inside the barn Ben lit a lantern and saddled his black ranger with its characteristic white-spotted rump. Titus turned an intelligent-looking face toward Ben and nodded as though anticipating a run.

"We're stayin' on the road, you know," Ben told him. "Not takin' any chances of you steppin' into a hole in a field. It's a pretty night. Maybe we'll see Hoot out there."

He led the horse outside, closed the barn door and mounted.

Titus pranced and Ben patted his neck with a smile. "Well, all right then." He nudged the horse's sides, and the animal shot forward.

This particular breed was not that old, descending from two horses presented to General Ulysses Grant by a Turkish sultan maybe twenty years ago. Bred from an Arabian and a Barb and then later crossed with a Quarter Horse, they were known as Colorado Rangers. Because if its pedigree, Ben had paid a pretty penny for the colt four years ago. He liked to imagine Titus's ancestors carrying sultans and princesses in exotic lands.

Titus carried him swiftly, sure-footedly anticipating the bends in the road and responding to the slight tension on the reins as they came within sight of Newton.

Ben reined his mount to an easy halt and viewed the lights of the city. Sometimes he thought about leaving Kansas behind. Making a start somewhere with mountains and cold rivers. Somewhere without the oppressive history this land held for him. But his older sister's abiding love and his feelings of responsibility toward his younger brother held him fast. Ellie told him he spent too much time living in his head, that he needed more than animals for companions. In his opinion there weren't many humans that were equal company or comfort. People were a disappointing breed.

The night breeze caressed his hair, and he gazed upward at the stars. Maybe Ellie was right. She was sure happy with her family and friends. Maybe he should try a little harder, work to discover and possess what was missing in his life.

Just the idea made his stomach burn. He leaned forward in the saddle and patted Titus's neck. "What *is* missing?" he asked aloud.

The animal's ears twitched.

A picture of his sister touching her husband's chin with a look of adoration flitted across his thoughts, followed by another disturbing image: Lorabeth standing beside the bed with the red-and-white quilt.

All Ben knew of family life was what he'd observed from the outside looking in. What he knew firsthand about men and women wasn't fit for a respectable person to think on.

Ben knew the dark side of men. He wasn't afraid of what they could do to him. He'd already endured more than his life's share of bad treatment, and he'd grown strong and capable in spite of it. He wasn't afraid of hunger or poverty or even the judgment of other people. He could take care of himself, and he didn't set much store by opinions or gossip.

What scared the wits out of him was that he was a man. And as a man what he was capable of. Choices were what set him apart. Good choices were what kept him from being like those others. He'd had no option but to kill once. But he could choose to live the rest of his life with honor and integrity, exercising self-control and challenging himself to become stronger.

But if what was missing was something inside him, he didn't know if he could fix that. Where did a person look to find a piece of himself?

* * *

Lorabeth's first full-time week couldn't have come at a better time. Ellie had been so tired and her body felt so weighted and achy that she was more than grateful to have her competent young helper close. She didn't remember this fatigue with her other pregnancies, but Caleb assured her each time was unique and that she had no reason for concern.

She felt positively slothful each time Lorabeth brought a tray to her in bed. Caleb spent as much time at home as possible, and even Ben stopped by nearly every day.

One morning midweek she'd asked Lorabeth to let the girls come play at the foot of the bed and later she read them stories while Lorabeth prepared ahead for the evening meal.

Ellie had just concluded *The Ugly Duckling,* and Anna was asleep on her shoulder when Ben leaned head and shoulders into her room.

"Is this a bad time?"

Ellie laid down the book. "Of course not. Come in." She gestured for him to come to the side of the bed.

He pulled the chair close.

"Would you mind laying her down in her own bed?" she asked, indicating the sleeping child.

With a grin at Lillith, her brother gently lifted Anna and carried her, cradled in his arms, from the room.

"You, too, sweet pea," she told the impish five-year-old. "Lie down for a nap and don't wake your sister. Kiss."

Lillith hugged her around the neck, pressing her sweet lips to Ellie's cheek before scampering from the bed. She nearly collided with Ben in the doorway, and when he hauled up short, she raised her arms for him to carry her, as well. He obliged her, hushing her giggles as he strode from the room.

Minutes later, he returned.

"You look refreshed today," he told Ellie, sitting beside her and taking her hand.

"I look tired and puffy, and you know it, but I don't want to talk about me today. Tell me all about your animals."

"Well, let's see. I told you I spotted Hoot the other night, didn't I? And the Olson brothers brought me a frog they think is sick. I've never done frog resuscitation before, but I think the little bugger's gonna live. Oh, and I've adopted a goat."

"Not a goat, Ben."

"She's a good companion around the place and she gives milk, so she's not just another mouth to feed."

"Companion, huh?"

She smirked and he grinned.

"I suppose you've named her?"

"Delilah."

"You've named a goat Delilah."

"It's a good name."

"It's a fine name, it just doesn't sound like it belongs to a goat."

"How many goats have you known?"

She met his pale eyes, and knew he was alluding to something from their past. "A couple, as you well know. Remember the goat Caleb kept when Nate was a baby?"

But that wasn't the same animal that had come to mind first. As a girl, she'd stolen out in the dark of night more than once to bring milk back to her younger brothers. There was a time when she'd grown a tobacco patch and rolled cigars to sell to the men outside the saloons just so she could pay for a few groceries. She'd stolen chickens from coops and vegetables from gardens, and still there'd never been enough.

"This is a good life," she said, never forgetting for a moment how fortunate they were.

"I can't explain what I feel when I look at those youngsters," Ben said, his voice thick with emotion.

"I know." He didn't have to explain. She knew well enough. The differences in their childhoods and those of her children were a universe apart. As far as from where they sat in this room to the outermost star. "The past has to be the past, Ben."

"It's where I came from, Ellie."

"But it's not who you are."

"I am who I am because of where I came from."

"*In spite of* where you came from," she said. "You'll never completely move on until you let go."

"Is that what you've done?"

"Yes."

"But you haven't forgotten."

"I can't erase the past, but I don't have to punish myself with it."

"Is that what you think I do? Punish myself?"

"Sometimes."

There was a light tap on the open door and Lorabeth carried a tray into the room. "I brought your lunch."

Ben straightened in his chair.

"I'm positively spoiled," Ellie said, smoothing the

covers in an attempt to find a spot on her nearly obliterated lap.

"You deserve it," Ben told her.

Lorabeth stepped forward to settle the legs of the wooden tray in an easy-to-reach position. She straightened and rubbed a palm against her apron. Her hair hung in a thick braid that draped over her shoulder. "If you haven't had lunch, I can bring you a sandwich and a glass of milk," she said to Ben. "You can eat with your sister."

"Much obliged, Miss Lorrie," he said, adopting the name the children called her.

At that Ellie observed the becoming color in her helper's cheeks with growing interest.

Lorabeth flashed an easy smile and hurried out.

Ben noticed a bunch of violets arranged in a tiny milk-glass jar on Ellie's tray. "She brought you flowers."

His sister smiled and raised the delicate blooms to her nose. "She's a godsend."

He gestured to the food on her tray. "Don't wait for me."

A few minutes later Lorabeth arrived with another tray and held it toward him. "Dr. Chaney had two pies delivered with the bread this morning. Would you care for a slice of peach or raisin, Mr. Chaney?"

Her eyes were the warm color of clear honey, and he liked the direct way she looked into his. "Ben," he replied.

Lorabeth held his gaze, and a flush crept up her cheeks.

"I'll get a slice later," he told her. "Thanks."

He noticed the way her hair shone in the sunlight from the window, then snared his thoughts.

"I'll take peach," Ellie said with a smile in her voice.

Lorabeth glanced toward Ellie with an embarrassed nod, then hurried from the room.

He picked up half a sliced beef sandwich, took a bite and caught Ellie looking at him. He chewed before asking, "What?"

She bit into a small shiny red apple with a satisfying crunch. "Nothing."

Half an hour later, Ellie was ready for a nap. Ben took both trays and carried them down to the kitchen where he found Lorabeth at the table scraping carrots. She laid down the knife and started to rise, but he waved her back down.

"Don't stop what you're doin'. I'm going to help myself to a slice of that raisin pie."

He poured milk from the ice chest on the back porch, then sat down with the full glass and a huge slice of pie.

"Ellie's going to nap," he said.

She nodded and continued to scrape carrots.

"I don't suppose it's a good week to make headway on those accomplishments of yours," he said.

She glanced up. "What do you mean?"

"You know, taking the long walks, reading all the books in the library…your train trip."

She dipped her head and raised one shoulder. "All that sounds foolish when you say it."

"It's not foolish," he disagreed. "I was just thinking that you're spendin' all your time looking after Ellie and the children."

She looked up, her hands falling still. "That's my job."

"But your free time," he mentioned. "Your free time is monopolized this week, as well."

"Mrs. Chaney needs me, and I'm pleased to be here for her."

"Maybe I could pick up a few books for you. At the library."

Her eyes widened in apparent interest.

"It's probably not as much fun as picking out your own. Caleb has a huge library, too. You could find a number of interesting subjects in there. I read through his books when I lived with them."

"I don't know," she said hesitantly. "I'm not family, and I wouldn't want to impose."

"Books are made to be read," he told her. "Caleb won't mind if you help yourself, but I'll mention it to him so you'll be assured. And I'll check out a few books until you can get to the library yourself."

"Why?"

"What do you mean?"

"Why are you doing that for me?"

"I appreciate you taking care of Ellie. And the way you do it is more than just a job," he said. "You do things from your heart. With kindness."

He had a moment's regret for saying something so personal. But the way she looked at him then, with surprise and pleasure, made him feel as though he'd said something important.

"The Bible does say that whatever I do I should do it as unto the Lord," she replied.

He took a drink of milk. "What does that mean?"

"I believe it means that each task, no matter how mundane, is a service unto God as long as we're doing it with pure motives and a right heart. No job is small or unimportant in God's eyes." She sliced the carrot lengthwise on the cutting board and placed it in a tin pan.

"Take scraping this carrot," she went on, holding up another. "It seems like an ordinary task, boring even, and perhaps it is. Some jobs are thankless but necessary. However, these carrots will nourish the Chaney family. The doctor is strengthened to go to work and save lives. Your sister is nourishing the child she carries and gaining strength to bring a new life into this world.

"The children are growing bodies and minds that will accomplish great things one day. Who knows?" Her vibrant expression lit her features. She'd been caught up in her passionate explanation, but she suddenly looked at Ben. "One of them could start a school or a hospital or give birth to a scientist that cures a disease or to a missionary who travels the world. We're just minuscule parts of an infinite picture."

Ben recognized all the joy and hope his own life was lacking. He envied her vitality and her optimism. She represented all the things he was starved for, and resentment and longing scared the spit out of him. He would never be that innocent again, never share her idealism. The fact that the inability was through no fault of his own dredged up reservoirs of anger.

Their eyes met for a heart-stopping moment.

No one had ever challenged his self-control as strongly as this woman did simply by being open and expressive. She stood for everything he strove for. And everything he wasn't.

Chapter Five

He leaned across the table and plucked a carrot stick from the pan. "I think I'm needin' one of these. Who knows what's in store for me this afternoon?"

He bit it with a resounding crunch.

Lorabeth raised one eyebrow as though concerned that he was mocking her.

"You've convinced me," he assured her. "Each task is important."

He chewed and thought of the various wild animals he'd treated and set free, wondering how his part in their lives affected nature. He didn't understand people who didn't feel compassion for animals or their fellow man, but he could understand Lorabeth's passion for the small tasks she performed every day. Everyone needed to believe they were making a difference in the world, that there was a purpose and a function for their lives beyond just getting through this hour and this day.

"Ellie asked me to come by again later," he said. His

sister never asked much of him, but she wanted him to check on Lorabeth and the children.

"Why is it you don't come for supper during the week?" Lorabeth asked out of the blue.

He shook his head as he considered her question. "Ellie asks me. Sometimes I accept. I guess I figure the weeknights are their family time."

"You *are* family."

He shrugged.

"I'll put a few more carrots in the pot."

Ben wasn't comfortable spending more time than necessary around Lorabeth, but if Ellie and Caleb needed him, he'd be here.

The rasp of the front doorbell caught their attention, and Lorabeth got up, wiping her hands on her apron. A moment later she returned.

"It's a man looking for you."

Ben strode through the hallway to the foyer where Matt Dearborn stood hat in hand, clearly uncomfortable in the Chaneys' expensively furnished home.

"Matt," Ben said.

"D'you have time to come by and look at my bay? Pennie's bloated and she's not eating."

"I'll come right now," Ben told him. "My other appointments can wait until later in the afternoon."

"Much obliged, Doc," the other man said with a look of relief.

Ben turned to find Lorabeth holding his hat. She extended it toward him.

He thanked her and followed Matt into the sunlight.

* * *

Late that afternoon, Ben finished his work at the Iverson ranch where he'd inoculated Pete Iverson's yearlings and examined a mare with matted eyes. He'd applied salve and left a tube with Pete after showing him how to pull down the mare's lid and squeeze a line of ointment into its eye once a day.

He mounted Titus and rode into town. The library was already closed as he rode past. He stopped for a few supplies at the mercantile. As a last thought, he asked Hazel Paulson for a couple scoops of jelly beans and tucked the bag into the pocket of his jacket after paying.

Relieved he didn't have to cook for himself, he rode toward his sister's, reminding himself this visit was at Ellie's request. He reined in and tied Titus to the post beside the front gate. The sight of all four youngsters and Flynn sitting in a row on chairs across the front porch brought him up short.

Flynn loped down the stairs, and the others followed. Buddy Lee followed at their heels, meowing. The children all spoke at once.

"Mama's having the baby!" Lillith said excitedly.

"Caleb's been up with Ellie since this afternoon," Flynn said.

"Mrs. Connor is here, too," Nate told him.

"I'm hungwy," Anna piped up.

"It's time for dinner," Ben said, guiding them back toward the house. "I'm hungry, too."

"Mith Lorrie'th fixing it by herthelf," Anna replied.

"Why didn't a couple of you help her?"

"David and me was helping, but she told us to watch Anna," Lillith replied.

Ben could imagine how much help David and Lillith had been.

He pointed to the swing in the side yard. "Why don't you girls swing while I go check on your dinner?"

Lillith and Anna ran down the stairs. Flynn accompanied Ben into the house. "How long does this baby stuff take?" Flynn asked with a furrow between his brows. "I don't remember it taking this long when Anna was born."

"I don't think there's a hard-and-fast rule," Ben told him.

He found Lorabeth in the overly-warm kitchen, strands of her honey-colored hair stuck to the back of her neck.

She glanced up from the bowl of potatoes she was mashing and gave him a quick smile. "Hello, Benjamin."

He opened the back door and the ceiling-high window to let in some air. Buddy Lee immediately shot inside, and Ben spent five minutes getting the cat out from under a cupboard and back out. "How are you faring?" he asked Lorabeth.

"Things got a little chaotic this afternoon. I ran an errand for Dr. Chaney and ended up getting supper started late."

"Flynn and I will help."

A look of relief crossed her features, but she said, "That's not necessary."

"Probably not, but we're helpin' anyhow. What can we do?"

"You can take the roast out of that pan and slice it. I didn't get the potatoes peeled in time to cook them with the meat, so I boiled them. The children like them better mashed, anyway. Flynn, will you please set plates around the table in the dining room? It will be cooler in there. Ask the boys to wash their hands and help you with silverware and napkins."

Ben removed the lid from the roasting pan, and the savory aroma of beef and browned carrots made his stomach growl. He found a large fork to lift the roast from the pan to a platter and sliced. A small piece fell to the side and he tasted the tender meat. "You're no stranger to a kitchen. This is perfect."

"I've been cooking since I was old enough to fire up a stove. What about you? You seem to know what you're doing."

"I've helped Ellie a time or two."

She moved beside him to spoon the carrots into a bowl. "Were you young when your mother died?"

Ben simply nodded.

"But your father had already passed away by then?"

Ben never lied. And he detested avoiding a question. He glanced to see if Flynn had returned, but his brother was still in the dining room. "Never had a father."

Of course *everyone* had a father. It just sounded worse to say he didn't know who his was.

She took the pan from him, placed it on the stove, and stirred flour into the drippings. Ben couldn't help noticing her efficient yet graceful movements. She wore a plain brown skirt and a white shirtwaist with her sleeves rolled back to her elbows. "Would you mind watching this for a moment? Just keep stirring."

He took over the gravy while Lorabeth scraped a

heaping mound of mashed potatoes into a serving bowl and made a well for a dollop of butter.

"Have you seen Ellie or spoken with Caleb?"

She nodded. "Her back was hurting something fierce when she woke up from her nap this afternoon. Caleb came around two to check on her. That was when he said it wasn't going to be long before the baby was born. I stayed with her while he went and canceled the rest of his appointments.

"She asked me to get the children from school, and once they were home and she'd seen and hugged them all, she told them to busy themselves. That was when Dr. Chaney sent me to get Mrs. Connor."

Sophie Connor was a friend of Ellie's. She'd been a Harvey Girl at the Arcade Hotel and restaurant before meeting and marrying the city marshal. Sophie had a couple children of her own. "Sophie's been down for water and tea a few times."

Lorabeth gave the gravy a final stir and used her apron to protect her hands from the hot handles as she poured the steaming liquid from the pan into a serving bowl. She reached for a ladle on a wall hook.

Ben unwrapped two loaves of bread and sliced both, stacking the slices on a plate.

"The carrots and green beans are warming back here," she said, taking bowls from the back of the stove.

Ben picked up the platter and followed her into the dining room. The boys had done a pretty decent job of setting the table.

"Nate, will you call your sisters now, please?" she

asked. "I'll go let Dr. Chaney and Mrs. Connor know that the food is ready and see if they want to eat."

Ben nodded and watched her head for the stairs, the braid swinging across her back.

The children were subdued as they took their seats around the table. Their parents' chairs were glaringly empty. Ben and Flynn served portions and cut meat into bites for the young ones.

Ben didn't give Lillith any green beans.

Lorabeth returned.

The kids looked at her and then at Ben. "Who's gonna say grace?"

Lorabeth asked a blessing for their meal and included a petition for Ellie's comfort and the baby's health.

Ben didn't look up, but the confident words of her softly-spoken prayer stayed with him throughout the meal.

Caleb arrived a few minutes later, his shirtsleeves rolled up and a look of preoccupation on his face.

"Mama's doing just fine," he told his children.

"When's the baby gonna come?" Lillith asked.

"When he's ready," Caleb replied. "It won't be long now."

"Maybe you should go back," David said with a frown of concern.

"Mrs. Connor is with her, and it will be a little while longer." He glanced at Lorabeth. "I'll send Sophie down to eat once I've finished."

"I saved some broth from the meat," Lorabeth told him. "When Mrs. Chaney is up to it, I'll take her a tray."

"That was a good idea. Very thoughtful, thanks."

Lorabeth nodded.

Caleb ate and left the table. It wasn't long until Sophie joined them. The pretty dark-haired woman was smiling and cheerful, assuring everyone that Ellie was indeed doing well.

Lorabeth asked Flynn to heat water and then she and Nate stacked the plates and washed pans and dishes. Ben and David dried while Lorabeth wiped the table and counters.

Nate and David had school assignments, so she settled them at the clean kitchen table. Minutes later she was pointing over David's shoulder to show him a step he'd missed.

Without missing a beat, she took cigar boxes from a shelf and set the girls to drawing and cutting.

Ben sat beside Lillith and pointed to a row of paper figures. "What's this you're makin'?"

"Miss Lorrie helps us draw pretty dresses for our paper dolls," Lillith told him. "She looks at the clothes in the catalog and then makes ours just like them."

"I never did things like this as a girl," Lorabeth told Ben with a sheepish shrug. "It's fun."

Ben knew all about missing out on things as a child, but he couldn't figure out how Lorabeth fit the picture. She had a respectable family, a concerned father, and lived in a nice home right here in Newton.

She had certainly stepped up and handled things for his sister's family this past week, and she'd knocked herself out to make sure the children's routines weren't upset. His admiration grew by leaps and bounds each time he was around her. She put her energy and talent to good use, and he acknowledged that.

Ben remembered the treats in his jacket pocket and excused himself to go get the bag. When he returned, he found a glass bowl in the cupboard and poured in the brightly colored candies. He set it on the kitchen table. "Each take five the first time to keep it fair," he told them. "And they can't all be the same color."

Anna stuck out her lower lip, but he'd done this before. "Others like red, too," he admonished, keeping his voice cheerful.

She looked up and tilted her lips into a cherubic smile, and all was well.

The candy made the rounds with each Chaney selecting five jelly beans until the bowl came to Lorabeth. She held it as though she'd been given a stolen diamond. Her wide tawny eyes looked to Ben in surprise. "They're for the children."

"Don't you like them?"

"I think so. A friend of my mama's gave me some a long time ago."

"Well, choose yours," he said with an encouraging nod.

Lorabeth carefully selected five and passed them on. She bit into the first one, and her broad smile gave him an odd hitch in his chest. She appeared every bit as childishly delighted with his surprise as Lillith and Anna.

Flynn came to the doorway and asked Ben if he'd read over an assignment for errors, so Ben gave Lorabeth a glance and headed for Caleb's den.

After watching him go, Lorabeth ran her tongue across her teeth to glean every last sugary bite. When the dish came to her again, she took five more candies and tucked them into her apron pocket for later.

Dr. Chaney entered the room and asked her for a cup of broth. She handed him a napkin along with the steaming cup. Preoccupied, he returned to his wife.

Lorabeth lit the lamps and lanterns and went upstairs to lay out the children's nightclothes and turn down their beds. Soft voices could be heard from behind her employers' closed door. The whole mystery of Ellie's pregnancy and this process of giving birth fascinated Lorabeth. All she knew about how babies were conceived she'd read in the Bible. "Caleb had 'known' Ellie" was vague and mysterious. All that metaphorical stuff about does and lilies in the Song of Solomon made it sound lyrical and lovely. The unknown was bewildering and alluring at the same time.

She escorted the girls to the outhouse and then washed their hands and faces in the wash room behind the kitchen.

"I want Ben to tuck me in," Lillith told her.

She sent them upstairs with a warning not to disturb their parents and sought out Benjamin. He and Flynn were seated in comfortable leather chairs in the doctor's handsomely furnished wood-paneled library.

"The girls asked for you," she said to Benjamin.

He stood easily, coming to his full impressive height. "Best indulge the little darlin's so they'll get to sleep."

"Are you set for tomorrow, Flynn?" she asked. Almost a full-grown man, Flynn was a student, as well. She'd never known anyone so cheerful or easy to please.

"I'm fine, Miss Lorrie," he told her with a grin.

She followed Benjamin from the room, and he

paused at the foot of the stairs for her to go ahead of him. She was reminded of the day she'd brought her things and he'd carried them to her room.

She led the way to the bedroom Lillith and Anna shared. The walls were papered with pale lavender violets, and the bureau and two small beds had been painted with matching flowers. Dolls lined the window seat and an enormous dollhouse occupied one corner. Lorabeth's breath had been taken away the first time she'd stepped in and seen the fantasy-inspired room created for their enjoyment.

Anna bounced on her bed and Lillith squealed at the sight of her uncle.

Lorabeth tucked Anna under her covers while Benjamin spoke with her sister.

"I am missing Mama," Lillith told him with a pout.

"It's only one night," he assured her. "She's busy, you know."

"Bringing us a sister," Lillith replied delightedly.

"Could be it's a brother," he reminded her.

"We got lots of them, but we only got me and Anna for sisters, so we need another."

"I want a puppy!" Anna called from her bed.

Benjamin looked across at her and grinned. "You'll have to talk to your mama and papa about that."

"Wake me up when the baby comes," Lillith told him in all sincerity.

Benjamin glanced at Lorabeth, but she wasn't familiar with the customs of this family and didn't know how to answer. She waited for him to reply.

"We'll wake you," he promised.

"'Night, Mith Lorrie," Anna said in her sweet baby voice.

"Good night, Anna."

Lorabeth traded places with Benjamin and he gave Anna a hug and kiss while Lorabeth spoke to Lillith. Finally she turned down the wick until the room was in darkness and padded toward the door.

Benjamin was right behind her, so close she could feel the heat from his body as she stepped into the hall lit only by a single reflecting tin lamp.

She was tempted to stop and experience the moment, but the door to Caleb and Ellie's room opened and Sophie came out carrying a tray. Lorabeth hurried to take it. "Can I get you something?"

"I can manage," she replied, keeping her hold on the tray. "But you must be exhausted. You've been working since dawn."

"I'm pretty tired," Lorabeth admitted. "I don't think I could sleep, though."

"Why don't you go out for some air?" she suggested. She turned to Benjamin. "Lorabeth needs a change of scenery. Ellie said she's been running after her and the children all week."

"It's no problem," Lorabeth assured her while the thought of getting out of the house appealed.

Sophie wasn't going to be put off. "No arguments now. Are the children all in bed?"

Ben explained that the girls were down and the boys would be next.

"As soon as Nate and David are tucked in," Sophie

said, "Flynn can listen for a problem. I'm here for Ellie and Caleb. Benjamin, take Lorabeth out for some air."

Lorabeth's body was physically tired, but she never slept more than five hours a night. She read until her eyes were weary, and then she fell asleep only to wake while it was still dark. The thought of a walk in the night air with the heavens stretching out above sounded far better than attempting elusive sleep. And the anticipation that she would go walking with Benjamin rejuvenated her immediately.

Lorabeth thanked her and turned to him. "If you want to send the boys up, I'll get a shawl from my room."

Several minutes later, man and horse stood silhouetted by the moon, both handsome, both restless. Benjamin said something to the animal, patted its neck.

"Where to?" she asked.

"We don't necessarily need a destination, but if you'd like a plan, we'll walk to the park."

"The park? Lovely!"

Lorabeth wrapped her shawl around her shoulders and appreciated that he didn't seem inclined to walk slowly on her behalf. Darkness had settled over the city, and the moon was a mere sliver of silver in the sky. A train whistle blew, a melancholy sound that reminded her of all the places she'd never been and all the things she wanted to do.

"Where did you attend university?" she asked.

"Chicago."

"Is it exciting, the big city?"

"It's bigger...all hustle and bustle like the train station."

She took a jelly bean from her pocket and extended

it to him. He shook his head, so she placed it on her tongue where the sweet flavor melted. "Did you visit museums and the theater?"

He nodded. A gas lamp cast his face into interesting shadows. "Sometimes."

"I read about Chicago in the *Florence Herald.* Dr. Chaney subscribes to that and the *Newton Kansan,* and sometimes he leaves them for us to use in the kitchen. I don't read them when I'm supposed to be working, of course. I wait until bedtime. And in the morning I return them to the rubbish bin."

"I'm sure Caleb doesn't mind you reading the newspapers."

"I asked his permission."

Of course she had. Her interest made it sound as though she'd never read a newspaper until recently. "Doesn't your father read the newspaper?"

"Oh, no. It's not edifying."

He'd sat through a good many of her father's Sunday sermons, but had never heard Reverend Holdridge express concern about people spoiling their minds with current events.

She glanced at Ben with a new look of concern. "Do you think less of me for reading a worldly publication?"

As though it mattered what he thought of her. "No. I read the news myself. Would your father disapprove of me reading it?"

"I couldn't say. He requires more discipline of himself and of his children than of others."

Benjamin didn't think it was undisciplined to read

the newspaper, but he didn't want to speak against her father or his convictions, so he said nothing.

They reached Broadway and neared the entrance to the darkened park. There had been gas lamps along the street, but in the one square block between Broadway and Seventh, there were only dark brick walkways, hedges and fading flowers lit by the moon.

"It's so dark," she said, her voice almost a whisper.

"Are you afraid of the dark?"

"I don't think so."

"We don't have to go into the park, we can walk around the outside…or we can head back."

"No. No, I want to go in." She took a forward step, but halted. "I want to, but it's a little frightening."

"Let's head back—"

"No." She extended her arm. "Just hold my hand, will you?"

Touching her was a liberty he didn't feel he should take. The time they'd spent together already was too much. His pulse thumped guiltily.

She was waiting. She would feel safe with him holding her hand, how ironic was that? This young innocent preacher's daughter trusted him to keep her safe. She was the most naive person he'd ever known. He wouldn't be the one to spoil that.

"Let's turn back," he said abruptly, and turned away from her.

She walked to his side, and he headed back the way they'd come.

"I'm sorry," she said, staying beside him. "I shouldn't have—"

"It's okay. Forget it."

The easy conversation they'd shared was behind, and it was okay, because he should never have let his guard down in the first place. Keeping it like this would be easier.

They walked in silence all the way back to the Chaney home where the only light from an upstairs window shone from his sister's room. He held open the front door, and Lorabeth entered into the foyer ahead of him.

"If you'd like to lie down, I can make up a bed for you," Lorabeth offered, always kind, always thoughtful.

"I'll wait in the library," he said, accustomed to holding back, keeping himself apart from others. "You go ahead and rest."

She moved toward the rear hallway.

"Aren't you going to your room?" he asked.

"I'm going to use the wash room first," she told him.

He turned away, feeling more foolish than ever.

Lorabeth drew water from the back of the stove and carried it to the wash room. She was exhausted, it was true. Every new experience was exhilarating, and she didn't want to miss out on a thing. Benjamin hadn't wanted to take her hand, that had been the problem, she guessed, and she felt awkward and ignorant. In her excitement, she'd made a blunder that had put a wrinkle in things between them.

She was confused, and confusion was an unfamiliar feeling. She was used to having things straight in her head. She'd always known what she wanted. Or she thought she'd known. She'd wanted more. A way out. A life without censor or deprivation.

And here she was, living in the town doctor's home,

privileged to a way of life she'd only dreamed of until now. She should have been content.

But she *did* want more. There was still so much to explore and dreams to indulge.

Benjamin stirred up all those dreams and longings she'd held dear for so long. He was the first man besides her father and brothers that she'd spent any time with, and he intrigued her.

He was waiting for her when she returned, and the sight created a warm glow in her chest.

She studied him in the golden flicker of the lamp that hung on the foyer wall. He had nice eyes, friendly but sort of sad, a straight slim nose and a generous mouth that rarely curved into a smile. Looking at him made her stomach feel funny.

A thin wail traveled down from the upstairs hall.

Benjamin's face tilted upward in expectation. The cry was the only sound in the enormous house. Seconds ticked by and their gazes met and held in expectancy. Gooseflesh rose along Lorabeth's arms and down her spine.

Finally the wavering cry ended, and a door opened and closed. Dr. Chaney appeared at the head of the stairs wearing rumpled clothing and a tired grin.

"It's a girl," he said, making his way down to where they waited, and Lorabeth had to move aside to let him pass on the stairs.

"Ellie?" The single name was Benjamin's only question.

"Ellie's just fine," Dr. Chaney assured him. "Tired but fine."

Relief crossed Benjamin's features.

"As soon as Sophie helps Ellie change and freshen up, you can go in and see them."

Lorabeth thought Benjamin might simply head on home now that he knew everything was all right, but he nodded and perched on the bottom stair to wait.

Dr. Chaney enlisted Lorabeth to help wake the children, share the news and ferry them one at a time from their beds to their mother and back. Each child was given a few minutes alone with their parents and new sibling while Lorabeth stood near the door and waited. More than once she saw Caleb and Ellie gazing upon their new child, on their older children, and sharing loving smiles.

Once Dr. Chaney leaned over Ellie and pressed his face to her hair as though she was the air he needed to breathe. The moment was so precious, so painfully intimate, that Lorabeth's heart ached with yearning for a similar bond, a tender belonging.

By the time the last child had seen the new sister, Lorabeth had dozens of tender images stored in her mind.

"I'll be heading home now," Benjamin told her after he'd seen his sister. He plucked his hat from a hook on the coat tree in the foyer. "I locked the kitchen door and checked all the windows."

"Thank you." A lonely ache had swelled in her chest until she felt close to tears for no good reason.

"Are you all right?" he asked.

She nodded. "Good night."

"Thanks for supper," he added.

"Thank you for all your help."

He settled the hat on his head and strode off the porch.

Lorabeth watched him mount the black horse that whinnied at his approach and listened until the sound of hoof beats on the brick street faded into the distance.

After turning down the remaining lamp wicks, she climbed the stairs to her room.

There'd been a time when she'd seen the bleakness and toil of her mother's days and dreaded growing up into the same kind of life. Her mother had known there was more, too. She'd been powerless to change things for herself, but she'd made certain to encourage Lorabeth to strive for more.

Now Lorabeth knew that one day she wanted her own home and a family. She'd worked for the Chaneys for two years, and in that time she'd had plenty of opportunities to be certain of what it was she wanted for her own life.

From her bedroom window, she gazed out into the dark night and tried to imagine where the park was. Why had she been so hesitant to go in? One of her dreams of freedom had been fulfilled this night, but she'd been afraid to plunge in all the way and dare the unknown.

Never again. She'd never again miss anything by holding back.

Chapter Six

～～～～～

Appreciating the physical exertion that same week, Ben tossed down hay from the top of a stack in the barn and forked it to the stalls in the rear. He'd put a lot of enthusiasm into commanding his head and his will into submission over the past several years. He worked to use his energy in good ways because he had to be a man of strong character.

His life had been all about self-control, but it had been too easy. He should have known. He'd never been tempted from his purpose or distracted by physical or emotional desires. Until now.

Lorabeth was his weakness. He recognized it. He resented it. She was all he valued and respected. She was pure and innocent.

Doubly dangerous because of her perfection. She stirred up responses that he had vowed never to allow.

The sound of a buggy alerted him to the presence of a visitor or a patient. Dropping the pitchfork with a flurry of swirling dust motes, he strode out into the sunshine and met the female driver who stepped down.

"Mornin', ma'am. Fine day for a ride."

Her straw bonnet hid most of her face from view as she turned to the rear floor of the conveyance and took out a crate covered with an afghan. "I've brought my Minnie for your help, Doctor. It seems the foolish girl has managed to get a fish hook stuck through her paw."

A loud mewl from inside the crate told Benjamin that the feline inside wasn't any happier than its owner.

He stepped forward. "Let's have a look at Minnie."

The woman held the crate forward at the same time she introduced herself. "I'm…I'm…" She flattened her palm against her chest and stared at him as though she'd seen an apparition. "Oh, my."

"Ma'am?"

"I'm—Susanne Evans," she said haltingly.

Ben took the crate, but her eyes didn't leave his face. "You're Dr. Chaney?"

"My brother-in-law is the medical doctor, as I'm sure you know. I'm the vet. Call me Ben."

He guessed her to be in her mid-thirties.

She had black hair and ebony-winged brows above green eyes. She was a striking woman, full-figured and apple-cheeked.

She stared at him. Then, as though realizing she hadn't let go of the crate, she jerked her hand away. "I'm sorry. It's just that…"

"What?"

Her skin seemed unusually pale.

"Are you all right, Mrs. Evans?"

She nodded.

"Do you want to come into my office while I look at your cat?"

She nodded.

"Do you need a drink of water or somethin'?"

She cleared her throat. "No."

He peeled away the afghan to have a look at his patient. The animal was a long slender Siamese with sleek silver fur, black ears and facial tinting and narrow blue eyes. "She's a beauty."

"She was a gift from my husband." Mrs. Evans followed him into the house and to the area he used for his office and examining rooms.

Ben spoke to the animal in a low comforting tone to gain its trust, petted her and fed her a tiny piece of jerky.

Mrs. Evans was now making him self-conscious with her stare.

He looked her in the eye. "Is there a problem?"

She shook her head without a word and glanced away. Her attention fastened on the glass jars where he kept treats for his patients.

"It looks like the candy counter at the mercantile, but with bits of jerky and—what's that?"

"Dried apple. When did this happen?"

"This morning. She got out when the children left for school and I found her in the shed where my husband keeps his fishing poles. I had to cut the poor thing loose from the line. Why the man left a hook on the line is more than I can figure out."

"She's gonna be just fine," Ben assured her. "Why don't you help me hold her."

Once he had the cat's trust, he hooked a short leash to her collar and secured her to the examining table.

"Look away and don't breathe this," he instructed Mrs. Evans.

Talking in a soft tone, he doused a cloth with ether and held it to the feline's nose. The cat tried to pull away for a panicky moment, but succumbed to the fumes and fell limp on the table.

The cat's owner released the pet and sat in a nearby chair to watch.

Ben quickly poured disinfectant over the paw, then cut the hook in two with a small pair of wire cutters. Once the prongs were disposed of, he pulled the hook out and firmly pressed a wad of cotton to the wound to stop the minimal blood flow, all the while aware of the woman's scrutiny.

Within minutes Minnie's paw was dabbed with ointment and bandaged. He washed his hands and placed his instruments in a pan of disinfectant.

"How much do I owe you?" Mrs. Evans asked.

"Two bits should do it," he answered, drying his hands.

She took a coin from her purse and handed it to him. "You have a gentle touch. Confident and capable."

"She's gonna wake up groggy and disoriented. Maybe mad as a hornet." Ben wrapped the cat in the afghan and handed her over like a sleeping baby. "I suggest you put her in the box and keep her there for a time so she doesn't hurt herself when she wakes up."

Mrs. Evans nodded and lowered the animal into the crate. "We're fortunate you chose to practice in Newton."

"Never thought about anywhere else," he said, picking it up for her and leading the way out of doors. "Family's here."

"Your parents, too?" she asked, following.

"No. My sister and her family and my brother."

He set the crate in the back floor of the buggy.

The woman's questions continued. "Have you lived in Newton your whole life?"

The way she kept looking at him made him uncomfortable. "No, ma'am. We grew up nearby though."

"Forgive me, but I've met Dr. Chaney—the other Dr. Chaney, I mean—and if you're not his brother, how can your name be Chaney, too?"

It was a logical thing to wonder. Sometimes Ben questioned taking the Chaney name and the respect and history that went along with it, like borrowing the name as though it was a pair of shoes that didn't fit.

"My brother-in-law adopted me and my brother," he answered simply.

"So…your mother…is she…?"

"She's dead. You wouldn't have known her."

That look of curiosity and suspicion that he hated to see in people's eyes made him angry. He found a lap blanket and tucked it around the crate, so the cat wouldn't wake up and escape.

"You must think I'm awfully rude," Mrs. Evans said.

Without comment, Ben straightened and assisted her up to the seat.

"It's just…"

He waited.

"I'd like you to meet my husband," she said finally.

He nodded. "I'm sure it'd be a pleasure, ma'am."

She gave him a last long look and shook the reins over the horses' backs.

Ben watched her go, shrugged off his irritation and went inside to clean up his exam room. It was still early enough to make a trip to the library.

"Ben, I want you to take Lorabeth to Zeta Payton's home social this Saturday night."

"What?" Ben looked at his sister. It was Sunday evening, and they were sharing a simple meal. The extended Chaney family had headed back to Florence a short time ago.

It had been Baby Madeline's first day at church, and the family was in good spirits.

Lorabeth had carried dishes into the kitchen.

"Sophie and I talked about this. The young people hold socials every Saturday night. They play games and the like. I've never known Lorabeth to take any time for herself. She even helps me all weekend and late into the evening. And I'm beginning to have my suspicions about her supposed mornings off."

"What do you mean?"

"I think she goes to her father's and does all their laundry and cleaning on those days."

Ben thought about it and remembered Lorabeth's mention of no time to go for walks or visit the library.

"She needs to get out and mingle with people her own age," Ellie added. "Working all the time isn't healthy. Please do this for me. I want to see her get out and have fun, and she'll be more comfortable if you're there to introduce her."

"I don't go to things like that," he objected.

"It won't hurt you, either," she insisted.

"Ellie, you know I'm not like all those others."

"Oh, you're too special to associate with the commoners?" she asked with a raised brow.

Caleb shot Ben a look that said he might as well give in and do her bidding while he was ahead.

Ellie asked so little of him, and Lorabeth was her right hand. He could do this for both of them. "Oh, all right."

Ellie smiled in satisfaction. "I'm going to get the girls ready for bed now."

Caleb rose from the table. "Nate and I will take care of the dishes."

Flynn had gone to visit friends for the evening.

"Lorabeth," Ellie addressed her when she returned, "take off your apron and get some air now."

Lorabeth glanced at her employers, immediately removed her apron and headed for the door.

Ellie stared at Ben pointedly.

He pushed back his chair and stood to follow her to the porch.

She was sitting on the top step, her forearms crossed on her knees. She glanced up at his approach.

He leaned against the column and studied the darkening sky. "The home social is at Zeta Payton's this Saturday night."

"What is that?"

He'd been a couple of times in the past. Those who attended had been classmates the short time he'd been in school in Newton and they invited him on occasion.

"They drink punch and play parlor games." He didn't like participating because he didn't know the children's nursery rhymes they took for granted in some of the games. "Kind of silly. You might know a few of the girls from school, though, and it would be a good chance to make some friends."

She was looking at him with an expression he couldn't quite decipher.

"Will you go?" he asked.

"A party? Have you invited me to a party? I've read stories about dances and social events, but the only activities I've ever been allowed to attend were church functions. I doubt I have the proper clothing. I would have to shop."

"Ellie will help you."

"We're going then? To a party? Young people and maybe…maybe dancing?"

"Maybe dancing," he answered with a lopsided grin.

She pressed her hands to her cheeks as though they stung. She dropped them immediately.

"What if my father finds out? He might make me go back."

"Caleb and Ellie approve, and they're serving as your guardians, aren't they?"

"I suppose they are at that."

"You're safe with me, and I could always assure him of that."

"I have to start thinking like an adult, don't I?"

He gave her a grin.

"There's another worry," she said. "I don't know how to dance."

"It's not hard," he told her. "I'll show you. Ellie will show you. Flynn's a really good dancer."

"Now? Will you show me now?" She stood expectantly.

With no music? And alone out here on the porch? Warning signals went off in his head, but he silenced them and straightened. How could he say no and dim the excitement in her eyes? She was eager and fragile, and he couldn't reject her. He could endure anything for Ellie and for the young woman who took such good care of his sister and her family.

So he did something he'd avoided, something he knew wasn't safe: he took her right hand in his left and placed it at his waist. He took her other hand and folded it in his while he rested fingertips on her back. He stood with Lorabeth in his arms, the scent of her fragrant hair under his nose.

Her nearness challenged his restraint, and there wasn't a man in all of Kansas who worked harder at self-control. He had to.

The fact that she'd never been held by a man or danced in his arms humbled him and gave him courage. At that moment there wasn't anything he'd rather do than teach her to dance.

Cicadas provided the background music, and he explained the steps and the count. She fell right into the pattern and followed him effortlessly. Each time they turned and passed before the light from the parlor window, the joy on her face took his breath away.

"I'm dancing!" she exclaimed, her voice breathless. She laughed, and the sound whittled away defenses he'd built for the safekeeping of his heart and pounded at barriers that protected his sanity. He felt an overwhelming desire to draw her against him and bury his face in her hair. His body reacted with purely male instincts.

Ben fought to rebuild that wall, mentally corrected himself and took a step back, releasing her. What was Ellie thinking? "I have to go."

She clasped her hands to her breast.

He opened the door and reached inside for his hat. "But I have something in my saddlebags for you."

"What is it?"

He went to the horse and withdrew the books he'd checked out of the library with her in mind. Carrying them to her, he placed the stack in her hands.

"You remembered." Her voice revealed awe. She closed her arms around the books.

"Just picked a few I thought you'd like."

"Thank you."

He looked away.

"I'll see you on Saturday, then," she said.

He hesitated. He'd made a promise. "Yes."

He couldn't reach Titus fast enough. A look over his shoulder showed him she was leaning against the pillar where he'd been earlier, watching him go.

He untethered the horse, placed his foot in the stirrup, launched himself onto the saddle and rode like the hounds of hell were on his heels.

Distance wouldn't help. He couldn't escape himself.

Chapter Seven

Saturday's plans were never far from Lorabeth's thoughts, no matter the task that week. On Thursday morning, Ellie readied the children, and they left them with Sophie Connor for a few hours so they could shop.

"I've always appreciated the shops in Newton," Ellie told her. "They buy for travelers and for the Harvey Girls who have spare cash and eyes for a pretty dress, so there's always a good selection."

Eva Kirkpatrick had an assortment of dresses for sale in her shop. "Ellie!" she cried, upon seeing the woman. "You look lovely. And you have a new daughter, I've heard."

"She's just perfect," Ellie told her. "Have you met Lorabeth?"

"I don't believe so."

Ellie made introductions.

"You're the reverend's daughter, then."

"Yes, ma'am."

"Lorabeth needs a dress for this Saturday. Something pretty for a social."

"Are those kids still doing those socials? I remember being that age." She led the way to racks of clothing along one wall. "You'll be easy to fit, Lorabeth. You're a perfect size, and though you're a little tall, I've left the hems out of most of these so they can be custom lengths. With your coloring, I'd suggest green or yellow. What would you like?"

Lorabeth was in awe of the lovely dresses Eva showed her, one after the other. There were so many to choose from! Time and again her eye was drawn to an ivory taffeta with a high neckline, a gathered yoke bodice and three layers of eyelet at the hem.

"I made this on a whim," Eva said, taking it out and showing them. "It's so feminine, isn't it? This wide sash cinches at the waist. Why don't you try it on?"

Lorabeth retreated to a curtained-off dressing room and changed clothing. When she returned, Ellie and the dressmaker stared.

"It's stunning on you," Miss Kirkpatrick declared. "Your hair and eyes are accentuated because of the soft color." She took the sash from Lorabeth and tied it around her waist. "Do you like it?" She turned her toward a full-length mirror.

An unfamiliar woman gazed back at Lorabeth. She looked feminine. She felt special.

"I think she'll need more besides this one," Ellie said. "Once the bachelors see her, she'll have invitations for every weekend evening from here on out."

Lorabeth blushed at the thought and the flattery. "How much is this one?" she asked.

"This one's my gift," Ellie told her. "Now pick out a couple more."

"I can't let you do that," she objected.

"You *will* let me," Ellie said, and she smiled as though she was thinking of something. "It's a gift to let you know how much I appreciate you."

"I already know—"

"No more objections. Find dresses."

Lorabeth was delighted to obey.

The day became even more interesting when Ellie escorted her to Aunt Tibby's Tea Parlor. They drank tea from rose-patterned china cups and saucers and ate delicate frosted cakes.

Lorabeth told Ellie about the books she'd been reading, stories that Benjamin had checked out of the public library for her. Ellie listened intently, a smile on her face.

Lorabeth's thoughts returned to the upcoming weekend, and her stomach fluttered in anticipation. How much more exciting could life get?

Ben didn't sleep well Friday night. He woke several times with recurring nightmares that left a bad feeling behind. He spent the following afternoon at the house in town. He'd experienced his first taste of family in these rooms, known his first measure of safety and acceptance. Here he clung to the good memories and drew strength and comfort.

It surprised him that Ellie didn't understand his need to keep this place he thought of as home. But then she had Caleb now, and she had learned security as a couple and a family.

Ben couldn't let go of this place.

He dressed and arrived at Ellie's promptly. He let himself in and found Caleb and Ellie in the study. Baby Madeline was sleeping in a bassinet a few feet from where they sat.

Ben strolled over and studied her miniature features. Another child to love and cherish. Another life couldn't make up for those lost in their childhood, though. He looked up and found Ellie studying him as though she knew what he was thinking.

"She's beautiful," he managed through the sheen of tears that blurred his vision.

"Ellie thinks she looks like you," Caleb said with a grin.

Ellie got up and came forward to lay her hand on his for a moment. When she looked up, the sadness he'd glimpsed was replaced with joy. "I'll go let Lorabeth know you're here."

Several minutes later, Ellie returned with Lorabeth.

Ben couldn't take his eyes from her, and he couldn't think of anything to say.

She was the most beautiful and captivating creature he'd ever seen. Her hair, looking soft and shiny, was swept from her face and hung in curls down her back. She wore a soft-looking dress in a color that reminded him of a new duckling, pale yet alive. Her tawny eyes sparkled with excitement.

And…anticipation. Ellie was looking at him, too. Caleb gave him a nearly imperceptible nod.

"You…um…" He stopped and caught himself before he stuttered. "You're beautiful, Lorabeth."

She beamed.

Ellie nodded approvingly.

"I'm so nervous," Lorabeth admitted, and pressed a hand to the sash at her unbelievably narrow waist.

"Nothing to fear," Ellie told her with a quick squeeze around her shoulders. "You're lovely and smart and you'll make lots of new friends in no time. You'll have all the fellas eating out of your hand."

Lorabeth's smile confirmed her unease had been set aside. She turned that heart-stopping gaze on Ben.

"Let's go," he said.

"I figured you'd enjoy walking," he told her as they stepped from the front porch. "The Paytons' is only about as far as the park."

"Next time," she said, "if you want to walk through the park, I'll go in."

He regretted his own hesitation that night. She'd led such a sheltered life and it wasn't fair to withhold simple things from her just to protect himself. "Next time," he told Lorabeth, "I'll hold your hand."

Another promise.

A train rumbled in the distance, and from inside one of the houses they passed a baby cried.

Ben extended his arm and she hooked hers through as they walked. The streets were lit by gas lamps, but the brick walks weren't perfectly even. It would be no hardship to be a friend to Lorabeth.

They strolled in companionable silence.

"Your sister gave me the dress as a gift," she told him after a few minutes.

"It's pretty."

"She's a wonderful person."

"I know."

"I never knew a family could be so caring."

"Your father cares for you," he pointed out. "He made a good home for you all your growing-up years, didn't he?"

"Yes, he did," she agreed.

"I'd have traded my childhood for one like yours in an instant," he told her.

She looked up at him. "What was wrong with your childhood?"

He shook his head, refusing to think back that far, let alone talk about it. "Never mind."

"I'm sorry to have sounded ungrateful. I didn't mean to. Everything is so new and exciting, and I don't have much to compare to."

"I should warn you," he said, changing the subject, "the punch at these shindigs is usually spiked."

"Spiked?"

"With liquor."

"Oh! Goodness! Isn't it wicked to imbibe in spirits?"

"Has some wicked aftereffects, I assure you. I don't set much store by drinkin' myself. Makes people do foolish things."

A buggy passed them, and passengers got out a few houses farther up the street.

"We're almost there."

She raised her hand to her hair in a self-conscious gesture.

Bright lights shone from all the downstairs windows, and the tinny sound of music reached them.

"What's that?" she asked.

"A Victrola."

"I've seen the advertisements, but I've never heard one. Do you know the song?"

Ben listened for a moment. "'Molly Malone.' It's an Irish folk song."

"How do the words go?"

Zeta opened the door of her parents' home and greeted them, sparing him. "Ben! What a wonderful surprise! And who's this?"

He introduced Lorabeth.

"Welcome, Lorabeth. Come in and meet the other guests."

The vivacious redhead drew Lorabeth into a large room where young men and women milled in groups. Benjamin stayed close beside her.

Lorabeth remembered Carrie Bennett and Frances Adler from school. She was introduced to a petite blonde named Jenetta Wisdom, as well as a handful of young men.

Carter Tibbs had wavy russet-colored hair and sparkling dark eyes. The slim young fellow attended church with his parents, so he was familiar, but Hobie Dearborn and Damian Wick were new acquaintances.

She clung to Benjamin's arm, unwilling to lose her safe connection.

"Where are your parents tonight?" Hobie asked Zeta.

"At the cattleman's club as usual," she replied. "Miss Pratt is our chaperone."

"I think she's referring to the Paytons' housekeeper," Benjamin supplied.

"Frances is apprenticed at the *Newton Kansan*," Zeta told Lorabeth.

"Oh, I've read it," she answered.

A couple of them laughed as though she'd made a joke.

She glanced at Benjamin. "I have."

He nodded with a smile.

"Let's have punch and sandwiches, and then I have some very special parlor games planned," Zeta suggested.

"What are the games?" Lorabeth asked quietly as they mingled with the crowd around the table in the dining room.

"Charades, guessing games, proverbs, things like that," he replied.

"I know a lot of proverbs," she assured him.

He gave her a weak smile.

"Is it liquor?" she asked of the punch.

He dipped a ladle, poured liquid into a small glass cup and tasted it. "Yup."

She glanced around the room. Studied the huge bowl with orange slices floating on top. Looked at the cup. The liquid was orange and fruity looking. She didn't intend to disregard her father's teachings and reflect poorly on him. Surely a sip wouldn't hurt. She'd promised herself never to hesitate and miss out again. "I'll have a little taste," she said.

Without expression he handed her the cup he'd just sipped from.

Lorabeth tasted the cold liquid. It was sweet and fruity and had a little sting that made her nose tickle.

Lightning didn't strike her dead. "It's quite refreshing."

Ben poured himself a cup from a pitcher of lemonade. She asked the question with her eyes and he answered with a shake of his head. Plain lemonade.

Benjamin handed her a plate and she followed him behind the line of guests, selecting a couple of dainty sandwiches. He led her to a long low divan and took her plate so she could adjust her dress to sit. He left and returned with a plate for himself.

Lorabeth was amused by the chatter around her and took pleasure in the playful banter. Her father would be appalled at the frivolous waste of time and money. There wasn't anything edifying about the evening thus far. She was loving it.

The hostess strolled past with a tray of full cups, and she traded her empty one for a full one. The second cup of fruity punch was even better than the last.

Benjamin finished eating and took their trays.

"Jenetta will keep track of forfeits this evening," Zeta announced.

"What does that mean?" Lorabeth whispered.

"Each time you lose, you add a forfeit to your tally. At the end of the games you have to pay."

"With what? I didn't bring any money."

"No, you pay with whatever the forfeit is at that time, like a song or a joke. The forfeits are just another part of the games."

"Oh, I see."

"We're moving into my father's study for the first game," Zeta said. "It's all set up."

The gathering merged down a hall and into a large room lit only by a flickering light. A sheet had been hung to divide the entrance of the room from the fireplace, she realized.

Murmurs and chuckles erupted from the crowd.

"This is a shadow game," Benjamin supplied.

They all walked around the sheet and took seats on chairs and the floor by the fireside.

"Draw a number," Zeta said, and passed a bowl of paper slips.

Lorabeth drew seven. Benjamin had twelve.

"Number one!" Carrie called. "Who's going to start?"

Jenetta jumped up and moved to the back side of the sheet.

Zeta motioned for Frances to get up. The girl took her hair down from its chignon, shook it out and tucked her arms close to her body and walked before the sheet.

Lorabeth realized then that Frances was backlit by the fire and only appeared as a shadow to Jenetta on the other side of the sheet.

"Who is it?" Zeta asked.

"It's Carrie," Jenetta guessed.

"No!" the gathering shouted.

"Lorabeth?"

"No!" they cried again.

"One more guess and you take a forfeit," Zeta called.

"It's you, Zeta."

"No!" they cried in unison.

Lorabeth understood the game and that Frances had

tried to disguise herself. The next fellow turned up his collar and tucked in his chin, but the guesser recognized him anyway.

"It's your turn, Lorabeth," Zeta announced. "Go take the seat."

Lorabeth walked around the sheet and took her place on the chair. After a few whispers and a thump, two figures loomed on the other side of the cloth. The taller one, obviously a man, leaned over the smaller one until their noses met and their shadows merged. She was so surprised that she slapped a hand to her breast. "Oh, my!"

"What are they doing back here?" Zeta called.

"They're, um, they're…" Her neck and face grew uncomfortably warm with embarrassment. "I think they're having a private moment."

The girls erupted in giggles.

"One of them is Carrie. Who do you think the other is?"

"Carter?" she asked, trying to recall everyone's names. "No!"

"Hobie?"

"No!"

"Damian, then."

"No, it's Ben!"

Ben kissing Carrie? She couldn't even comprehend it. "Come see!"

Lorabeth got up with her heart pounding and made her way around the white curtain.

Benjamin and Carrie weren't even touching. They faced each other, but stood in such a way that their shadows reflected an embrace.

The young people burst into laughter.

"It's such fun to play that prank on someone new," Frances said, coming to link her arm through Lorabeth's.

Lorabeth couldn't explain the relief that flooded over her or the embarrassment that climbed her cheeks and made it difficult to meet Benjamin's eyes. When she finally dared, she noted he wore an amused expression.

The guests filed back to the dining room where they filled their cups. Lorabeth held hers out for Zeta to ladle punch in.

"This was Ellie's idea," Benjamin said near her ear. "If you're not comfortable, we can leave anytime. I won't mind."

"Oh, no. I like it," she assured him and sipped her drink.

"Men are going to flatter the ladies now!" Zeta called.

The females in the room murmured their enthusiasm over that suggestion.

"Lorabeth," Zeta told her. "The requirement is that each young man will go from one lady to the next and say six flattering things about her. But tonight—" she paused for effect "—he cannot use the letter *L*."

The males groaned.

"We'll go around the room and, Carter, you're first."

Lorabeth watched with interest as Carter complimented a fair-haired Ida Hunter with statements such as, "Your hair is shiny" and "You are very good at charades." When he used the word *helpful* a chorus of voices tagged him with a forfeit.

Carter reached Lorabeth, and she smiled expectantly. The etiquette books she'd read had advised her it was inappropriate for a lady of quality to encourage flattery from a young man, but flattery was the object of the game.

"You—" Carter caught himself and started over. "Your…oh, my…your finger work—that's it! Your finger work at the piano is very good."

Everyone laughed at his frustration to get his meaning across.

"Thank you," Lorabeth said.

He grinned. "You are, um, you have good manners."

"Thank you," she said again.

"Your hair is a unique and an attractive—shade."

No one had ever said that to her before. "Why, thank you, Carter."

A few of the guests chuckled, and Lorabeth realized she didn't need to thank him each time. She blushed.

"Your eyes are incredibly—"

"Forfeit!" the cries came.

She was disappointed he'd used an *L*. She wondered what he'd meant to say about her eyes.

And so the game went, with the young men tripping over their tongues. When it was Benjamin's turn, he told Zeta her party was nice and that the sandwiches were good. He told Frances Adler she wore a becoming shade of rose. When he got to Lorabeth, she waited expectantly.

"You make me…um…with you I, um, you make my face happy."

Lorabeth laughed at his avoidance of the word smile.

"You're kind and generous."

Her cheeks warmed. "Thank you."

"You catch on to new things fast."

"Like croquet?" she asked.

He grinned. "You're sweet and innocent and not at— not the—not jaded or affected."

"How many was that?" someone asked.

"You have a good heart," he added.

"One more," Zeta said.

"You're the prettiest woman I know."

One of the ladies beside Lorabeth sighed.

Lorabeth blushed to the roots of her hair, and Benjamin took his seat beside her.

Conversation swelled around them, and she looked over at him. "Truly?" she asked.

"I don't say things I don't mean, even in a game."

"Thank you."

"What's good for the goose is good for the gander," Zeta called. "The ladies will compliment the gentlemen now." Carrie Bennett began, making rounds and earning three forfeits. Frances was next, but she made it all the way around the gathering without a penalty.

When it was Lorabeth's turn, her heart fluttered. She didn't relish making a fool of herself, but that seemed to be the sport of the evening and everyone took it with good nature.

She approached Carter first, because she knew him from church.

"You are prompt," she told him.

He nodded in amusement.

"You are good to your mother."

A few guests "awed" at that comment.

"Your—" She stopped herself before she said clothing or always. "Your *attire* is fresh and neat."

Pleased with her first attempts, she smiled and glanced at the accepting expressions of the others. For the rest of the young men she commented on their smiles and clothing, earning a forfeit when she told Hobie he made her laugh.

She reached Benjamin and her mouth went dry. So many things came to mind when she looked at him, but none of them were appropriate for a game and most of them contained *L*s. She smiled, and the corner of his mouth inched up in return.

"That," she said, pointing to his mouth, "thing you do is very handsome."

He raised his brows in wordless response.

"You're good with—the young ones."

He nodded.

"You're a good teacher."

But so much more than that.

"And a good friend."

"Two more!" Zeta called.

"You don't judge. You're smart—and kind-hearted."

The gathering clapped as she finished. Lorabeth gave Benjamin a last look before moving on to Damian and commenting on his neat appearance and shiny hair.

By the time they played Grecian statue, everyone had enough forfeits to make the party finale interesting.

Zeta placed a fish bowl in the center of the room on an oak pedestal.

"Draw as many slips as you earned forfeits," she instructed.

They plucked folded slips of paper from the bowl, and Zeta explained they would go around and pay them one at a time. Hobie was first, and he had to recite a poem.

He chose a silly one about a cat in a rowboat, and the game moved on. Carrie's first forfeit was to give something she was wearing or holding to another person. She took a handkerchief from her pocket and gave it to Carter.

Jenetta's forfeit was to crawl on her knees like a kitty and rub against the legs of the person beside her.

Beside her sat Damian, and he quite enjoyed Jenetta's catlike performance.

Benjamin unfolded a slip of paper.

"Kiss a person of the opposite gender," he read.

Lorabeth widened her eyes at that request. She'd thought the kitty had been risqué!

Benjamin seemed to consider his options for a moment, then got up and walked across the room to lean over Carrie Bennett and kiss her right on the lips!

The crowd applauded, and Carrie blushed. Benjamin returned to his seat beside Lorabeth without meeting her eyes.

Frances Adler caught the attention of the room with her next forfeit. "Five minutes in the coat closet with the person of your choice."

Laughter and surprised comments erupted.

"Parker," she said, crooking a finger. Lorabeth couldn't remember hearing his last name.

He was tall and dark-haired with a lock that fell over his forehead in a becoming manner.

Zeta opened the coat closet and closed the door behind them.

Lorabeth glance at Benjamin. He met her eyes and raised an eyebrow.

"Watch the time," Zeta instructed Ida.

Lorabeth's first forfeit was to recite a proverb backward, and she was relieved because proverbs were something she knew forward and backward. She thought it through first, then said, "Rubies above far…is price her for…woman virtuous…a…find…can… who?"

Laughter rang out as the friends deciphered and approved of her rendition.

"How does that go?" Ben asked while the others were occupied.

"Who can find a virtuous woman? For her price is far above rubies."

"That Solomon knew his stuff, didn't he?" Benjamin's next forfeit was to give away a possession. He took a pocketknife from his trouser pocket and handed it to Lorabeth.

The utensil was warm, the bone handle worn smooth from use. She held it self-consciously.

Jenetta and Parker were released from the closet and took their seats amidst jeers and cheers. Jenetta smiled as though quite pleased with herself, and Parker wore a wide grin.

Lorabeth stumbled reading her next forfeit. "K-kiss a beau on your left."

Frances was directly to Lorabeth's left and next to Frances sat Parker.

"Parker! Your lips are getting a workout this evening!" someone called and the others all laughed.

Lorabeth looked at Benjamin. His expression didn't give away what he was thinking, but he did say, "You don't have to. It's just a game."

"She has to draw two if she refuses this one," Carrie reminded them.

Lorabeth hadn't expected anything like this. She

wished she could kiss Benjamin and not this other fellow, but she wanted to play the games and do everything the others did. She stood on legs that trembled and moved around Frances's knees to stand before Parker.

He smiled up at her. He was handsome and friendly looking. Her stomach quivered nervously. She'd seen Ellie and Caleb share a kiss now and then, and she knew they enjoyed it.

Taking a deep breath, Lorabeth leaned forward until she was face-to-face with Parker. His brown eyes held little gold flecks in the lamplight.

She feared closing her eyes because she didn't want to miss her target or fall headlong over him, so she kept them open and touched her lips to his.

His lips were warm. Not unpleasant feeling at all. Not what she'd expected, either. But the contact was too intimate for this public display. Her cheeks burned.

Spectators applauded.

Lorabeth straightened, returned Parker's smile and went back to her chair. This time she avoided Benjamin's gaze.

Ben would have left an hour ago if Lorabeth hadn't assured him she was having a good time and wanted to be there. He wouldn't have come at all if Ellie hadn't insisted.

The games had become a lot more risqué since the last time he'd joined this bunch.

He sure as hell hadn't been about to kiss Lorabeth in front of these people, and he hadn't expected her to kiss a man. He should have known, though. She was open to experiencing all the things she'd missed, and the activities here were beyond her limited experience.

He wished the forfeits were over so they could leave.

Several more kisses and a few badly sung nursery rhymes and it was time to go.

Benjamin thanked their hostess and led Lorabeth out the door. The fresh air felt good on his face. He took off his jacket and slung it over one shoulder.

"Are you chilly?" he asked.

She shook her head.

They walked along the brick path, hearing guests leaving and buggies pulling out behind them.

Benjamin reached for Lorabeth's hand. She didn't resist.

"I feel like walking a little farther," he said.

He led the way to the park and guided her along the darkened paths. "Scared?" he asked.

"No."

They reached the center of the park where stone benches shone pale in the moonlight. He released her hand.

"Were you shocked?" he asked finally. "At the games?"

She giggled. "I *was* pretty surprised."

"I don't think Ellie knows exactly what goes on at those house parties."

"If my father knew, he'd be holding a prayer vigil on the street," she said.

"He'd be disappointed in me for takin' you, I know that," Ben added.

Lorabeth sighed and tipped her head back to study the heavens. "He's disappointed a lot."

"What did *you* think?"

Her laughter was spontaneous and light. "It was fun." She turned in a circle, then faced him, her features composed. "Why did you pick Carrie?"

Silence yawned between them.

"For the kiss," she clarified unnecessarily.

He thought about how to answer.

"Didn't you want to kiss me?"

Chapter Eight

Ben's stomach dipped. "I didn't want to kiss you like that. Not in front of everyone."

"Oh." She wrapped her arms around herself. Seconds passed. "That was my first kiss."

Damn. He shook his head in self-disgust. "I should have kissed you. Even in front of everyone. I should have kissed you so I would have been the first."

"It wasn't a real kiss, was it?" she asked.

"What do you mean?"

"It couldn't have been as real as when two people care about each other and choose to kiss because they want to, not because it's a silly forfeit, like a riddle in a game."

Lorabeth deserved a special kiss. A kiss as perfect as she was. "You're right. I don't think it was a real kiss."

"Good."

"Are you cold?"

"A little."

He settled his jacket around her shoulders. The scent

of her hair drew him like a bee to a sweet flower. He leaned over her and inhaled the scent of Lorabeth.

"Don't you want to kiss me?" she asked.

"Oh, I want to."

She paused a moment before asking, "Then why…?"

Ben dipped his head and brought her chin up on the knuckle of his forefinger to capture her mouth and hush her questions.

Her mouth was a sweet discovery, her lips soft and pliant beneath his. He wrapped her close in his embrace and she fit against him perfectly, her curves pressed to the plains of his body. His chest swelled with expectancy and his thoughts of reason dimmed as pleasure took over his senses and feeling ruled out hesitation. He loved her honesty, admired her zeal for life…but most of all he appreciated her innocence and purity. She was a fresh clean breath of air in a stagnant world.

She was light in the midst of darkness. She was unspoiled and naive, and he loved those things about her.

His body reacted quite naturally, and he eased himself away from her so as not to spoil this moment.

She raised a hand to his cheek, and the touch of her fingers made him feel clean. Young again.

He caught her hand and pressed his lips against her skin, tasting her, absorbing her goodness.

"That was a real kiss, wasn't it?" she asked breathlessly.

His eyes closed tight against the night, against the world. "Yes."

"I liked it," she said in her usual childlike straightforward way.

"I liked it, too," he answered.

"And I like being alone with you like this," she admitted.

He knew three or more cups of Zeta's punch were making her giddy and he had a responsibility to her, to her father. "Lorabeth…"

"What?"

He shook his head almost imperceptibly. "It's unsafe for you to be alone with just any man. You know that, don't you?"

"My father warned me enough times."

She couldn't understand, and he didn't want to shatter her illusions. "You wouldn't be safe here like this with anyone besides me. I need you to understand that."

"All right. Will you kiss me again next time we're alone?" she asked.

He leaned away from her then, steadying her before he released her. "I'll have trouble resisting."

She smiled in the moonlight. "I hope we're alone a lot, then."

"You don't know what you're saying…or what you're hoping."

"Maybe not. But I want to learn."

It was obvious she wanted to learn—about everything. And it was apparent he would be doing battle with himself at every turn. He took her hand. "Let's get you home."

They were silent most of the way. When they reached Ellie's, Ben walked Lorabeth to the front door and watched as she used the key Ellie had given her.

"This is the first time I've used a key."

"Are you going to tell Ellie?" he asked her.

"About what?"

"About the parlor games."

She pushed open the door and turned to him. "Do you want me to?"

He shrugged.

"If she asks directly, I'll tell her, of course."

Of course she would never lie.

"But if the subject never comes up—and why would it?—then I won't say anything. I never knew it would be so enjoyable to be around others that way, just to have fun for the sake of fun."

The pleasure on her face could have lit the night. How refreshing to see her delighted with such simple things. She was unique and special, and her eagerness scared him.

She moved inside and stood back from the doorway. "Are you coming in?"

He thought of mentioning next week's social, but couldn't make himself say the words. Like a coward, he shook his head.

"Good night," she called behind him.

Titus had been tethered near the back gate. Ben loosed him, walked him out to the street and mounted.

Looking back at the house, only one light was on, and it shone from the side of the house on the second floor.

Ben urged the ranger to walk toward the fence that bordered the acreage and watched as a shadow fluttered behind the curtains of that upstairs room.

His insides knotted at the thought of Lorabeth preparing for bed. Undressing…washing…brushing out her hair.

He'd never seen a woman perform any of those nighttime rituals, but his imagination was filling in the blanks.

It was a domestic scene he pictured, a scene where man and woman shared a home and a bed....

What did he know about domestic? He'd grown up in a shack with no food and a mother who drank herself blind every day. What did he know about men and women other than whores and men with twisted desires and unholy unions...perverted desires? He'd witnessed sex in exchange for booze money. He knew about lack of responsibility. About lust. He knew how men cheated on their wives under cover of night. He dreamed crude distorted dreams that disturbed and aroused.

Ben didn't know the first thing about decent men and women except what he'd observed between Ellie and her husband. There were good men in the world, but all he understood for sure was weakness, and he'd made a stubborn vow never to show any. Without self-control he was nothing.

By allowing this association with Lorabeth, he was placing himself in a position he'd shunned all his adult years. He had chosen not to be the kind of man he abhorred. He'd held himself apart. He'd never let himself weaken or lose control.

And unleashing those desires was a weakness and a danger.

The weight of the burden he carried had increased. That experience with Lorabeth scared Ben more than he cared to admit. He stayed away from his sister's house that week. He didn't want Ellie asking him to take Lorabeth to another home social.

* * *

Saturday arrived and Ben spent the day in town. He used his time and energy refinishing the kitchen floor and replacing boards near the thresholds.

As evening came and went, he prepared himself a simple meal of fried eggs and toasted bread with the strawberry jelly Ellie had given him.

He was exhausted at bedtime, but lay atop the covers wide-eyed with his head reeling. Finally he tugged on his denim trousers, shirt and boots and grabbed a jacket from near the door. A walk would do him good.

The town hadn't gone to sleep yet. Buggies traversed the streets and about half the homes had lights burning behind their windowpanes.

He walked all the way to Ellie's corner and stood behind a forsythia hedge where he could see the house and the lights. The room he knew belonged to Lorabeth was dark. He pictured her asleep, wondered if she'd missed him that week.

A horse drew a buggy toward the house from the other direction and pulled up before the gate. Not an unusual occurrence to see a patient call on Caleb at odd hours.

A tall man climbed down and reached back up to assist someone to the ground. A wife or daughter perhaps.

The woman's laughter arrested his thoughts, and Ben squinted through the darkness for a better look. She gathered her skirts and walked toward the door, the man close behind.

Lorabeth!

His head spun for a moment, the surprise scattering

his thoughts. Her room was dark because she had been out with a gentleman caller!

And Ellie had encouraged this?

Anger welled in his chest. Lorabeth was too naive to be cavorting with the likes of the young men in this city. She had no idea of the vulnerable position she was placing herself in.

She was too impressionable to be out alone.

Ben held himself in check, not wanting her to know he'd been standing here as they arrived. She would think he was jealous or overly interested.

What about Caleb's responsibility? Caleb had made a promise to her father to see to Lorabeth's well-being. The reverend would never approve of this.

The couple was standing on the porch now, and the roof hid them from the moon and the streetlamps. Ben couldn't see what was happening, but the front door hadn't opened.

It didn't take this long to say a courteous good-night and take your leave.

Ben strode out onto the walk and under the trellis where the path led to the house. His steps were loud and hurried.

He made out two separate shadowy figures just as Lorabeth called, "Benjamin?"

"Evenin', Lorabeth. Who's that there with you?"

Carter Tibbs approached the edge of the top stair and reached for Ben's hand. "Evenin', Ben."

"We've just come from Ida Hunter's," Lorabeth told him, excitement lacing her voice. "Her home is nearly at the edge of town, and it's beautiful! Her mother made candies and there was a tray of caramel-covered apples on sticks."

Enthusiasm poured from her as she shared everything she'd seen and done. "Hobie was funny tonight! One of his forfeits was to act like a pig!" She laughed.

She shared her excitement with him as though he was her closest friend and she couldn't wait to tell him. "We played pantomimes and blindman's bluff. It was quite fun. I'm sorry you missed it."

"I had work to do," he told her, but he was sorry he'd missed it, too. Sorry he'd missed her reactions. He'd cheated himself by holding back.

"Well, perhaps next time," she said just as friendly as you please.

"Definitely," he replied, with a pointed look at Carter.

"What are you doing here so late?" she asked.

Carter seemed curious for an answer, too.

"I was going to speak with Caleb if he's still up," he replied.

She seemed to accept that explanation. "I see. Thank you for accompanying me," she told Carter. "It was a lovely evening."

"Thank you for agreeing to be my partner," he replied. "You've taken to the group like a duck to water. Everyone likes you."

Ben should have stayed behind the hedge.

He should have stayed at home.

He should have shown up this week and invited her himself.

He shouldn't be standing here humiliating himself in front of Carter Tibbs. "Good night, Tibbs. See you in church in the morning?"

Carter nodded and backed toward the top stair.

"Good night, Lorabeth." He returned to his buggy, picked up the reins and guided the horse away.

"Come on in and we'll see where Caleb is," Lorabeth told Ben.

"If he's not in his study, I'll just talk to him in the mornin'."

The study was dark as Ben had suspected it would be.

"Lock the door behind me," he told her.

"Good night, Benjamin."

He closed himself out on the porch and listened for the turn of the lock and the sliding of the bolt.

Carter certainly hadn't wasted any time inviting Lorabeth to be his escort. Ben wondered why Carter had the impression that Lorabeth was free to accompany just any person who asked her.

Lorabeth *was* free to accompany any person who asked her. The admission hit him over the head like a well-aimed two-by-four. Benjamin's stomach knotted, and the night air was suddenly too close to breathe comfortably.

He didn't want to want her.

What kind of man refused to acknowledge his desire for a woman and yet denied anyone else the privilege?

He'd pondered what was missing inside him. Was it the ability to be like other people? Was it confidence? Was he dishonest with himself? He fought down the irrational feelings of helplessness and set a determined course toward home.

Ben didn't sleep well that night and awoke with the same thoughts on his mind.

* * *

Lorabeth was seated at the piano when he arrived at church to sit with his family. He acknowledged her smile with a nod and slid into the pew beside Flynn.

Lillith immediately scooted down from her father's lap to work her way in front of Flynn's knees and ease her fanny up until Ben tugged her onto his lap.

He kissed her ear and smelled the delicate scent of her hair. Ellie's children gave him hope. Their lives and happiness were slowly changing his jaded view of the world. They were delicate treasures, and he loved them wholeheartedly. "Mornin', sweet pea."

Confident of her welcome, Lillith snuggled in comfortably until the hymns began and he urged her to stand. She took his hand and sang along while he held the hymnal low, even though she could only read a few words.

Lorabeth was wearing a blue dress with matching ribbons in her hair. She sang along with "When the Roll is Called Up Yonder," her gaze only occasionally touching the songbook in front of her. When the singing was over, she took a seat beside her brother in the front row, and Reverend Holdridge approached the pulpit.

Ben seated himself again and Lillith tucked herself into a comfortable position with her head under his chin.

Ellie glanced over and smiled. Baby Madeline slept soundly on her lap, and on her other side Nate and David fidgeted in their seats.

Ben loved Sundays. He loved seeing his family all dressed in their best and enjoying the service. Loved going back to the house with his belly growling and helping set the table and see to the children. He loved family dinner and games and being around Caleb's parents.

He'd always felt as though he was sharing the benefits illegally somehow, as though this family life he so desired wasn't truly his. Somehow Lorabeth's presence exposed those insecurities for the truth.

He wasn't like all of the Chaneys—he was wired differently. Ellie would disagree because she'd made the needed adjustments and become like them.

Ben had never learned how. He knew where he came from. He knew where he wanted to go. He just didn't know how to get there—how to set aside the burdens that weighed him down. Was he even worthy to keep company with people like the Chaneys? Was he right to feel unworthy yet protective of someone like Lorabeth? He stored the doubts in a little cubbyhole in his mind and ignored them.

The reverend read the story of Joseph and how his jealous brothers sold him into slavery, and Ben's thoughts drifted to the kiss he and Lorabeth had shared. Her father would run him out of town on a rail if he knew.

Last night rose up and taunted him. Which was worse? Ben sullying Lorabeth's innocence or another man making the attempt?

The other man, of course.

He couldn't stop himself from turning and seeking out the man who'd been on his thoughts all night and this morning. He located the Tibbs family on the other side of the church, a few pews back.

Carter's parents appeared engrossed in the message. Carter's older brother and his wife stole secret looks at each other and held hands. Carter was studying the front pew where Lorabeth sat with her younger brother on her left and her older brother and his wife on her right.

Carter's intense gaze traveled from the front of the church to fasten on Ben. He cast a barely perceptible nod. The greeting wasn't as much of a hello as it was acknowledging the competition.

A warning that had been flickering to life inside Ben burst into flame. For now his focus zeroed in on protecting Lorabeth. He could best do that by keeping her safe. By not neglecting her or forsaking her to the wolves in sheep's clothing.

He wasn't completely fooling himself. He couldn't deny that the idea of being Lorabeth's guardian appealed to him on more than one level. He accepted the challenge in that moment while his gaze was locked with Carter's.

The reverend summed up his message with a prayer. With Lillith on one arm, Ben quickly made his way to the front to escort Lorabeth from the church.

A short time later they were riding toward home in the buggy Caleb rented on Sundays. Lorabeth was seated with Lillith and David on either side of her, and Ben had sandwiched himself in the rear with Flynn and Nate. Anna was asleep on his lap.

A thought occurred to him in that instant—an awful thought. What if Lorabeth *preferred* Carter Tibbs's company to his?

"Did you hear me?" Lillith asked over Lorabeth's shoulder.

"I'm sorry, what?" Ben asked.

"I said why did God make fleas? Mama said I should ask you 'cause you know all about animals."

He thought that one over, seeking logic and finding none. "Maybe Lorabeth should answer that one. She knows more about God than I do."

Lorabeth turned to give him a look that said, *Thanks a lot.*

Caleb and Ellie exchanged amused glances in the front. Ben gave Lorabeth an innocent smile. Her tawny gaze held a measure of amusement.

"Some things we just don't know," Lorabeth replied easily. "God is much wiser than all of us, so if He thought fleas were a good idea, who are we to question Him?"

Ben was highly impressed when Lillith calmly accepted that answer and resumed her seat.

He made sure he maneuvered his duties so that he was in the kitchen with Lorabeth as she took a ham from the oven and placed it on a platter.

"I'll slice," he offered, reaching for a knife.

She used a masher on a pan full of potatoes and whipped them until they were fluffy.

"So you had a good time with Carter last night?" he asked as though it was of no concern to him one way or the other.

"Mr. Tibbs is quite nice. Did you have a chance to say hello this morning?"

"We acknowledged each other." He stacked slices of meat. "I trust he was a gentleman."

"Very much so. He was attentive and thoughtful."

"Lorabeth."

His serious tone caught her full attention. She turned a wide-eyed gaze on him.

"I'm concerned for you. You're not used to the pranks and the games. You've led a very sheltered life."

"Why are you concerned?" She frowned. "Are you disapproving of me wanting to make friends and have fun?"

"Of course not," he answered quickly. "It's just that, well, I'd feel responsible if anything were to happen. I introduced you to these people. You're too unworldly to know the dangers."

She raised her eyebrows. "What are they?"

The deeply buried memory of a dark night many years ago throbbed to life, seizing Ben's mind and voice. All the helplessness and horror flashed into his awareness now. At a loss for words, he was relieved when Ellie joined them, her clothing changed.

She donned an apron. "My, aren't the two of you an efficient team?"

She squeezed Ben around the waist affectionately and gave Lorabeth a little hug from behind.

Lorabeth turned to her in obvious surprise.

"I'll pour milk and make sure the hooligans are washed and have the table set," Ellie said, sweeping toward the back porch and the icebox.

Ben and Lorabeth worked in silence until Ellie returned with two pitchers and carried them to the dining room.

Gathering his thoughts, Ben finished with the ham and wiped his hands clean. "The dangers are probably beyond your understanding," he told Lorabeth. "Men aren't always who or what they seem. One of them could seduce you before you knew what had happened. Or…or worse."

Lorabeth was stirring the contents of a pan on the stove, but she turned and stared at him. "Worse?"

He remembered the screams. The feeble cries. "Ignore your innocence and your wishes and compromise you."

She gave him a puzzled look. "That's pretty unclear."

His anger was actually apprehension for her safety now that he thought it through. "All the more reason to be careful."

"You're truly afraid for me?"

Now that she'd put it so baldly, he had to admit it. "I am."

"You know more about these things than I, Benjamin. I trust your judgment. I do so enjoy the home socials. So should I stop going?"

"No. It's important to you. I'll take you. I'll take you anywhere you want to go."

Like the wolf guarding the sheep, he thought momentarily, then dashed that nagging worry away. He would keep her safe.

"That's kind of you."

"No, it's selfish." He'd be honest. She was honest.

"Because?"

"Because I don't want to worry about you."

Ellie returned and peered over Lorabeth's shoulder at the smooth dark gravy. "Perfect."

She reached into a cupboard for two china gravy boats and then helped pour.

"Are you as hungry as I am?" she asked Ben.

"Pretty hungry," he answered.

They picked up the platters and bowls and proceeded to the dining room.

The wind had increased, bringing with it rain that tapped on the steamed-over windows in staccato bursts. The sound of geese overhead was a reminder of winter ahead. Inside it was warm and comfortable, and all seemed right with Ellie's world.

With an overwhelming sense of satisfaction, she looked from her husband to her brothers and children. Madeline lay sleeping in her wooden cradle in the corner of the room. Ellie dabbed at her eyes.

"Something make you sad?" Caleb asked, leaning close to take her hand and touch a fingertip to her cheek.

She shook her head and smiled through the sheen of tears. "Something makes me very, very happy," she said. "You've made me happy, Caleb."

He kissed her forehead and squeezed her hand. "I love you."

Their family swelled around them, laughing, passing food, and Caleb turned to take the warm roll Anna was pushing at him.

Ellie glanced from her husband to her brothers. Flynn was as happy and carefree as a lad his age should be, thanks to Caleb. And thanks to Ben.

She turned her attention to Ben, and her pleasure dimmed ever so slightly. The picture of him as a skinny, terrified eight-year-old flitted across her memory, replaced by images of formative years and teen years, and his contorted and perspiring, gaunt face the night he'd offered his life in exchange for hers.

She probably understood her brother better than he

knew himself. He thought he had all his ducks in a row. He held himself in strict judgment to prove he was a person who mattered. Being hard on himself somehow made up for their past and the sins of others.

Ben took slices of ham for himself and Lillith and sliced Lillith's into bite-size pieces. Each of these children had cut through his defenses right to his heart. How much more would it take for a woman to do the same?

Ellie's gaze moved to Lorabeth. Ben had never shown interest in a particular woman before, and Ellie understood his hesitation. He'd seen too much during his formative years, things that had skewed his perspective of men and women. He wouldn't want to do the same things he hated in others.

Inside Ben was a tender heart seeking acceptance, a wounded soul needing fulfillment. Caleb's love had mended Ellie's emotional wounds. Love would do the same for her brother.

Chapter Nine

Ben felt so much better about the situation with Lorabeth that he slept all night without the recurring dreams that normally haunted him, dreams in which he was helpless to protect the people he loved. This morning he awoke refreshed. As a rule he liked Mondays because they represented a fresh start on a week.

He was making rounds of his caged patients when a familiar buggy pulled close to the barn. He recognized Suzanne Evans. She had a man with her this time.

The tall, sandy-haired fellow assisted her to the ground and they walked toward Ben. The man wore an expression of puzzlement and concern. Something about him, about the impressive width of his shoulders and sheen of his fair hair in the sun struck Ben as oddly familiar, though he knew he'd never laid eyes on the man before. Unexplainable apprehension nagged at his gut.

"Mrs. Evans," Ben said, striding forward. "Is Minnie in trouble again?"

"No, Doctor. I've brought my husband."

"I'm not a people doctor, ma'am. That's my brother-in-law's job."

"I know," she answered. "Wes isn't ill."

Ben's attention traveled from Suzanne to the man standing beside her. That strange and uncomfortable sensation crept up his spine and raised the hair on his neck. "Who are you?"

"Maybe we should sit down," the man suggested.

Stiffly, Ben pointed to the front of the house, and Suzanne headed for the porch. He followed a few steps behind Wes. "Chairs are dusty," Ben said. "Don't sit here much."

"It's all right." Suzanne took a seat.

Ben waited for Wes to follow suit, then perched warily on a painted bench.

The man took a breath as though fortifying himself. "Was your mother Sylvia Foster?"

The air left Ben's lungs. He stiffened his spine and narrowed his gaze. How would this man know that? "Who are you?"

"Well…" His disturbing eyes moved from his wife to Ben. "I think I'm your father."

The words hung in the air. The drone of a bee was the only sound save the pounding in Ben's ears. "I don't have a father."

"Everyone has a father," Wes answered.

Ben had thought the same thing a hundred times, but a biological fact didn't make a family. Ben stood and moved to the bottom of the stairs as though preparing to get away. "What are you trying to pull?"

Suzanne spoke up then. "I'm the one who asked Wes

to come here and see you for himself. You two are the spitting image of each other." She gestured by jutting an upraised palm toward her husband. "*Look* at him!"

Ben's instincts were on alert. He didn't want to look, he didn't want to recognize any such thing. He knew the circumstances of his conception, and he didn't need to imagine them. But the oddly familiar sense he'd gotten at first sight of Wes nagged at his peace of mind.

Wes hadn't moved from his perch on the wooden chair, though his body was rigid. The man had hair the same color and texture as his own; his eyes were the same shocking blue that startled Ben each time he looked into a mirror. The man's hands were large, his fingers long, nails flat and blunt. Looking at Wes's hand was like looking at his own, except for the added years.

Ben had always known that his father could have been any of a hundred men. It should be no surprise to discover a man who looked exactly like he would in twenty years.

"My mother was a whore," he said flatly. "If what you say was true, it wouldn't say much for you."

He glanced at Suzanne, realizing she was learning that her husband had paid a cheap whore for sex.

"Wes and I have been married eighteen years," she told him as though guessing his thoughts. "And the situation wasn't what you're thinking."

The anger and resentment that were never far below the surface welled up in a ball of rage in Ben's belly.

"Your mother was Sylvia Foster, wasn't she?" Wes asked. "You have an older sister named Ellianna."

Ben's gaze shot to Wes, and he placed one foot on

the bottom stair in a move toward the man. "What the hell do you know about her?"

"I told you I knew your mother."

"And my sister? You knew my sister?"

"Saw her when she was a tiny little thing is all."

"Get off my land."

"Dr. Chaney, please listen," Suzanne begged.

"You don't have anything to say that I want to hear," he told Wes. "My mother was a whore. If you knew her, that's your sad story. I don't need it, thanks. I don't know what you want from me or why you came here, but I don't want anything to do with you."

With a pained expression, Wes glanced at his wife. She shrugged and stood to reach for his hand. He took it and they moved past Ben into the yard. The man paused and turned his head to the side as though he wanted to say more. Apparently he thought better of it and continued on to the buggy.

Ben strode to his barn and waited for the sound of horses and harnesses to assure him they'd gone.

He looked at his hands and found them shaking. He curled his fingers into fists and pressed them against his eyes.

Years of safely guarded emotions clawed at his soul like demons gaining a foothold to scramble out of a pit. He knew where he came from. He'd dealt with it. He couldn't change it. He didn't need anyone except his family. Ellie. Caleb—the Chaneys who'd become his family by choice—*because they wanted him.*

He sure as hell didn't need the hellish reminders that man wanted to dredge up, and Ben refused to acknowledge Wesley Evans as his father and buckle to the depravity of being sired by a whore.

What would it prove?

Ben replaced hay in stalls and pens, then untethered Delilah the goat and let her follow him as he worked. The animals were his solace; helping them had healed him. He spoke to them—nonsensical things, important things—as though purging himself of all the confusion and anger could heal him. Delilah was a good listener, and followed him from barn to house.

He donned a jacket and pulled up the collar against a late-afternoon chill. Minutes later a galloping rider approached from the road.

Ben recognized Riggs Webb, son of the Arcade Hotel manager.

"Ice wagon ran over Mrs. McKinley's dog, Doc!" Riggs managed out of breath. "She's hurt bad."

"I'll grab my bag," Ben called. "Can I take your horse and you follow with my wagon?"

He was only a few minutes away from town, and the dog still lay in the street when he arrived. A small crowd milling around the injured animal parted when he arrived.

The dog wasn't bleeding from his head or mouth, but his back legs looked crushed, and the high-pitched whine was pathetic. Ben filled a hypodermic needle and immediately gave the canine a sedative.

Mrs. McKinley sobbed into a lace hanky. "Beau was right beside me in my garden. I was covering my bulbs with straw. Then he heard the dismissal bell and ran toward the schoolhouse. He likes to follow the children home, you know. Can you help him, Dr. Ben?"

Mrs. McKinley lived right beside Ben's house in town, and Beau greeted him with a friendly yip and a visit each time he saw Ben come and go.

"I'll do my best, ma'am."

The ice truck was stopped several feet away. "Somebody fill a gunnysack with ice and bring it to me."

Robbie Rentchler hurried to do Ben's bidding, and Ben placed the ice on the dog's hindquarters. "Help me get him on this blanket so I can take 'im to my place."

Robbie helped him, and they placed the now-unconscious dog in the back of the wagon.

Mrs. McKinley cried like a little girl who was losing her best friend. Eva Kirkpatrick had come out of her dress shop, and she draped an arm around the woman's shoulders to comfort her. "Why don't you come in and I'll make us some tea? Benjamin will let you know how Beau is doing."

Ben thanked her with a nod and took the dog home.

The most serious injury was a broken hip. He worked on the animal through the evening, setting the bone and keeping him sedated while he made the cast and let it set.

He believed the animal would make a recovery, but he wasn't sure how well he'd be able to get around afterward.

Eva drove Mrs. McKinley out to see the patient that evening. Ben greeted them and offered them cups of coffee.

"How come no woman has caught your fancy yet, Benjamin?" Eva asked in her friendly manner as they sat at his kitchen table. She glanced around the spacious, obviously little-used room. It looked pretty much like it had the day he'd moved in.

He shrugged good-naturedly. When he'd first come to Newton, Caleb's first office had been above Miss Kirkpatrick's dress shop. Ben had been Caleb's helper until leaving for college, so he'd had plenty of opportunities to get to know the kindhearted woman. "Don't know, Miss Eva. None compare to you, I reckon."

She laughed. "None compare to that sister of yours is more likely."

"That woman is a dear," Mrs. McKinley agreed. "Taking on all she has, what with you boys and Dr. Chaney's son, and now her own children. Watched you boys grow from skinny young things to strappin' men under her care, I did."

"I don't know if you can entirely credit Ellie with their remarkable size and strength," Eva chided. "Heredity may have had something to do with it."

Her friendly remark jolted Ben's thoughts back to the man who'd been there that morning. He and Flynn had survived *in spite of* family origin, thanks to Ellie.

Mrs. McKinley waved away Eva's comment and added another spoonful of sugar to her coffee. "I'll be so lonely without Beau tonight," she said, and a tear rolled down the thin pale skin of her cheek. "He sleeps across the foot of my bed and keeps my feet warm even in the dead of winter."

"Why don't you come stay the night with me?" Eva suggested, patting the elderly woman's arm. "We'll play a game of cribbage in front of the fire."

"That's kind of you, dear. Thank you."

Ben took them to see Beau again before they left. The mutt was awake and raised his head and thumped his tail at his mistress's attention. Ben took it as a good sign that the animal was alert, though he planned to keep him sedated and resting for several days until he let him go home.

Beau was the focus for his thoughts and attention the next two days and nights, and Ben was glad for the distraction. When he felt the animal was recovered enough so that Mrs. McKinley could care for him, he drove the wagon to town and got him settled.

Ben ate supper at the Arcade and once it was dark, rode to the Chaneys'. He let himself in the front door and stood in the foyer listening to the heartwarming sounds of life and family. This was what was missing in his house. Children's voices carried from upstairs. It was bedtime.

He found Flynn in Caleb's study.

"Hi, Ben! I heard about Mrs. McKinley's Beau." They'd been neighbors with Mrs. McKinley for years, and it was a family joke to call the dog Mrs. McKinley's Beau. "How's he doin'?"

"I think he's gonna be all right. Where is everyone?"

"Caleb got called out. Ellie and Lorabeth are upstairs. I'm finishin' my studies."

"Would you mind askin' Ellie to come talk to me in the kitchen when she's finished?"

"Don't you want to go tell her yourself?"

"I don't want to get the kids all excited. I'll just wait."

"Okay." Flynn left and returned a few minutes later. "She said she'll be down shortly."

Ben watched Flynn tally a row of figures and eventually wandered into the kitchen, where he pulled out a chair and waited. He considered pouring a cup of coffee, but apprehension made his stomach refuse that idea. He needed to find out whatever Ellie knew, but he was afraid of what the facts might be. She would be straight with him; she always had been.

A few minutes later Ellie showed up. She leaned over him to smooth his hair and press her face to his temple in a motherly gesture.

Ben caught her hand. Emotions welled up and he fought for control.

With her hand still in his, his sister sat on the bench beside him. Her look flickered over his face and hair. "Something wrong?"

He dropped his gaze to the tabletop and composed his thoughts and his words. "Had a visitor a couple days ago."

"Who was it?" she asked.

"Man name o' Wes Evans." He brought his attention to her face to observe her reaction. "Ever heard of 'im?"

Ellie's lifted brows and slow blink showed a measure of surprise. "Wes? What did he look like? What did he want?"

"Matter of fact, he looked a lot like me."

A floorboard creaked overhead and the clock in the hallway chimed, but neither of them flicked an eyelash as they stared at each other.

"Do you remember him, Ellie?"

"Vaguely. She—" they never called her mother "—had a friend named Wes for a time. I was too little to remember much. He was kind, I think. I don't recall things being so bad around that time. They got worse later. Ben, what did he want?"

"A week or so ago his wife brought her cat for treatment, and she stared at me the whole time. I know why now. Apparently she went home and told her husband she'd seen me. I have no idea what that conversation must've been like…but she brought him to see me."

Ellie stared at him wide-eyed.

"He thinks he's my father."

She blinked a few times. Opened and closed her mouth. Gripped his fingers and then let go to press both hands to her breast as though her heart was a speeding train threatening to jump the rails.

"Why would he admit to that?" he asked. "Why would he tell his wife he fathered a kid with a whore?"

She shook her head, apparently trying to reason or remember. "What did you say to him?"

"I told him to leave me the hell alone."

"Oh, Ben." She stared at him wide-eyed. "We haven't talked about this for a long time. I think about it every day. I don't need to take it out and beat myself with it, too."

"You're the one who said I shouldn't punish myself with the past."

She conceded with a begrudging nod. "But you're the one who told Caleb the truth about Winston and what he did to me—what *she* let him do to me—because you wanted to stay with Caleb so badly, remember? You told him that night after Winston came after me again."

"I doubt I'll ever forget."

"So we admit the truth, but we don't punish ourselves with it," she insisted.

"The truth is our mother was a whore and we don't know who our fathers are," he said bluntly.

"But if you had a chance to know," she said, her voice intense now, "would you take it?"

He looked at her. "A man like that isn't worth opening a vein for, Ellie."

"Can you be sure what kind of man he is?"

"He was one of *them*."

She closed her eyes. A tear slipped beneath her lashes, and the sight made his chest ache.

"Ellie."

"I'm not sad for me, Ben, I'm aching inside for you." She opened her eyes. "You're the only one who can decide if you want to give this man a chance or not. If you want to know the truth. If you can handle it."

"What good would it do?"

"I don't know. And neither do you. But you have a chance to find out." She stood and gazed down at him. "You're not him. You're not any of them. Maybe that's what you'd learn. Or maybe you'd learn he's not the piece of dung you've believed he is all these years, and you just don't want to stop hating him because hate is easy."

Her words found their mark and sank in. He placed his elbows on the tabletop and laced his fingers over the lower half of his face.

Soft footsteps sounded, and Lorabeth stepped into the semidarkened kitchen. "Oh, I'm sorry. Am I interrupting you?"

She turned as though to leave.

"No," Ben said before she could go. "Come on in."

He got up and turned up the wick on the wall lamp.

Lorabeth held a book against her midriff. "I was going to make some tea and read."

"I'm tired," Ellie said with a weak smile. "If you'll excuse me, I'm heading upstairs." She leaned over and pecked Ben's cheek with a light kiss.

"'Night, Ellie."

Lorabeth laid the book on the table, pumped water into the kettle and stoked the fire in the stove. "Will you join me?"

"Sure."

The water boiled and she poured it over leaves in the teapot, then let them stand while she got cups from the cupboard. "How's your patient?"

"News sure travels," he answered. "Dog's doin' well."

"There's no home social this week because the Iversons are holding a dance at their place. A barn dance, Ellie called it. She and Caleb are planning to go, and she said her mother-in-law will come stay with the children so I can go, too."

The harvest dance was a yearly event, but his thoughts had been elsewhere, and he hadn't given the festivity any consideration. "Will you let me escort you?" he asked.

She gave him a bright smile. "I would love that. This will be our chance to really dance, won't it?"

He nodded. "It will."

She poured their tea and set the sugar bowl in front of him. "Is everything all right?"

"What do you mean?"

"You're awfully quiet."

"I've just had a lot on my mind."

"Of course. I liked all the books. I'm reading this one a second time."

"I'll return them and bring you more."

Her smile showed her delight. She appreciated small things, things others would deem inconsequential. He liked that about her. He understood. He knew what it was like to miss out on things others took for granted and to be grateful for them when they were finally yours.

Recent events had ripped open emotional wounds and shed light on unresolved fears he had never wanted to face. Maybe he didn't want to face the truth about Wes because it would place some of the responsibility on himself. Responsibility to accept and understand and forgive instead of hating and blaming. He needed wisdom to put his life in order.

Chapter Ten

"Can I ask you a question, Lorabeth?"

She picked up her cup and blew lightly across the surface of her tea. "Sure."

He absently stirred a spoonful of sugar into his. "What does the Bible have to say about fathers?"

"Well, all the stories about fathers are stories of men who loved their children. Men like Joseph and Abraham and David. The apostle Paul tells us we're supposed to honor our fathers and mothers."

"Yeah, I heard that. What about parents who don't deserve honor?"

She frowned and a little crease formed between her brows. "You ask tough questions, Benjamin."

"Does your father deserve honor?"

She nodded. "I respect him and I respect his position as my parent. I may not have always agreed with all of his mandates, but I recognize his right to have those opinions and make the rules."

Ben rested his elbows on the table and leaned toward

her. "What if he'd been cruel to you and your brothers and sister? What then? What if he'd never provided for you or even cared if you lived or died?"

She brought her gaze to his in the lamplight, and he hoped his emotions and confusion weren't plainly displayed on his face.

"My father taught me to always take the verses in context, so let's look at that one in its context."

He shrugged. Did she mean she needed a Bible?

"Children obey your parents in the Lord, for this is right." Obviously she didn't need a Bible. "Honor thy father and thy mother, which is the first commandment with promise—that it may be well with thee, and thou mayest live long on the earth."

He was gonna die any minute if that promise held true.

"And ye fathers," she continued. "Provoke not your children to wrath, but bring them up in the nurture and admonition of the Lord." She sipped her tea and set the cup back in its saucer. "I suppose if my father provoked me and neglected me, I wouldn't be bound to honor him."

After a moment, she added, "Maybe I haven't done so well in that department lately."

"Mothers, too?" Ben asked as though he hadn't heard her.

"Probably the same would hold true for either parent."

"I don't want to put myself in that place," he said at last. "If I couldn't be a good parent, then I wouldn't want to have young ones. It's too risky."

Lorabeth prayed she knew how to answer Benjamin's questions correctly. His face was etched with deep concern and confusion, and intuitively she knew this was an important conversation. She'd never heard him or his sister talk about their parents, and the one time she'd asked, he'd told her he'd never had a father.

"Some people's best is better than others. I'm no expert," she told him with a shrug.

"I didn't ask you because you're an expert," he said. "I asked because you're a friend and you're smart about that kind of thing."

I asked because you're a friend. She'd known he thought of her as a friend, but hearing him say it tweaked her confidence. "Perhaps if you need a wiser answer you could ask my father. Ellie has invited him to dinner this Sunday."

"Your brother, too?"

She nodded. "We're often asked to dinner after church, but my father rarely accepts. I suspect he did this time so he could gauge how I'm faring here."

"I'd like to know your brother better," he told her. "I'll think about talkin' to your father. I think he's a fine preacher, don't get me wrong, I just don't know if I want to, well, ask him questions like this."

"That's okay," she answered.

"Thanks for answering," he said.

"I'm pleased to talk with you anytime, Benjamin."

A vivid blue fire blazed in his eyes as he studied her. His perusal warmed her skin and made her stomach flutter. She felt a connection to him that she'd never experienced before, something special and tender and exciting. She didn't want to miss out on a moment with him.

Getting up from the bench and moving to the other side of the table, she perched beside him.

"Thanks for caring about me," she told him.

"A lot of people care about you, Lorabeth."

"Your reasons aren't family obligations, though. It's not the same."

He had a full lower lip that curled up becomingly when he smiled, and that smile had a powerful effect on her, especially right now when she was so close to him. "No, I don't suppose it is," he said.

"You don't feel toward me like you feel toward Ellie, do you?"

His expression sobered. "Sure don't."

It felt right to raise her hand to his face and rest her fingertips against his cheek. It was an intimate touch, that brush of sensitive skin against the rough texture of his jaw. Foreign. Forbidden. Exciting. She moved her fingers and experienced the rasp of his beard with a jolt of sensation that shot through her body.

His nostrils flared as though her scent disturbed him, and a muscle ticked in his jaw.

"This is dangerous, Lorabeth." His low voice was almost a growl.

"Because you want to kiss me?"

He nodded without speaking.

"I wouldn't mind."

He turned and took her head in both hands, pulling her to him for a meeting of lips more greedy and less delicate than the last time. The kiss detonated, setting off a robust clamor in her heart and a throbbing rush of heat to her limbs. She wanted to climb onto his lap and make herself part of him.

Lorabeth's senses reeled. Nothing had ever prepared

her for this rush of desire, for the desperate craving she had for this man. She wanted to belong to him, possess him, crush him to her and never let go.

She draped one arm around his neck and curled the fingers of her other hand into the front of his shirt. Benjamin wrapped his arms around her and pulled her right up beside him, hip to hip, breasts crushed against his ribs, where he held her tightly.

His tongue darted across her lips, and Lorabeth parted them, meeting his tongue with eager thrusts and surging passion.

Benjamin moved his body away and bracketed her face with his hands, staring into her eyes, his chest heaving.

"Oh, the wonder of it," she whispered. "The beauty and *perfection*. Did you know? Did you know it could be like this?"

He shook his head.

She didn't want him to release her. She didn't want the moment to disappear. "Don't let me go," she pleaded.

"I have to leave."

"Hold me a moment longer."

He crushed her against him, her ear to his chest, where his heart pounded in a frantic rhythm. Lorabeth knew in that moment that she didn't want this overwhelming need for him to be snatched away or criticized or met with disapproval.

Her existence had purpose now. Benjamin Chaney's presence made colors brighter, made scents sweeter, and the fact that he wanted her buoyed all her dreams and desires and made her want to shout with gladness.

"Benjamin," she whispered. "You make me feel alive."

He threaded his fingers into her hair, and the way he held her made her feel precious.

After a few minutes Benjamin ended the embrace and gave her a final sweet kiss before standing. "I'll come for you Saturday evening," he told her.

"I can hardly wait," she answered.

She walked him to the front door and bolted it behind him. Parting the lace curtain on the long foyer window, she peered into the darkness, trying to make out his retreating form.

She couldn't see anything, so she turned down the last lamp and ran up the stairs to her dark room where she hurried to the window and caught a glimpse of him as he rode beyond the trees and nudged the horse into a gallop on the street.

Was he her answer? Was Benjamin the husband she'd prayed for? Could he be the mate she'd dreamed of so many times? He'd been places beyond her tiny world, had seen things he could share with her. He was educated and kind, as endearingly handsome as she'd dreamed for, but he wasn't taken with himself. In fact, he was attentive and unselfish. He'd shown her things she'd been curious about, had already introduced her to a way of life she craved knowing.

Would there be anything wrong with hoping he was the husband she'd waited for? What would her father have to say about him? she wondered. Benjamin had attended their church on a regular basis for years. He had his own veterinary practice and a home—two homes for that matter! What kind of objections would stand in the way of something she wanted with all her heart?

She lit her lamp and studied her reflection in the mirror over the washstand for a moment. It might not be good to want this too badly, Lorabeth reminded herself. Even if her father came up with an objection, Benjamin might not have the least inclination to marry her.

The chance made an ache blossom in her chest. She may not be the woman of his dreams. She thought about Zeta and Jenetta and Carrie and their lovely dresses and the way they knew all the games and had so many friends. Frances and Ida had pretty smiles and fashionable hair. Why would Benjamin choose her over any one of them?

She unbuttoned her shirtwaist and plain skirt, stepping out of them and turning back to the mirror in her cotton undergarments. As plain as all her clothing, as all her belongings. She'd dressed her little wards many mornings and undressed them at night, and even the children wore drawers and chemises with delicate lace and pastel ribbons.

She took the tie from the end of her braid and brushed out her hair until it crackled and shone. She separated the mass into three sections, then stopped herself. She let the tresses fall over her shoulders and down her back and turned this way and that to see herself in the mirror.

Taking a fresh nightgown from a drawer, she flipped it out and changed. White cotton. Plain and practical. Like her life.

Lorabeth padded to the bureau and opened her top drawer. Under more cotton chemises and ironed hankies was a small wooden box Simon had made for her. She opened it and looked at the layers of bills.

If offer card is missing write to: The Harlequin Reader Service, 3010 Walden Ave., P.O. Box 1867, Buffalo, NY 14240-1867

NO POSTAGE
NECESSARY
IF MAILED
IN THE
UNITED STATES

BUSINESS REPLY MAIL
FIRST-CLASS MAIL   PERMIT NO. 717-003   BUFFALO, NY

POSTAGE WILL BE PAID BY ADDRESSEE

HARLEQUIN READER SERVICE
3010 WALDEN AVE
PO BOX 1867
BUFFALO NY 14240-9952

Her brother Jubal had convinced her to start an account at the bank, so this was only a small portion of what she'd earned working for the Chaneys the past two years. She'd barely touched her wages in all that time. Her father had paid for clothing and food. Meals were provided and her needs were met here, too. Occasionally she purchased shoes or a hair comb, but the amount spent had never been much. She'd never had an opportunity or a reason to spend this money. Or an inkling of what to spend it on.

Lorabeth had an idea. She closed the box and the drawer.

Turning up the wick on the lamp, she nestled into the comfortable chair with her feet curled beneath her and picked up the book she'd left there. She could have clothes as feminine and pretty as the others—shoes, too. She could be the woman of Benjamin's dreams.

Chapter Eleven

"Can I ride with you and Lorabeth?" Flynn asked. He had his fiddle case tucked under his arm.

Benjamin stood in the foyer in his best black trousers, white shirt and tie, waiting for Lorabeth.

"Of course you can," she said from the top of the stairs.

She gathered the hem of her dress and descended as gracefully as anything Ben had ever seen. The dress was the color of a fresh summer peach, with lacy stuff at her neck and on the cuffs. The closer she got, the more clearly he noticed how the shade complemented her skin and made her eyes look dark and luminous.

"Holy cow, Miss Lorrie!" Flynn exclaimed. "You look beautiful!"

"Thank you, Flynn."

Ben nodded his agreement.

Caleb ushered Nate and David down the stairs. "Papa's ready to take on you two boys in a checker championship."

Ben had seen Matthew and Laura's buggy out front, the horse still harnessed. "I brought my rig," he said.

"We're taking my folks'," Caleb replied.

Ellie came from the hall that led to the kitchen, carrying Madeline wrapped in a light blanket. "Your mother's baking cookies with the girls," she said to Caleb. "I need to grab a shawl."

Madeline was still too small to leave behind for that many hours, and she slept most of the time, anyway, so she was coming along.

Lorabeth took her shawl from over her arm and draped it around her shoulders. "I made pies," she told Ben.

Flynn picked up the crate that must hold her covered desserts, handed it to Ben, and they made their way to Ben's buggy. While Ben stowed the pies, Flynn helped her up to the seat.

"What kind are they?" Ben asked, taking up the reins. "The pies."

"Pumpkin. Do you like pumpkin?"

"One of my favorites."

Lorabeth had to sit close in order for Flynn to fit on her other side, and the cramped space was no hardship. He enjoyed her presence beside him, her sweet fragrance reaching his senses immediately.

"Where do the animals go when people are dancing in their barn?" Lorabeth asked.

Ben exchanged a look with Flynn, and his brother looked away as though the countryside suddenly held particular fascination.

"The farmer herds them all into pens and corrals and pastures while he cleans out the barn during the day. He leaves them there for the evening."

"And they don't mind?" she asked.

Flynn wouldn't look at him.

"The cows and horses? No, I don't think they mind."

"Do the Iversons have a Victrola?" she asked.

Ben wondered what difference that made, then figured it out. "There are musicians," he told her. "Plenty of local talent in these parts."

Lorabeth looked to Flynn. "That's why you've brought your violin? To play with the musicians?"

Flynn nodded with a grin. "Yes'm."

"Well, this will be more of a treat than I'd even imagined."

"Wait till you see. All the schoolgirls line up near the front to watch 'im," Ben teased.

"Nah, they don't," Flynn replied, and a smudge of ruddy color tinged his lean cheek.

"Wait and see," Ben told Lorabeth.

She laughed at their good-natured joking.

Lorabeth asked questions about the farms and fields they passed. The purple and red streaks across the skies disappeared into inky darkness as night descended. The lights from the Iverson barn were visible as they approached from the road.

"This makes me think of Simon," Lorabeth said softly. "I do wish he could share in things like this." She reached over and grabbed Flynn's hand, and Ben turned to observe her expression of excitement and apprehension. He glanced at her hand clenching his brother's and felt a stab of possessiveness.

Even though he was a young man, Flynn was one of her charges, he chided himself. And surely Flynn reminded her sharply of her younger brother. His own hands had been occupied with the reins. He pulled the horses to a stop and looped the reins around the brake handle.

Flynn had stepped away from the buggy so that when Ben got around to the other side, Lorabeth was waiting for him. Ben bracketed her waist with both hands, and she stepped off the stair. He lowered her to the ground and immediately took her icy hand.

"Are you scared?" he asked, rubbing it.

"Only a little."

"Nothing to fear," he assured her. "You'll be the prettiest girl there."

Her gaze shot to his in surprise.

He smiled and went to get her desserts. They followed Flynn toward the barn.

Two woodstoves warmed the interior, which still held the smells of hay and livestock. Makeshift tables had been constructed along the west side in front of empty stalls, and already their surfaces were covered with trays and bowls of food. Ben held the wooden box out to Lorabeth, and she lifted out her pies and placed them on a table with a dozen delicious-looking varieties. Ben stored the container.

A keg sat on a workbench in the rear by the other set of doors which were closed in deference to the cool night. A crate of clean, empty jars stood on the floor beside it.

The platform that the townspeople took turns storing between dances had been constructed on the right, and J.J. Jenkins had brought the piano he had painted red a few years back.

A hum of conversation filled the building, which probably held forty people already. Flynn headed straight for the platform and the other musicians who were tuning up in a splendid clash of notes.

"Lorabeth! What a gorgeous dress!" Carrie Bennett came up beside them and ran an appreciative gaze over Lorabeth's costume. "Did Miss Kirkpatrick make that for you?"

"She did," Lorabeth answered.

"Lorabeth splurged this week." Ellie joined them, Madeline swaddled in her arms. "Isn't she a vision in that color?"

Carrie nodded.

"I'd better go make sure Caleb knows what to do with the sandwiches I brought." Ellie hurried away.

"A few of the others are already here," Carrie said. "You two must come sit with us." She motioned for them to follow and led the way to the open area beside the platform where several chairs were gathered. Hobie and Carter stood to greet Lorabeth and Ben.

Ben didn't like the way Carter looked at Lorabeth.

"These dances are so passé," Zeta said, joining them, and pulled a long face. "But it's a tradition and all, so I come with my parents."

"I *like* the dances," Carter said.

"Well, we can still have entertainment of our own fashion." Carrie leaned forward. "I have an idea."

"What is it?" Zeta asked.

"Why don't we put all of our names in a hat and draw for dance partners throughout the night?"

"Will you keep the boys and girls separate or might a person draw their own gender as a partner?" Carter asked with a frown.

"You could draw a person of your own gender," she replied with a twinkle in her eye. "And if you don't dance with the person you drew, you have to pay a forfeit."

Murmurs rippled.

Ben didn't like the idea and he didn't mind saying so. "I brought Lorabeth tonight, and I intend to dance with her. If she wants to accept invitations, that will be her choice, but count me out of the mix."

"I'd rather not play this evening, either," Lorabeth said, and her agreement pleased him.

He stole a glance at her, and she offered him a smile and took his hand.

"Have fun," Ben said to the others who quickly formed a circle to plan their evening's entertainment.

Half a dozen musicians had gathered. The man holding the guitar tapped out a rhythm and they jumped into a song.

"Are you hungry?" Ben asked. "I didn't have supper, so the food tables look pretty good to me."

"I'll eat with you."

He grabbed two tin plates from a stack, and they selected their fare. He led her to several long tables made out of planks and sawhorses, where they seated themselves so they could observe the goings-on. Ben ate one of Ellie's sandwiches and a chicken leg while Lorabeth picked at a little sandwich she'd made of cheese and ham.

Deputy Sanders and his wife, Amanda, were the first on the dance floor, joined soon after by several other couples. Lorabeth watched with interest. "Do you know them?"

"Yep. That's Owen Sanders, one of Marshal Connor's deputies. His wife used to be a Harvey Girl. She and Sophie and Ellie are all friends."

"Do they have children?"

"Don't reckon I've heard. You might ask Ellie. Not hungry?"

She glanced over. "Not so much."

He could see she was itchin' to get out on that dance floor. He could really go for a cup of coffee and a piece of cake, but first things first. He wiped his mouth on a napkin. "Want to dance?"

Lorabeth turned to him. "Oh, yes!"

He took her by the hand and led her into the throng of couples moving to the lively strains of a song she'd never heard. She glanced at the others beside them, then tried to move the same way they were.

"Don't think about your feet so much," Benjamin told her, holding his elbows out and his back straight. "We'll just do an easy count. Think about moving toward the side and then back this way. One two three four, one two three four."

It only took a few minutes for her to fall into the pattern and feel comfortable dancing. Benjamin's patience and gentle guidance touched her. One by one he was giving her experiences that had been out of her reach. Lorabeth felt part of this community for the first time. No longer was she the preacher's invisible daughter. She wished Simon could be here.

By the next song, she laughed and spared glances at the other dancers and the musicians. Fiddle under his chin, Flynn grinned at her as his fingers flew, and he wielded the bow with expertise she hadn't imagined he possessed.

"How did your brother learn to play like that?"

"Caleb's dad first taught him to pick, and then Ellie got lessons for him. He's quite the fiddle player, isn't he? Look there." He nodded in the direction he wanted her to turn.

A row of schoolgirls with ribbons tied at the end of their braids stood beside the platform, some talking behind their hands, others swaying to the music. When Flynn played a particularly difficult sequence of notes, they clapped and cheered.

Lorabeth met Benjamin's amused gaze with a laugh. "It's just as you said!"

His expression was warm as he studied his brother. "He's gonna be a fine man. Caleb and Matthew have been good influences."

"What about you?" she asked. "You're closer to him than anyone, aren't you?"

His bright blue eyes seemed to darken somewhat at her comment. "He'll grow up better'n me."

"I don't know that there are any men finer than you, Benjamin."

His gaze locked on hers. "I've never enjoyed myself at one of these the way I am tonight," he told her.

The music slowed, and a few of the dancers left the floor, but Benjamin placed his arm behind her back and gave her a reassuring smile. She could smell the starch in his shirt, feel the controlled strength of his arms, and her heart beat as fast as it had when he'd kissed her. She could remain like this forever and never tire of his arms around her.

A couple of songs later he said, "I know you could probably do this all evenin', but I need somethin' to drink."

"I'm thirsty, too."

He poured her a jar of lemonade and sweetened a cup of coffee for himself. Caleb and Ellie were sitting side by side, the baby on Ellie's lap, watching the dancers when Benjamin and Lorabeth approached.

"I'll hold Madeline for a while," she told Ellie. "You two go dance."

"This is your night, Lorabeth," Ellie objected.

"And I'm having a wonderful time," she said. "But we're going to rest and have our refreshments, so you two take some time for yourselves."

Ellie handed Madeline over with a grateful smile, and the two of them threaded their way onto the floor.

Madeline was awake, and had probably just nursed, because she looked sleepy-eyed and content. She blinked up at Lorabeth and the side of her tiny wet mouth slid into a grin. Lorabeth kissed her soft warm head and placed her over her shoulder, snuggled in the blanket. The baby smelled like fresh laundry, warm milk and possessed a sweet fragrance all her own. Her slight weight was a welcome presence against Lorabeth's breast.

Benjamin sipped his coffee and looked at her with an expression she couldn't quite decipher. Someone had placed two slices of layered white cake with a berry filling in front of them.

"You going to try that?" she asked.

"What about your pumpkin pie?"

"I can make you one anytime. You may never get to try this again."

He picked up a fork and took a piece of cake, but instead of eating it, he held the bite toward her. "You first."

She opened her mouth and took his offering, sweet and delicious with a mouthwatering raspberry bite. "Mmm." She chewed slowly and swallowed. "Delicious."

"More?"

She nodded.

He fed her several more bites before trying the cake himself, then started on the second slice. "Are you having a good time?" he asked.

"I am." A couple caught her attention. "Look."

He turned his head.

Carrie and Ida were dancing together, laughing as though they were schoolgirls. Parker and Zeta worked their way through the crowd to find a spot beside them. Lorabeth was glad Benjamin hadn't wanted to play their silly games tonight. She was delighted to have him all to herself.

Someone moved up beside Benjamin then, and she glanced up at Carter. "Care to dance, Lorabeth?" he asked.

She looked from Carter's boyish face to Benjamin's. She'd been content right here, but she didn't want to be rude.

Benjamin's expression was unreadable, but he reached for Madeline and cradled the baby in the crook of his left arm as capably as you please. "Go ahead. I'll stay here until Ellie comes back."

Madeline gazed up at him with a little furrow between her brows, then sleepily closed her eyes. Obviously content, she moved her lips in an endearing little sucking motion.

With a puzzled look at Benjamin, Lorabeth stood and followed Carter to the dance floor. Just as they reached an opening, the music changed to a slow song, and Carter took one of her hands and placed his other at her waist.

Lorabeth tried to peer around his shoulder to see Benjamin.

"Are you and the doc exclusive?" he asked.

"I'm not sure what you mean."

"Has he voiced any intentions? Asked you not to accept offers from other men?"

She shook her head with regret. "No."

"So I still have a chance, huh?"

She glanced up at him. "A chance to what?"

"Win you. Be in your favor. You know."

She didn't know. She'd never been in a position to accept dance offers or invitations of any sort. If there was some kind of unspoken protocol, she wasn't aware of it. "Exactly what does being in my favor involve?" she asked.

Carter's complexion reddened. "Why, courting, Lorabeth."

She blinked. "Courting?"

She knew what it meant. A gentleman sought out a lady's favor by spending time with her. A few of the books Benjamin brought for her had been fictional novels with story lines where the gentlemen romanced their intended wives.

"What does courting involve, exactly?" she asked.

"Invitations to dances and socials. Gifts. Kissing, of course."

"Everyone is kissing at the home socials," she thought aloud. "It hardly seems special in that setting."

"I would have to agree," he answered. "But kissing is different in private."

Indeed it was. "If a gentleman kisses a lady in private, is he courting her?"

"Quite likely," he replied.

Lorabeth fell into the steps of the dance, turning at every opportunity to seek out Benjamin. Occasionally they moved his direction, and the crowd parted enough so she could spot him where she'd left him, the baby nestled on his arm.

He'd kissed her more than once. Was that courting?

The music ended, and she moved away from Carter and headed back to the table. She reached for Madeline, but Benjamin said, "She's fine."

Hobie came by and handed Benjamin a jar filled with dark liquid and foam on the surface.

Lorabeth glanced at his retreating back, then at the jar. "What is it?"

"Beer." He turned and set it untouched on the table behind him. Then he met her gaze, apparently reading her curiosity. "Wanna try it?"

"May I?"

He picked up the jar and handed it to her.

She raised it to her lips and the pungent yeasty aroma met her nostrils. She drew her head away and blinked. Determined to taste it, she held her breath and took a sip. The unpleasant taste made her shudder.

Benjamin grinned and pointed to her mouth.

"Oh." She flicked her tongue across her upper lip.

"Like it?" he asked.

She shook her head. "Not especially."

She glanced from his face toward the crowd and back. He was studying her. Their gazes locked. His fell to her mouth. Embarrassed, she looked away.

Zeta came by with a tray and handed Lorabeth a jar of lemonade.

"Thank you. This is more like it." She'd worked up a thirst, and the beer was awful. She took a long drink. "Oh!"

"Spiked?" Benjamin asked with a raised brow.

"Uh-huh." She set it on the table. "These people enjoy their strong spirits, don't they?"

Caleb and Ellie returned, and Caleb took Madeline from Benjamin.

"Oh, that looks good," Ellie said, spotting the full glass of lemonade. "May I?" She reached for it and took a deep swallow before Lorabeth could say anything. Her eyes watered, and she fanned herself with a hand. "Oh, my."

Benjamin laughed. "That's what Lorabeth said."

She quickly set the glass back down. "Go on, you two," Ellie said, waving. "Have fun."

Benjamin took Lorabeth's hand, and they made their way back out. After dancing to a few brisk tunes, the music slowed again. She loved the way Benjamin's hand rested at her waist, the way she could smell his hair and clothing and feel the warmth of his body. "I don't want to dance with anyone but you," she said.

"Good." He studied her, his gaze touching her hair, her eyes. "I don't want you to dance with anyone but me."

Was this what Carter had asked about? "Benjamin?"

"Yes."

She wanted to know about exclusiveness and court-ing, but she couldn't form words to ask.

In the split second while the strains of a song dwin-dled away and dancers parted and headed toward the sides of the room, Benjamin's demeanor changed. His body stiffened and his face looked pinched.

"What's wrong?" she asked, concerned.

He took her hand and led her toward the chairs. "Nothing."

She studied him, but he avoided her eyes. She turned her attention to the others in the room, but couldn't figure out why he'd suddenly become tense and withdrawn.

Ellie came to stand beside Benjamin then, and the two of them looked at each other, then at the crowd of dancers.

"Is something wrong?" Lorabeth asked again.

"No." Ellie turned away and joined a gathering of women that included Miss Kirkpatrick.

Benjamin seemed to be studying someone, but Lorabeth couldn't figure out who or what had changed his mood.

With a sick feeling growing in his belly, Ben watched Wes Evans escort his wife from the dance floor toward the side, where several youngsters greeted them. Two were blond-haired girls around ten or twelve with braids and calico dresses, another a dark-haired boy of maybe fourteen or fifteen who resembled Suzanne.

A startling realization flooded over him. Uneasiness riled his nerve endings and set his heart racing. A few of those children in that gathering obviously belonged to Wes and Suzanne.

Ben had siblings he hadn't known about.

One of the girls elbowed the other, and they laughed. Wes leaned forward and said something to the young man, resting his hand on his shoulder as he did so.

At the sight of the Evans family's interaction, Ben turned away. Those children led normal, happy lives, were well fed and had nice clothing. Their parents treated them lovingly. No doubt they had a decent house and attended school.

Ben couldn't bear the overwhelming envy and sadness that enveloped him. He drew a breath and gathered his composure.

"Do you want to leave?" Lorabeth asked from beside him.

He glanced at her concerned expression and nodded. "If you don't mind."

"I don't mind."

Ben found Lorabeth's wrap draped over the back of a chair and nestled it around her shoulders. "We're headin' out," he said to Caleb.

His brother-in-law nodded.

The crisp night air held the scent of fall.

"That was fun," Lorabeth said.

Ben helped her up to the buggy seat. "Glad you had a good time."

"Where are you spending the night? I mean, at which house?"

"I like to spend Saturday night in town. I'm closer for church in the mornin' that way, but I really need to go check on the animals tonight, so I might as well stay out there."

"I'd enjoy riding along if you want to go tend to them now, then come back to town."

"You wouldn't mind?"

"Not at all."

"All right, then." He headed the horse toward the outskirts of Newton. "There's a lap blanket back here," he said, reaching under the seat and pulling out a Hudson Bay blanket. "Air's nippy tonight." He wondered what Evans did for a living.

She covered herself. "Look at all the stars."

He scanned the expanse of dark heavens with its winking lights. "Pretty, isn't it?"

Ben couldn't think much past Wes Evans's appearance at the harvest dance. Had the man attended local dances before? Had he recently moved to Newton from Florence? Ben had been born in Florence, and he didn't remember seeing the man before now. Suzanne would have spotted Ben sooner had they been at the same activities. Ellie would have recognized Wes. Or would she?

His head spun with questions, and for once Lorabeth was silent and contemplative.

The picture of those youngsters was burned into his mind. Half brothers and sisters? As close in blood relation to him as Ellie and Flynn. Did they know about him? Of course not. Wes hadn't known about him, and Ben was sure the man hadn't hurried home to tell them he had an illegitimate son.

How could Ben go on living in this community if that man and his entire brood were going to show up unannounced every time he turned around?

They reached Ben's property, and he pulled the

buggy up in front of the barn. He must have been sitting with the reins in his hands and the night closing around them for a few minutes before Lorabeth spoke, startling him out of his reverie.

"Are you all right, Benjamin?"

He glanced at the reins and tied them. "Yeah. Just tired, I reckon. Come inside the barn with me. I'll light the stove there and you can keep warm while I check the animals."

"Don't go to any trouble," she told him. "You don't need to light a fire just for me."

He helped her down and escorted her through the side door where the familiar scents of hay and animals enveloped them.

Delilah bleated from her pen.

"What's that?" Lorabeth asked.

"That's Delilah." He let out the goat, and it sniffed Lorabeth's skirt and shoes, then tried to nibble the hem of her skirt.

Lorabeth squealed and tugged the fabric away. "What's she doing?"

"Bein' nosy. Delilah, leave Lorabeth's dress alone."

Ben checked the occupied cages along the inside wall, made sure each of the animals had food and water, and examined a few healing wounds. A pigeon ruffled its feathers and pecked at the grain in its dish.

"What's wrong with the dog?" Lorabeth asked.

"That's Hoover, Marshal Vidlak's huntin' hound. Got his hind leg caught in a trap. It's nearly healed now."

Hoover stood with his black nose against the wire door, his tail wagging.

"What about her?" She pointed to a calico cat with a gold and black face.

"Him. Almira Wheeler found him in the alley behind her shop. He was skin and bones, pretty scraped up."

Lorabeth placed her hand on the front wire of the cage, and the cat backed into the rear corner. "Are you afraid, kitty?"

"He doesn't even let me pet him, and I've been feedin' him for a couple of weeks."

"What's his name?"

"Doesn't have one. He's a stray."

She bent to peer into the cage. "You look like a Mittens to me. Your paws are all a different color fur than the rest of you."

"Not a very manly name for a tom," he commented.

"He likes it."

Ben came to stand beside her and studied the animal. "How can you tell?"

"His ears stood up when I said it. Watch. Mittens?"

Sure enough the feline twitched his notched ears and gave her a superior green-eyed stare.

"What will you do with him?"

"Let him go, I guess. There are already half a dozen barn cats around here. Another won't hurt. Takes care of the mice."

He was standing close enough behind her to detect the soft floral scent of her hair. Instead of the braid she wore during the week, she had fashioned her hair so that it hung in rippling waves down her back. Every time his hand had brushed it that evening he'd experienced a twinge of longing.

"Your hair is so soft and shiny," he told her.

She straightened and turned so that she was looking at him over her shoulder. "I had it trimmed this week. And Ellie helped me do an egg treatment."

"Eggs? Really? What do eggs do?"

She smiled. "Make it shiny, I guess."

They stood that way for a moment.

"You can touch it if you like."

He didn't need an engraved invitation. Ben reached tentatively and took a tress between his fingers and thumb, noticing the cool, silky texture. Then he threaded all five fingers into the mass and brought it to his nose. He touched the satin smoothness to his lips.

Lorabeth turned so that she was facing him and watched his expression, obviously not caring if her hair was mussed.

"Nice," was all he could say. He released her hair and grazed his fingertips along her jaw.

Her eyelids fluttered shut and trembled before sweeping open and fixing him with a yearning gaze. He could get lost in the depths of her tawny eyes and never want to find his way out.

Without hesitation he leaned forward and touched his lips to hers.

Chapter Twelve

She inhaled and sighed as though taking in the essence of him. He loved kissing her. He'd never realized this simple expression would be so tender and feel so wholesome and right. Her lips felt good against his.

The rightness was because she was pure and innocent and her reactions were chaste. A man like Carter might take advantage of that. Ben cared too much about protecting her.

He backed away. "Ready to go?"

"Aren't you going to show me your house?"

"Not much to see," he said with a shrug. "But sure."

He turned down the wicks to extinguish the lanterns and made sure she pulled her shawl around her shoulders before leading her out and across the yard to the house.

"I use the back door." He opened the screen door with a creak of hinges.

He found matches and lit the lamps as well as a lantern he could carry to show her the rest of the house. "This is pretty much how it looked when I bought the place," he told her. "Haven't done much except clean it up and stock the pantry."

Lorabeth followed him as he led her into a hallway and showed her the dining room, the tiny parlor and his bedroom. The rooms were clean, the furnishings practical and serviceable, but there wasn't really much of himself here.

"It's nice," she said, as though feeling obligated to comment.

"It's just a place to work." With a shrug, he led her back to the rear door. "The house in town is more like a home."

"Will you show me?"

"If you like."

He took her hand to lead her across the darkened yard to the buggy and helped her up. Lorabeth pulled the blanket around her shoulders for the ride.

"Time to get winter coats out," he commented.

"I've ordered a new one from Miss Eva's catalog," she told him. "It has a matching hat and a fur-lined muff. Quite fashionable."

"Sounds warm. And pretty."

The horse pulled them toward town.

"I have several paintings for you to choose from," Ben said. "Never got around to bringin' 'em to you."

"Paintings?"

He nodded. "Remember when you moved your things into your room? I told you I had pictures for the walls that Ellie had left behind. You're welcome to 'em."

"I might like one or two," she replied.

The house was dark, of course, though next door Mrs. McKinley's lights were burning in her downstairs windows. Ben pulled the buggy back to the carriage house and took Lorabeth's hand again.

Enormous spirea bushes flanked the back porch stairs, their blooms long gone. Ben unlocked the door and lit lamps.

He observed Lorabeth's reaction to the enormous kitchen with its long trestle table and scarred chairs. The floor was smooth and shiny from the recent refinishing. Ben gestured to the brick chimney. "There's even a fireplace. The pictures are in the dining room. I leaned them up against the wall."

She followed him as he carried the lantern and lit more lamps.

Lorabeth knelt to the framed paintings along the wall and looked from one to the next. "They're all lovely," she said. "Why didn't Ellie take them?"

"I think Caleb's first wife might've picked 'em out. Ellie bought more for the new house when they moved."

"Oh. I see." The paintings Benjamin offered her were done in beautiful colors and of various subjects. She passed over the country scenes, drawn to a depiction of two young girls sitting in a meadow. Their skirts made circles around them in the grass as they created dainty flower chains. "I like this one."

"Good. It's too girly for me."

She glanced up at his smile. "How about this one?"

She pointed to a portrait of a young girl wearing a bonnet. A bluebird had perched on a nearby limb. The colors were red and blue with soft white accents.

"Good choices for your room." He picked them up. "I'll put them near the back door."

He took her farther into the house, then, showed her a large parlor with an expanse of windows, and a study with bookshelves built along the walls and a heavy dark wood desk. A framed oil painting of hunting dogs hung over the fireplace.

"Bought that one myself," he told her. "Brought it back from Chicago."

"I would love to see Chicago."

"Newton's a big city itself, you know," he told her. "Some of the towns along the railroad are made up of a train depot, a livery and a couple of saloons."

"Truly?"

He nodded.

"I guess it's not necessarily the big city I want to see as much as the world outside of my small existence."

"Your dream of takin' a train trip," he remembered aloud. "Did you ever think about workin' at the Arcade? Those girls get free tickets to wherever they want to go."

"My father wouldn't even consider allowing me to work there. Or to go to a university. It took months of assurance for him to let me work for your sister."

Ben nodded thoughtfully. "He was protectin' you."

"He was smothering me," she said, and then immediately regretted her words. "I'm sorry, I shouldn't have spoken so unkindly. You're right, he always had my best interests in mind." She shivered and rubbed her palms together.

"Want somethin' warm to drink?" Benjamin asked. "I can make coffee."

"Do you have milk and cocoa? We could have hot chocolate by the fireplace. I can do it."

He nodded. "I'll help you start the stove and then set a fire in this grate."

It was obvious that Benjamin had spent more time and energy making this place a home than he had the other house. Even for a bachelor's home, the kitchen was well stocked and the cupboards held matching dishes and adequate cooking utensils.

She found mugs and a tray and carried their hot drinks to the study where Benjamin had a fire blazing. She set the tray on the braided rug and they seated themselves on the floor.

"I would spend all my time in here if this was my house," she told him.

He took the mug she held toward him. "It's my favorite room. It was Caleb's study when they lived here."

Lorabeth imagined the house filled with voices and laughter, the smell of Sunday dinner in the air. "You're blessed to be part of the Chaney family."

His gaze traveled to hers.

"Dr. and Mrs. Chaney have something rare and special," she said. "You mentioned Dr. Chaney's first wife. I don't remember her."

He looked at the fire for a moment. "Matthew told me she was never happy here. She wanted to live in a big city."

"I don't want to live in a big city," Lorabeth told him. She didn't want him to think she'd be a discontented wife. "I'd just like to see one."

"She died after Nate was born. He needed someone to take care of Nate and that's how he and Ellie met."

"Was your mother alive then?" she asked.

"No."

"You must've been pretty young then. Where did you and Ellie and Flynn live?"

Ben took a sip of his drink before forming a reply. "Ellie was workin' at the Arcade."

"That's right. She was a Harvey Girl."

He nodded. "Flynn and I were working on a farm near Florence."

"Working? You were just children."

"The state gave us to a foster family."

She hadn't known anything about that. "So this other family took care of you?"

"I don't really want to talk about it." His tone revealed pain she was sorry to dredge up.

"Sorry, I didn't mean to pry."

"You weren't pryin'." But he didn't say any more on the subject.

Would talk of his growing-up years always be off-limits?

"I enjoyed takin' you to the harvest dance. I was real proud to dance with you."

"I wasn't very good at it."

"I didn't mean because of your dancin' ability, I mean because of what a fine woman you are."

His high opinion, along with the radiating heat from the fire, warmed her through and through. She draped her shawl over the arm of the chair behind her. "Just a simple Kansas girl," she said with a shrug. "Never been farther than Topeka, and I don't know beans about much other than gardening or keeping house."

"Now, that's not so."

"No? What else do I know about?"

"Croquet and paper dolls and playin' the piano. Flynn said you help him with his mathematic assignments. You kiss bumps and bruises. You're wise and honest. And I've personally seen you talkin' with a cat."

She laughed. "Yes, of course. Cat language is one of my gifts."

"Just one of many," he added. "This is probably the best hot cocoa I've ever tasted."

"It isn't."

"It is." He paused, ducking his chin as though he was embarrassed. "I bought somethin' for you...."

Her heart lifted in expectancy. Gifts were unheard of in her upbringing. "What is it?"

"You might think it's silly."

"I won't. What is it?"

"It's not much really. I was just thinkin' of you when I was in the mercantile." He got up and went to the desk, where he opened the top drawer and took out something flat and rectangular. He carried it back and sat across from her, extending the object.

"What is it?"

"Look."

She accepted it and read the blue wrapper. "Chocolate. Made in Switzerland."

"Do you like chocolate?"

"I think so. I've never had one of these. I use cocoa powder to bake."

"Well, unwrap it and try it."

"Right now?"

"Why not?"

She carefully peeled away the wrapper and tin foil, exposing a solid bar of chocolate.

"Go ahead. Break off a piece," Benjamin said.

She did, then placed the bite in her mouth and let it melt on her tongue. Lorabeth closed her eyes. Chocolate was a hundred times better than jelly beans! It melted into a creamy-textured delight.

After swallowing, she ran her tongue over her teeth and the roof of her mouth. "Imagine," she said. "The people in Switzerland must try this every day while they're making it."

"Gonna share?"

She extended the wrapper for him to break off his own piece. He chewed slowly.

"Could be they do," he replied. "In between bites of cheese, o' course."

They laughed together over that.

Lorabeth put another bite of chocolate in her mouth. This time she chewed.

Benjamin reached between them to touch his thumb to the corner of her lips. A twig in the fire snapped and a log hissed. She met his eyes with a yearning desire to have more and know more…to have it all. "Thank you for thinking of me."

"Seems I can't *stop* thinkin' about you, Lorabeth."

"What is it you think of?"

"Your smile. Your shiny hair." His gaze caressed her lips and hair. "About kissin' you."

"I think about that, too," she admitted.

He leaned toward her and she met him halfway. They

both moved in closer, and Lorabeth rested her fingertips on the front of his shirt.

With their lips nearly touching, she said, "Sometimes
I think about you so much, nothing else seems real."

Their lips met, and Lorabeth noticed the warmth,
tasted the chocolate. His kiss was too gentle and unset-
tling for the hunger that quivered inside. She hooked her
arm around his neck, and he responded by folding her
into a hard embrace.

She loved the feel of her breasts crushed to his hard
chest, his strong arms banding her. She'd never been this
close to another person, never felt lovable or desirable or
wanted. Benjamin's embrace awakened her body to the
hard planes of his chest and the wild beat of his pulse under
her palm. She wanted to hold on to his solid presence,
press herself into his heart and make herself indispensable.

He tore his mouth from hers to trail fiery kisses
across her chin and down her neck. Lorabeth let her
head fall back while shivers of pleasure washed across
her shoulders and encompassed her whole being. If
she'd been standing she would have collapsed in a heap.

Benjamin brought his lips back to hers, and she
eagerly framed his face in both hands. He leaned over
her, and this time their bodies lowered from where they
sat until they lay side by side, Benjamin's welcome
weight pressing against her.

Giving herself over to yearning, she threaded her
fingers into his hair, along his scalp, and pressed one
hand to the back of his head. He trailed his fingertips
down her neck and brought his hand to the front of her

dress. At the feel of his touch against her breast, Lorabeth's heart raced.

His touch was as lyrical as a poem and his mouth as
sweet as the ripest fruit. *Set me as a seal upon thine
heart,* she prayed. *Make me his.* He'd become her heart's
desire. *I am my beloved's, and his desire is toward me.*
The fact that he desired her was amazing. Almost too
good to be true.

Lorabeth cherished the perfection of being in his
arms, the tender way he held her. Her senses were more
acute than they'd ever been. She smelled the soap he'd
used that day, felt the heat of the fire along her side, saw
the golden glint on his hair and lashes.

All her yearning, magical dreams were coming true.
Her secret yearnings were being fulfilled one by one,
and it was even better than she'd hoped. Benjamin was
the man she'd prayed for.

His thick silken hair in her hands was a sensual thrill.
Lorabeth trailed her fingers through it, along his neck
to his jaw.

She wanted to touch more of him. She caressed his
broad shoulders through the crisp fabric of his shirt,
loving the solid feel of muscle beneath smooth warm
flesh. He was so much broader and stronger than she,
creating a perfect foil to her softness.

Benjamin cupped his palm around her breast and
kneaded in a gentle yet breathtaking fashion. She'd never
imagined that intimacy could feel so good and so right.

She loved the feel of his lips on hers, the weight of
his body along her side.

Benjamin drew his mouth away and dropped his head

into the crook of her neck. His breath fanned her skin there, sending shudders through her body.

"I prayed for you," she whispered.

Ben raised his head. "What did I need prayer for?"

"No, I mean I *prayed* for you," she said again. "For God to send you to me."

He wasn't so sure he was God's answer to anyone's prayers. The way he felt toward her right now wasn't exactly holy. He'd wanted to kiss her again, had craved a taste of her, but it wasn't enough. The feelings he had were taking on new proportions.

She was a preacher's daughter, raised in a strict environment and protected her entire life. Until now. Until she'd met him.

A pulse of concern beat in his heart. Her father had entrusted his precious daughter with Ben's family. He'd turned Lorabeth's safety over to them, and Ben didn't want to give in to becoming the kind of man he'd vowed never to be. How could he protect her when he was the one she needed protection from? All he wanted right now was to touch her all over, take her up to his bed and make her his.

Heat engulfed him, and he moved away, taking her hand and helping her to a sitting position.

"I should get you home," he managed.

She straightened her clothing and hair, and the sight of her breasts beneath her dress speared him with want.

"I know all about self-control," she told him. "My whole life has been about self-control. I've had my fill of holding back and living up to other people's expectations."

He glanced at her in surprise. Her lips were pink and

swollen from their kisses, and he wanted to capture her mouth again, but he looked away instead. He knew all about self-control, too. He was a master at it.

He'd worn belligerence like armor as a youth, hadn't trusted a soul except Ellie until Caleb had come into their lives. Impotent rage had been his constant companion until he'd had to let it go or lose his mind. He may be jaded and pragmatic, but he wasn't living an illusion or pretending to be anything other than who and what he was. And what he was scared the hell out him most of the time. More so now than ever because he'd learned how weak he really was. Lorabeth had revealed his weakness. And it was her.

He wanted her.

But she was so unaffected and eager and beautiful that she scared him. She was a butterfly emerged from a cocoon and riding the winds of waking up to a whole new world that had opened before her.

She was bright and eager and trusting. Too trusting.

What would happen if he didn't shield her? He had warned her, and he could continue to warn her, but warnings weren't experience.

"Tell me what you asked God for," he said, sitting back with one knee in front of him like a barrier.

"Well, someone handsome," she said hesitantly, "though that wasn't the first trait or the most important, but I didn't want a man I didn't find appealing. I hope that's not shallow of me. But I didn't want a vain person, of course. I asked Him for a husband filled with life and passion who would show me everything I'd been missing."

"Husband?" Ben asked, hearing that word above all the others.

"Carter said what you and I have been doing is courting. And courting suggests marriage, does it not?"

He hadn't planned to court her, hadn't thought the words in his head, but he'd wanted to monopolize her, keep her to himself. Was he courting her?

Her idealism and romantic hopes touched him. She was open and guileless. She thought *he* was what she'd been praying for. The thought made his chest ache at the probability of disappointing her. She had no idea.

She needed a protector, though, and he saw himself as that person. He definitely wasn't the worst man she could end up with. He would respect and honor her the way she deserved, the way her father would approve of. He could take care of her and make a home for her.

At the thought of Lorabeth in this home with him, of them eating meals together in the kitchen, of her playing a piano in the parlor, a wondrous hope bloomed.

He could buy her a piano for the parlor.

The firelight cast one side of her lovely face in shadow, and he leaned forward to place his knuckles under her chin and turn so he could see her eyes. She was lovely. The most angelic-looking woman he'd ever known.

They couldn't go on the way they had been, because he couldn't trust himself. And he couldn't back away. Ben could become worthy of her if he tried hard enough. There had been changes taking place in him ever since he'd met her. Changes for the good. If he was as unacceptable as he'd always believed, she wouldn't be so drawn to him. What was it about her that made him a better person?

"You really believe I'm the answer to your prayers?"

She nodded. "I've known it for some time."

He already knew she was the perfect woman for him. "Then I'll talk to your father tomorrow."

A joyful glow touched her face. Her smile reached his heart. "Oh, Benjamin, you will? You truly will?"

He nodded.

Her smile dimmed. She leaned toward him and grasped the front of his shirt. "He *must* approve of you, Benjamin! He has to!"

He didn't know what to say to that. He'd never thought about it. Never faced a father whose daughter he wanted to marry. He was respected in Newton, was well able to care for her. Unless the man could see into his past or miraculously knew of the shame of his birth, Reverend Holdridge didn't have any reason to deny Ben.

Lorabeth's desperation didn't have much basis for Ben. Not because he was a great catch, by any means, but because she could have her choice of any man she wanted.

A sick feeling dropped into his belly. What if the reverend *didn't* approve?

He couldn't think on that.

"It will be all right," he told her.

"You don't know him the way I do," she said. "He expects perfection in all things."

He took hold of both her arms by her elbows. "What is the worst thing that could happen?"

She blinked. "That he wouldn't approve of you?"

"That he thinks I'm an unsuitable mate for you. What then?"

She studied him without a reply.

"Would we say, 'Well never mind then' and forget about it?"

"No!" She shook her head.

"What then? What if he hates me?"

"He doesn't hate you."

"Suppose."

He could tell she was thinking it over, and he knew the moment she came to the realization he'd hoped for. "I would marry you anyway. That is if you wanted me to. And we would have another preacher marry us."

Overwhelming emotion rose up, and Ben had to take a deep breath in order to talk. "Okay. The worst thing that could happen is that you would have to choose to defy your father. Could you do that, Lorabeth?"

She raised a hand to rest along his jaw and her eyes sparkled with unshed tears as she replied, "I would."

He urged her closer and kissed her gently, with a new expectation and level of excitement. Lorabeth wanted to marry him. This beautiful innocent perfect woman.

This house would truly be a home again. He would be a good husband. He would protect and love her.

"I'd better get you back now, so you can get a good night's sleep and be fresh for tomorrow."

"I don't need much sleep," she told him. "I'll be praying tonight."

He got up and took her hand to help her stand. Couldn't hurt to have a wife with so much fervor when she prayed, could it? He found her shawl and banked the fire.

If Ellie was asleep when he took Lorabeth home, he would wake her. She would be the first to hear his plans.

Chapter Thirteen

Lorabeth played the piano with an extra flourish the following morning. She planned to do everything she could to be on her father's good side that day.

She had told Benjamin the truth. She wanted her father's blessing more than she could say, but she wanted Benjamin as her husband even more. It would break her heart not to remain in the reverend's good graces, but she would make a new life. There were many people who cared for her.

When Benjamin had arrived that morning, her stomach fluttered at the sight of him, broad-shouldered and tall, as he entered the building and strode to the pew which was as yet unoccupied.

She'd met his eyes across the room, and they shared a private look, a look that conjured up the heat and sensations of the night before. Lorabeth's body tingled remembering the way he made her feel with his kisses and touches.

And he would make her his wife. Soon. She would

know all the mysteries and pleasures of being a woman then. She would taste life and know it was good.

Benjamin turned and greeted Kate Jenkins and her son, J.J., then took a seat. It was only a minute or so later that the rest of the Chaneys filed into the church.

The congregation sang and Lorabeth's father took the offering, then preached on David defeating the giant in his life. The giants they faced today were sin and corruption, he told them, but Lorabeth was too distracted to pay much attention.

As the service ended, Simon turned to her. "We're having dinner together."

She smiled. "Yes."

"I miss you, Lorabeth."

She hugged him. "I miss you, too. This will be fun. I can't wait for you to get to know the Chaneys and see the fun they have. The afternoon promises to be warm, so Dr. Chaney and Benjamin can show you how to play horseshoes."

"I've heard the other boys talk about playing. Do you know how?"

She frowned now that she thought about it. "Only the men throw horseshoes."

"Suppose Father will object?"

"It truly doesn't edify, but it sure looks fun," she answered. "Maybe he'll stay occupied long enough for you to give it a try."

Simon grinned.

"I'll be helping Ellie with the meal and the children," she told him. "I want to show Father I'm not remiss in my duties. He must be pleased by what he sees today."

* * *

The whole time Lorabeth removed the jackets from the potatoes that had baked while they were gone and stirred together potato salad, she wanted to drop what she was doing and run to watch for her father to arrive. Because she wanted him to know she took her duties here seriously, she stayed put. She would hear the doorbell, she reminded herself.

When it rang, she dropped the spoon she was using to stir the creamed peas.

Ellie looked up from slicing a ham to give her a knowing glance. "You're as jittery as a long-tailed cat under a rocking chair. Are you upset that I asked your family to dinner?"

"No, I'm delighted. Just a little nervous. I want Father to be pleased."

"Well, calm down, dear. Go ahead and join them if it helps you feel better."

"No, I need to be in here helping you. Dinner will be served in a few more minutes and I'll see what's going on then."

Lorabeth avoided Ellie's delighted gaze and used some of the squash a patient had given Dr. Chaney to make a casserole while Ellie sliced fresh bread. She wanted to ask if Benjamin had told her their news, but she didn't want to take the privilege from Benjamin if he hadn't. She should have asked him.

Once the table was set, Ellie sent Lorabeth to call people. She found the girls in their room playing baby dolls, scooted them downstairs, then located the boys and finally found the men in Caleb's study. Her father's somber presence in his pressed black suit seemed out of place in this house where laughter rang and children played. He was sitting on one of the leather side chairs, his expression unreadable.

"Dinner is ready," she said, wishing for a moment to speak alone with Simon.

Dr. Chaney gestured for Lorabeth and her father to go before him. The men followed her, and Ellie showed the reverend to a seat beside her and placed Simon next to Flynn. The boys knew each other from school, and Flynn grinned amiably at his dinner companion.

It was the Chaney family's habit to bow their heads and wait while Caleb said grace, and this day was no different. Lorabeth was delighted for her father to observe how the children automatically waited for the prayer.

After the amen, the quiet was immediately broken as Lillith asked if there were green beans and Nate exclaimed over the bowl of potato salad.

Lorabeth sat with her hands folded in her lap, glancing from her father to each child who piped up. David said something to Nate, and the two of them chuckled. No one had ever spoken without permission at the reverend's dinner table.

Ambrose showed no expression, however, silently taking the platter of meat as it passed and spearing a slice.

"Lorabeth?" Benjamin had taken to sitting beside her on Sundays, so he was the one offering her creamed peas.

"Oh." She took the bowl and added a spoonful to her empty plate. She passed the dish on to Simon. He met her eyes and she saw the same dawning awareness that she'd experienced her first meal at this table.

Mealtime was not a somber occasion nor a time for children to be paralyzed for fear of making a mistake. Dinner was for sharing, an occasion when family members talked about their week, their lives, and enjoyed each other's company.

Her father cut his ham into same-size pieces and buttered a roll.

From beside him, Ellie's sharp-eyed gaze traveled from Benjamin to Lorabeth. "I enjoyed the sermon this morning," she told the reverend.

"Thank you, Mrs. Chaney."

"Do you work all week on a message like that?" she asked.

"I have my messages planned out a month in advance."

"How interesting." She offered him salt and pepper. "I'm so glad you could join us today. We've been wanting to have you and Simon over for a long time."

"It is our pleasure, Mrs. Chaney."

"Your daughter has been such a blessing to this family," she told him. "I don't know what we would do without her."

The statement held a double meaning for Lorabeth, as though Ellie suspected that doing without her might be a future possibility. She met Lorabeth's gaze and her eyes held a twinkle.

"Idleness has never been Lorabeth's downfall," the reverend replied. Which left a question remaining in Lorabeth's mind that he did believe she had a downfall.

"My brother Benjamin is a hard worker, too," Ellie added. "He earned only the highest grades at the university."

Lorabeth's father nodded. "That is admirable."

"He was my husband's assistant every afternoon even when he was going to school here in Newton," she went on.

Caleb gave his wife a questioning look at that comment.

Lorabeth sensed Benjamin's discomfort with the topic.

"I help my dad now," Nate said. "I sterilize his instruments and make sure his bag is ready in case of a 'mergency."

"And a fine job you do," Caleb told his son. The meal was about halfway through. "We won't have many Sundays warm enough to play outdoors," he added. "What will it be today without Nana and Papa?"

"I thought the girls and I would work on our knitting," Ellie said. "That will leave you fellas to entertain yourselves."

"How about horseshoes?" David asked with a bright-eyed expression. "Teams. An' Flynn can be on my team."

Flynn was the best horseshoe player in the family, rarely ever missing the stake.

"That sounds about right," Caleb said. "Reverend, how's your horseshoe arm?"

Lorabeth's father hadn't spoken or smiled once during the meal so far, and at the direct address he laid down his fork.

Lorabeth's heart began a jittery beat that made her head light. She, too, laid down her fork and wiped her lips on her napkin. She sought out Simon and their gazes met across the table. Was this where he'd admonish that their day and their talk and games were all folly and not respectful of the Sabbath? Would she be embarrassed in front of everyone? Would she be forced to make a choice she didn't want to make?

Lorabeth's last bite of ham stuck in her throat like a rock.

Ambrose Holdridge leveled his gaze on Caleb and cleared his throat.

"I was hopin' the reverend would go for a ride with me." Ben's suggestion drew all eyes. His palms were already sweating. "I'd appreciate some of your time, sir."

"Certainly, young man. My calling is to be available to my flock."

"Well, that's settled then." Ellie gave Ben a satisfied smile and offered the reverend another roll.

His sister had been casting impatient looks from Ben to Lorabeth throughout the meal. She'd been ecstatic when he'd told her of his plans to ask the reverend's blessing on a marriage between him and Lorabeth. Nobody knew him better than Ellie, so she knew how nervous he was right now.

By the time they'd eaten apple pie and had coffee, Ben's heart was racing. He'd never spoken to the reverend in private. They had nothing in common, save Lorabeth. The man had to know what was on Ben's mind. But his stoic expression never changed enough to tell the difference between curiosity or anger, so it was impossible to guess what he was thinking.

Why had it suddenly become so important that the man approve of him? Lorabeth said she would marry him regardless. Because her father's blessing was important to her.

Without a word, Lorabeth stood and cleared plates

and glasses from the table. Her occasional surreptitious glances clued Ben that she was even more wary than he of her father's reactions.

He got Reverend Holdridge's coat from the tree in the foyer and shrugged into his own. He led him out of doors, Buddy Lee mewling at their heels, and to the buggy he'd brought that day. "I'd like to show you somethin'. Won't take long."

"Very well."

Ben directed the horses toward his house several blocks away and stopped the team on the street.

"This is my house."

"Dr. Chaney used to live here as I recall."

"Yes, sir."

The reverend climbed down and followed Ben up the brick walk to the porch. Lorabeth had been Ben's first visitor. Ben noticed now how solitary the bentwood rocker appeared. He used his key to unlock the door and ushered Lorabeth's father into the foyer.

"I kept a few of the pieces of furniture that Caleb and Ellie left behind, but it looks a mite empty, I guess. The house has three fireplaces. Last year I bought a Glenwood kitchen range. It's back here."

The reverend followed, nodding at each item Ben pointed out on the way through. "Handsome home," he said finally. "Not excessive or ostentatious like some I've visited."

"I like things simple," Ben agreed. "I have another property, too, where I work. Here's the range. Cast iron, and it has two hearths, see here? One in front and one on the left. Trim and hearths are nickel plate. Oven is airtight so it holds the heat and doesn't get the kitchen all hot in the summer."

He was rambling, so he clamped his mouth shut.

"A good range," the man said with a nod.

Ben showed him the other rooms, and finally they stood in the study. Ben couldn't help but think of what had taken place between himself and this man's daughter the night before. He was going to make that right, though. He hadn't wasted a minute.

Reverend Holdridge raised one eyebrow nearly to the center of his forehead. "What is on your mind, Benjamin?"

Ben resisted the urge to clear his throat and risk sounding even more nervous. "I didn't just bring you here to show you the kitchen range. I was, uh, tryin' to show you somethin' about me. This place means a lot because it's the first home I ever had."

The reverend didn't reply.

"The Chaneys—Caleb and his family, I mean— were the first people who ever cared about me and Ellie and Flynn."

"I don't know how you came to the Chaney family."

How would the truth affect the good reverend's opinion of him? A lie stuck in Ben's craw. Last night he'd lain awake thinking about this, had dreamed that Ambrose Holdridge had whipped him with a cane. The memory of that dream wafted in his thoughts.

"After our mother died, Flynn and I went to a foster home." That was the truth, the honest-to-God truth. "Finally Ellie married Caleb and they took us in." Ben had never told the true story to anyone—not even Lorabeth, the woman he intended to marry. He didn't want to reveal it now, but if he wanted to marry this man's daughter, the reverend needed to know. And Ben couldn't be less than honest in this crucial situation.

"I never knew my father," he said. "Ellie and Flynn and I each have different fathers. Our mother didn't care if we lived or died, and most of the time I thought death would've been a whole lot kinder."

Reverend Holdridge seemed to be taking in that information.

The most critical question he'd ever asked of anyone formed and Ben worked to get it past his lips. "Are the circumstances of a man's birth important to you?"

The man's mouth was set like a deep slash across his face. He didn't have many lines in his skin, and Ben figured that was because he never smiled. If this was where he'd earn disapproval, Ben was prepared. If his family history was the deciding factor, did he want his blessing based on a lie?

On the other hand, he didn't intend to lose Lorabeth over something he couldn't help. "If genealogy matters, I probably don't hold much esteem in your eyes."

"Jesus's genealogy is traced all the way back to Adam," the reverend replied.

Ben thought about that. "Wasn't Rahab in there, somewhere? A harlot?"

The reverend didn't reply, but he looked at Ben with dawning appreciation.

"I have a successful veterinary practice. I don't have debt. I'm not a drinkin' man. Or a gambler."

"One would think you were trying to sell me something."

"I am."

"What do you want from me?"

"I'm tryin' to sell you on the fact that I'm responsible and hardworkin'."

"I already know those things about you, Benjamin."

Ben glanced away and gestured for the reverend to have a seat. That's when he realized they were still wearing their coats. It didn't matter now. He had to get to the point. "I'm just gonna say it." He took a breath and his heart hammered. "I want to marry your daughter, and Lorabeth and I want your blessing on our marriage."

Heat rushed into his face and his heart pounded in his chest the very second the words were out. What could he expect from a man who had raised and sheltered and taught a young woman the way he had? Lorabeth had assured him she would marry him anyway, but this moment was momentous—life-altering—to both of them.

Chapter Fourteen

Lorabeth had offered to do the dishes while the girls worked on their scarves and hats and the males played horseshoes. She was drawn to the side porch every five or ten minutes to see how Simon was doing. He and Flynn were a team against Caleb and the younger boys, which seemed pretty fair, considering Flynn was the best and Simon was just learning.

From the laughter and jibes that were flying between the two teams, it appeared that Simon was fully enjoying himself. The sight blessed Lorabeth's heart to no end. Just the fact that her father had accepted the invitation still astounded her. They'd been on pathetically few visits to other people's homes during her growing-up years, and she didn't remember ever getting to join in the families' leisure activities. Leisure was synonymous with idle hands, and the Holdridge siblings knew how their father felt about idle hands.

Flynn looked over, spotted her and waved. Simon

turned his attention, too. She gestured for him to come and raised the hem of her skirt to descend the stairs.

"I haven't got one to actually hook on to the stake yet, but I've struck it several times." He beamed with delight.

"Good for you!" She clapped, excited that he was having such a good time doing the things ordinary people did all the time. Sobering, she leaned forward and said, "Simon, I want to tell you something."

"What?"

"It's about Benjamin and Father. Benjamin asked him for time alone so he could ask him for his blessing."

Simon waited as though not quite understanding.

"Benjamin asked me to marry him."

A look of surprise quickly turned into sheer joy. "I can tell you're happy about it."

"I am. I've never been this happy. I just want Father to approve."

"Why wouldn't he? Benjamin is an acceptable mate. Father approved of Ruthann's choice."

"You're right. Benjamin is more than acceptable." She gave her brother a quick hug. "Go have fun."

He grinned and jogged back to the game in the side yard.

She returned to the house, finished drying the pans and put them away. The clock in the hallway chimed. It had barely been an hour since Ben and her father left, but it seemed like forever. She couldn't bear to imagine their conversation one more time, so she rubbed glycerin into her hands and located the girls in the parlor. Flynn had laid a fire for them, and the flames were warming the room. Madeline had just started to fuss.

Lorabeth crossed to where the baby lay on a palette on the floor and scooped her up. "Is she hungry?"

"She shouldn't be," Ellie replied, "but if an hour has passed since her last feeding…" She shrugged and smiled.

"Maybe she just wants to see what's going on with her big sisters." Lorabeth carried her to a chair beside the sofa where mother and daughters sat and turned Madeline so she could see them.

Ellie looked at the contented baby and laughed. "Maybe she just knows it's Sunday, and on Sunday there's usually someone who wants to hold her."

"Well, we can do something about that, can't we, sweetie?" Lorabeth nuzzled Madeline's fine hair and kissed her ear.

Ellie's hands fell still on the red yarn in her lap. Tears came to her eyes. "Thank you for loving my children."

Her remark surprised Lorabeth. She did love these children. She loved all of the Chaneys as though they were her own family. "They're easy to love," she replied. "Thank you for treating me like one of you."

"You *are* a part of our family," Ellie answered. "I can't imagine you not being in our lives, and not just because of the things you do for us."

Lorabeth couldn't imagine it, either. The possibility that she might soon become a real member of their family humbled and amazed her.

Ellie was looking at her as though she was waiting, as though she knew there was something life-changing in Lorabeth's next words.

"Ellie?"

"I'm listening."

Lorabeth took note that the girls were sitting right there listening, too. But she and Ellie had developed ways to communicate in front of the younger ones without them being aware of what they were saying. She chose her words carefully. "The noun we were just using…"

Grinning, Ellie nodded and lent a feeble effort to her pearl stitches so the girls wouldn't catch on.

"The likelihood of that becoming more so is real."

Ellie seemed to think a minute. Her hands barely stilled before she said, "One of my siblings mentioned his intentions."

Lorabeth nodded. "A proposal was suggested."

Ellie smiled with approval. "Was the proposal all you'd dreamed of?"

Lorabeth glanced at the girls who had picked up on their mother's excitement. "Affirmative."

"What's formative mean, Mama?" Lillith asked.

"The way the stitches are made, darling. Dinner today was important. And the ride…"

"More important," Lorabeth replied.

Ellie grinned. "Our favorite canine physician…"

"Conversing with our mutual man of the cloth," Lorabeth answered.

Ellie gave her an encouraging look. "It will go well, you'll see."

"What, Mommy?" Lillith asked. "What's a mammoth claw?"

"It's like a Danish roll, dear." Ellie smiled at Lorabeth, and the two of them broke into giggles.

Ellie got up and knelt in front of the chair where Lorabeth sat holding Madeline. "I couldn't be happier."

Careful of the baby, Lorabeth leaned into a hug with tears blurring her vision.

Ellie sat back on her heels. "He seemed so anxious. Are his fears justified?"

"Our mutual mammoth claw will insist that everything be proper and orderly in his sight."

A look of concern passed Ellie's features.

"Not to worry," Lorabeth told her in a whisper. "I love him. We will be married with or without my father's blessing."

Her words didn't seem to assure Ellie if her eyes were any indication, but she managed a smile and patted Lorabeth's hand. "Good for you."

"Do you know what the Bible says about husbands and wives?" Ambrose asked Ben.

Ben was glad he'd studied those parts. "I do, sir. It says that a husband should love his wife the way Christ loved the church."

"Do you know what that entails, son?"

Ben had given it a good measure of thought. "I reckon it means that a man should love his wife enough to die for her."

A beat of silence passed between them.

"And is that how you love my daughter, Benjamin?"

"Yes. I'd give my life for her, sir."

"She is unspoiled," the reverend said. "I trained her up in the way she should go. She believes I am a harsh taskmaster, but I raised my daughters to be good wives and God-fearing women."

Ben should have taken off his coat. The room was sweltering. "You are a good father."

"I have prayed for her to have wisdom in all things."

Benjamin waited, perspiration prickling under his starched collar.

"I prayed for her husband to be a man of faith, a disciplined man. A good man."

Benjamin met his eyes, surprised in that instant to find them the same golden-brown color as Lorabeth's.

"Are you that man?"

Ben's heart chugged to a stop and then started again. He thought over Lorabeth's options. He knew exactly what bad men were like, and he'd disciplined himself to be the best man he could be.

"I'm not perfect, sir, but I believe I can be that man."

"I believe you can, as well," the reverend agreed.

Ben absorbed those words slowly.

"She will remain untouched until your wedding night. Becoming one flesh is a solemn and holy occasion."

Ben's head buzzed. "Of course."

"You will honor her and value her above rubies…and kitchen ranges."

The man's expression hadn't changed, so that hadn't been a jest. "Of course."

Ambrose wasn't a man who minced words. "You have my blessing."

Ben jerked out of the chair and extended his hand. "Thank you, sir! Thank you."

The reverend shook Ben's hand and then pulled his

own back when Ben clung too long. "You will set a close date for the wedding. Paul said it is better for a man to marry than to burn."

Ben would have to think on that one some. "Soon," he agreed.

"Let us return then."

"Yes, sir." Ben led him toward the front door.

As relieved as he was with the reverend's faith in him, doubt still crowded in. He couldn't fail this man who'd placed his trust in him. And he couldn't fail Lorabeth.

But his prevailing doubt remained. He'd taken a man's life. He'd been justified, vindicated in the eyes of the law. Ben never let that demon out and he couldn't now. Not when the stakes were so high. He couldn't afford to give himself qualms. His measure was yet to be proven.

The sound of footsteps on the front porch alerted Lorabeth and Ellie that Ben was back. With a smile, Ellie took Madeline from Lorabeth's lap. "Not that I don't trust you…"

Lorabeth ignored her jest and watched the doorway. Frozen in place, she waited.

Caleb appeared first, and her heart sank. The boys all clambered in next and took seats around the room. Simon settled beside Flynn on the floor. Where was Benjamin?

Her father appeared next, his face as inscrutable as ever. Her heart pounded in anticipation anyway.

Benjamin entered. And he was wearing a smile!

"I asked everyone to come on in," he said.

Ellie slipped her hand into Lorabeth's and gave it a squeeze.

"I have a piece of news," Benjamin said.

Lorabeth remained on her chair, unmoving.

"The reverend has given his blessing, and Lorabeth has agreed to marry me."

For one split second, deafening silence encased the room. And then chaos broke loose. Lorabeth jumped up and ran toward Benjamin. He met her halfway and she wrapped her arms around his neck. He cupped her head in his palm and looked into her eyes. She could hardly see him through the blur of tears.

Ellie ran up and crushed them both in a hug. Madeline, somewhere in the middle, broke into a whimper that led to a full-blown howl. Caleb came and took the baby while Lorabeth backed away and let Ellie embrace her brother.

Lorabeth turned and crossed to her father who was standing behind one of the settees. She laid her hand on his arm. "Thank you, Father."

"You and God are the ones who made the good choice," he replied.

The Chaneys had all flocked around Benjamin and now turned to envelop Lorabeth in their hugs. Over Flynn's shoulder, she spotted Simon on his knees before the hearth, a look of wonder on his face. She gave David a last hug and went to her brother. "Happy for me?"

He stood to his height several inches above her. "It's like you said, Lorabeth." Awe tinged his voice. "And you will be one of them."

"I'll always be your sister, and I'll always be here for you."

"You didn't need to say that. I know you."

They embraced, and Lorabeth was glad she and Simon weren't as standoffish with each other as her father had always been with them.

She turned to find Benjamin watching her, waiting for her, and her heart leaped. "You'll have a new brother," she told Simon.

"Will you have Sunday dinners at your house?" Simon asked.

"I hadn't given it any thought. Why?"

"Because if you do, I might get to play horseshoes again."

She laughed. "You can count on it."

She hurried to Benjamin, and he took her hand. Her heart was so full, she didn't know how much more joy it could hold. All of her dreams were coming true.

Chapter Fifteen

They set the wedding date for three weeks away. Plenty of time to make arrangements, Ellie had assured Lorabeth. Plenty of time to make a gown and address invitations and plan the menu.

Lorabeth went from euphoria to nervous exhaustion and back several times a day in the weeks that followed, and it became even more difficult to sleep.

Benjamin arrived one afternoon, scolding Buddy Lee back out the kitchen door when the cat tried to get in around his feet.

Lorabeth had been stirring together a recipe of rice pudding to set in the oven for that night's supper. "Benjamin!"

She wiped her hands on her apron and hurried to greet him. Smiling, he gave her a brief hug and a chaste kiss.

He looked around and discovered they were alone. "I couldn't sleep last night."

"Me, neither. But then I never sleep much."

"You don't?"

"No. What were you thinking?"

"There's so much we haven't talked about. I think we need to spend a little more time together." He didn't remove his coat.

"We haven't made the final arrangements yet," she answered. "I have a list."

"Let's go somewhere and talk," he said. "I want to surprise you today."

"Well…"

Ellie came into the kitchen. "Go. Take her. She needs a free afternoon."

Lorabeth didn't waste any time removing her apron. "I'll change and be right back."

"Wear something nice," he suggested.

Ben watched her hurry from the room.

"Are you hungry?" Ellie asked. "There are a few pieces of chicken left from last night."

He shook his head. "I want to take her to supper. Can you manage without her?"

"I'm going to have to learn, aren't I?"

He looked at her. "What do you mean?"

"I doubt she'll want to stay as many hours a day as she does now after you're married."

"Probably not." He said what he'd been thinking. "She doesn't have to work at all if she doesn't want to."

"I'm not going to scold you for stealing away my help," she said with a smile. "It will work out."

A few minutes later Lorabeth returned wearing a dark green dress and carrying her new coat. "I'm ready."

"Ellie and I were talkin'," he said as he helped her into it. "After we're married you won't have to work unless you want to. But if you'd like to spend a few hours a day or a few days a week helpin' Ellie, it will be all right with both of us. We want you to do what pleases you."

"I…I can't imagine not being here," she said, a furrow between her brows. "But of course I'll have another house to keep, won't I?"

"We'll work it out," he assured her.

"'Bye, Ellie," Lorabeth said with a little wave. Ben led her out of doors where his buggy waited. "Where are we going?"

"I thought we'd browse a few of the shops this afternoon, then have dinner together."

"Not come home, you mean?"

"That's right. I want to take you to the Arcade Hotel's dining hall. Ever been there?"

She shook her head. "Where Ellie and Sophie used to work? Does Ellie know?"

"I told her."

"What a treat this will be!"

The first place he took her was Miss Tibby's Tea Parlor. He'd never been there himself, but he knew the ladies liked it. Ben felt completely out of place as they sat at a table with white linen and ate tiny frosted tea cakes and sipped from delicate china cups, but he wanted Lorabeth to have all the experiences she'd longed for.

"We'll live in my house in town, of course," he said. "I'll ride out every day to work at the other place."

Her smile displayed her pleasure. "It's a beautiful home. I can't believe I'm so blessed."

"I want to talk about some new pieces of furniture," he told her.

After tea, they strolled the boardwalks along Main Street and Broadway, browsing in clothing stores and a tailor's.

Eventually they reached the mercantile. The crowded store was bustling with activity. Dirk Paulson was gathering supplies for a dusty cowboy, and Tubs McElroy, the bartender from the Side-Track, was looking at boxes of cigars. Two women were comparing colors of cloth and thread while three small children clung to their skirts.

One of the women glanced up and recognized him. "Dr. Ben! How unusual to see you in town of an afternoon."

"Hi, Mrs. Henley."

The woman admonished one of the toddlers to wait for her and walked toward them, her curious gaze flitting to Lorabeth.

"Have you met Lorabeth Holdridge? Her father is the Congregational preacher."

"Hello, dear."

"Pleased to meet you," Lorabeth said.

"Lorabeth and I are to be married in two weeks."

The other woman overheard and joined them to ooh and aah. Lorabeth's blush was so pretty that it made Ben's chest ache.

Eventually the women went back to their shopping and Ben showed Lorabeth the catalogs. "What kind of rugs and curtains would you like in our rooms?"

"I'm sure what you already have is serviceable," she replied.

"But we should have new for our new life together."

Her eyes shone with interest and surprise. "All right, then. Let's look."

They scoured the pages for colors and fabrics and selected rugs for the parlor and bedroom. They ordered bolts of fabric for curtains to coordinate.

"How long will these take?" Ben asked Hazel Paulson who ran the store.

"They come from the factories by rail and usually don't take no more'n a week or two," she replied.

"Is there someone who can come measure windows and make the drapes for us?"

"You're in luck. My daughter Beverly is the best drapery maker in town. Her place is 'round the corner."

"There's been nothing in that front hall since I've had the house," he thought aloud to Lorabeth. "Let's choose a hall rack. Maybe one with a mirror."

Instead of a huge piece, they both liked a golden oak hall seat with storage inside and a separate matching mirror with hooks for coats and hats.

"Our first purchase," he told her with satisfaction. "Now. Let's select a bedroom suite."

"Benjamin, is that a wise expense? Don't you have a bed and chests of drawers?"

"All hand-me-downs," he replied. "Not good enough for our new life. Let's see how expensive they are." He flipped through the pages of a catalog, past tables and desks and bookcases until he found iron bed frames and on the next page found sets. "Look at this one," he said, pointing to the full-page depiction entitled, High-Grade Bedroom Suite with Ornate Hand Carvings.

"I don't even think I could sleep in a bed that costs that much," she whispered.

"It's not that much," he told her. "I earn that from nearly every rancher in the spring when I do inoculations and exams."

Her eyes widened in surprise. "You're rich?"

"I guess to some people I'm rich. *We're* rich," he corrected. His ability to afford a home and all they needed was a far cry from his humble beginnings. "How about this one, then? See here, it says exceptional value."

"Three hundred and ten pounds," she read over his shoulder. "How much will it cost to ship?"

He turned to look at her.

She gave him a hesitant smile. "A good wife is frugal."

"I'm thankful that you'll be lookin' after our household, then. You'll do a good job. Isn't frugal also buyin' good quality and makin' the best deal possible? We're not spendin' money foolishly here. I want to provide these things, Lorabeth. It's why I worked hard in school and sacrificed to start my business. So I never had to be poor."

"In that case," she said, "I've always admired Ellie's armoire."

Ben smiled. "Well then, that'll be my wedding gift to you."

They were among the early diners at the Arcade that evening. The wood-paneled walls, elegant chandeliers and white linens caught Lorabeth's attention immediately. Gleaming silver coffee urns lined one wall, and girls in immaculate black dresses and crisp white aprons bustled about with trays.

A man in a black suit led the way to a table, and one of the girls handed them menus. The table was set with sweating glasses of ice water and pressed napkins. Lorabeth studied the menu in awe. She had no idea what a blue point was, but it came served on a shell. She read the list: filets of whitefish with madeira sauce; young capon; roast sirloin of beef au jus; pork with applesauce; stuffed turkey; salmi of duck; prairie chicken with currant jelly; sugar-cured ham; pickled lamb's tongue; and lobster salad au mayonnaise.

She raised her gaze to Benjamin's. "They have all this food ready to bring us?"

He nodded. "Pretty incredible, isn't it?"

"Where do they get all this?"

"Fred Harvey pays his chefs more than anyone else in his employ. I hear some of 'em are from France. Food arrives fresh every day by train."

"Have you ever eaten lobster?" she asked.

He nodded. "Had it once when Caleb brought us here for Ellie's birthday."

"Pickled lamb's tongue?"

He shook his head and grimaced.

"So the fish is fresh from the coast? That's what I'm having. I've only eaten catfish and trout."

The waitress took their orders and brought them coffee. After she'd moved to another table, Lorabeth said, "Everything is so elegant. It's all just perfect."

"All the Harvey Houses along the Sante Fe are set up the same. All staffed with attractive young woman like these."

"You've eaten in more than one?"

He nodded. "A couple along the railroad. One right in Florence."

"Sometimes I think I'm going to wake up and all this will have been a dream." She folded her hands on the edge of the table. "It's almost too good to be true. *You're* almost too good to be true."

"I'm not that special," he answered.

"You are to me."

"I find *that* too good to be true." He winked.

She smiled, and he placed his hand on top of hers.

Movement caught his eye and he noticed the waiter leading a family to a table on the other side of the room. He immediately recognized the man's hair and wide shoulders. All the heartwarming confidence the afternoon had generated evaporated as the Evans family took seats around a table.

Ben looked away sharply. He tried to push Wesley Evans out of his thoughts so he could get on with his life, but fate kept throwing the man and *his whole stinkin' family* in his face.

Part of the rage he'd directed toward the world for so much of his younger days surfaced, and being so angry scared the hell out of him. Men were capable of terrible things when they were angry or drunk, and Ben never got drunk.

He studied Lorabeth's serene countenance as she admired their surroundings. The same peace she possessed was his desire. She was perfect for him in so many ways. He relaxed somewhat just looking at her. Her calming influence would always be a balm to his spirit.

Tell her. Get it out. Secrets are destructive and you'll

lose her trust. The voice in his head wouldn't be silenced, and the clincher was, Ben knew his conscience was right.

The waitress served their food. Lorabeth tasted her fish and her lashes drifted down over her incredible eyes. She opened them and Ben read her delight. "I've never tasted anything like this," she said.

Ben cut a slice of his ham. He had to tell her about Evans. He'd told her father, thinking *that* had been the most difficult thing he'd ever done. This would be worse. This woman he held in such high esteem would know his sordid secrets.

He worked at making the most of their meal time together, refusing to look over and be tortured by Wes Evans eating with his perfect little family.

The waitress offered them dessert, and Ben was hoping to leave, but Lorabeth's eyes lit up at the mention of cheesecake. He realized in that moment that it was a good thing she was an unselfish and sensible woman, because he doubted he'd ever be able to say no to her.

Once it arrived, she offered him a bite, and he leaned to accept the morsel from her fork. She gave him a bashful smile and a flush rose in her cheeks.

Ben made up his mind not to be run off, and they sipped coffee until Lorabeth was ready to leave.

He paid, leaving the waitress a generous tip, and helped Lorabeth into her coat.

"I need to talk to you," he said as they left the Arcade.

"What about?"

He stopped and turned to her. The wind had picked up since that afternoon and a brisk chill swept around their ankles. "Somewhere where we'll be alone."

He led her to where they'd left the buggy, and drove to his house. Once inside, they hung their wraps, and Ben laid a fire. He stoked the range and pumped water for coffee. "I made a fool of myself showin' your father the house," he told her.

Lorabeth wandered the room as though taking better note of the layout. "You couldn't have made too big a fool of yourself. He approved of you."

"He liked the range."

She cut him a glance.

"It's your kitchen now," he told her.

"I'm going to love everything about it. About the whole house, and…" She paused in her inspection of the room to study him. "I'm going to love everything about being your wife."

At those words new heat burst to life in Ben's body. He busied himself getting down mugs.

Lorabeth seated herself on one of the benches that flanked the long table. "What did you want to talk about?"

He didn't like his reactions. His childhood made him feel inadequate, and letting her see the inadequacy made him vulnerable. He didn't want to tell her, didn't want to be less in her eyes.

He had to.

"Ellie and I don't talk much about where we came from," he began. "How we grew up."

"I noticed."

"Some things are too painful to talk about."

Her lovely eyes held understanding. "Are you sure you want to now?"

He nodded, then shook his head. "No. I don't want

to. But I have to. I have to tell you this so that it's not between us."

Lorabeth was curious about the past and the family that Ellie and Benjamin had been evasive about. She would never have pried, but she was interested.

Benjamin didn't meet her eyes as he told her the circumstances of his birth, how he and Ellie and Flynn didn't know who their fathers were because their mother had been a prostitute.

Lorabeth absorbed that information and tried to process it. "Prostitutes are in the Bible. I just didn't know any lived around here."

"Yeah, well, it's an age-old profession for sure," he said.

"I'm sorry to be dense," she told him, feeling completely ignorant. "I can't even imagine what you're saying."

"You're not dense, Lorabeth. Decent young ladies don't know about things like that, and that's good."

"Does my father know?"

"I told him."

"I see. Well, what your mother did can't be held against you, Benjamin."

"What my mother did made me who I am today," he argued.

"No." She reached to take his chin in her hand and turn his face so she could look him straight in the eye. "What you did with your life, going to school, attending college, coming to church, becoming a veterinarian—those are the things that made you who you are today."

"Hold those kind thoughts until you hear the rest," he said.

Lorabeth rested her arm on the table and leaned toward him. "There's more?"

Benjamin got up and strode across the kitchen and back, displaying his agitation. "There's so much more, it would make your head hurt hearing it all. And you don't need to hear it all. But you need to hear this." He walked back to where she sat and stood beside her.

Lorabeth had to look up.

"The man who fathered me approached me a few weeks ago. His wife had seen me and suspected I was his son." He went on to explain the events of the past several weeks.

Lorabeth's heart broke at the pain in the words he chose so carefully so as to disguise the hurt. She couldn't even imagine the life of poverty and shame that was his childhood, but he had lived every moment of it. And now he knew that all the while he'd been struggling for existence, there had been a man out there—a father living a comfortable life. A father with a respectable wife and legitimate children he loved and for whom he provided while Benjamin and his siblings had gone hungry and cold. That knowledge had to be eating a hole in his heart.

"It wasn't fair to keep it from you," he told her. "You should know what kind of man you're marryin'."

"I know what kind of man I'm marrying." She reached and took his hand. "You're nothing like the woman who gave birth to you, Benjamin. You're a good kind man. You take your responsibilities seriously."

She got up and moved to place her hand over his heart and looked up into his eyes. "More important, you have a pure heart and a lot of love to give." They stood like that while the coffee perked on the stove, the aroma filling the warming room.

Benjamin's eyes closed and he dropped his forehead against hers. A moment later he hugged her close. Finally Lorabeth leaned away and asked, "Why did Wes come to see you? What did he say?"

Ben released her and took a seat. "Didn't really say anything."

"He came to see you, but didn't have anything to say?"

"I—well, I didn't give 'im much of a chance."

She sat and covered his hand with hers. "What do you mean?"

"I ordered him off my property. Said I didn't want to talk."

"Maybe you should have listened, Benjamin. Maybe he wanted to apologize."

"He can't make amends for my life."

"No, but he can ask your forgiveness. And even if he doesn't ask, you can forgive him."

Benjamin pulled his hand away. "You don't know what you're askin'."

Lorabeth paused, unsure of how much to say or if she had the right, but his misery was so complete that anger and resentment had to be eating him up. She stayed seated while he poured coffee and set mugs on the table, then placed a sugar bowl between them and sat. She calmly spooned sugar and milk into her cup and stirred.

"You've asked more than once about what the Bible says on different subjects," she said.

He sighed and pursed his lips as though he didn't want to hear what was coming.

"So I know you think it's good advice."

He said nothing.

"I wouldn't presume to tell you what to do, Benjamin, but I will tell you what the Bible says about forgiveness."

"Turn the other cheek?"

"That if we want to be forgiven, we have to forgive."

He met her eyes then. She didn't see any resentment, for which she was relieved. "You think I should talk to him."

"You didn't let him talk, did you?" she answered.

He raised a palm in a supplicating gesture. "He can't explain away my childhood."

"No, he can't. But you learned how the truth eats away inside and needs to come out. Maybe it's the same for him."

"I don't owe him anything."

"Forgiveness is a gift, Benjamin."

He studied her, his expressive blue eyes taking in her face and hair before softening. "I asked for this, didn't I? Marryin' a woman so kind and wise?"

Their hands met on top of the table, his large and warm around hers.

"Will you come with me?" Ben asked. "To talk to him?"

"I'll always be here for you," she assured him.

He believed her. He didn't know what he'd ever done

to deserve someone so wholeheartedly good and kind
and generous, but he was grateful. And he vowed he
would never take her devotion lightly. He was going to
be the man she deserved.

Chapter Sixteen

Benjamin visited the town hall to read the directory of Newton residents and businesses and discovered Wesley Evans's home address.

He told Ellie what he was going to do and gathered Lorabeth to accompany him the next evening. He drew the buggy before a modest home in the Third Ward.

"Accordin' to the dates recorded in the city directory," he told Lorabeth, "he bought this place less than a year ago."

He helped her down and she took his hand as they approached the front door. Ben raised and lowered a brass knocker several times. Lorabeth squeezed his fingers. Her reaction to the truth about his mother still took him by surprise when he thought about it. Could she care for him so much that it didn't matter? Or was it her nature to be forgiving of all?

The door opened. One of the young girls he'd seen with Wes and Suzanne stood in the opening. Two platinum-blond braids hung over her shoulders. Her eyes were startling blue—like his own. "Can I help you?"

"I've come to see your father."

"Come on in." She opened the door wide and ushered them into a small hallway. "Have a seat in the parlor and I'll go get Daddy."

Ben and Lorabeth entered the room she'd indicated. The furnishings were not new, but had been well cared for. Needlepoint pillows rested in every sofa and chair, and delicate lacy antimacassars were pinned to the backs.

Solid footsteps along the wooden boards of the hallway alerted Ben to someone's arrival.

Wes Evans halted in the doorway, surprise evident on his face. He composed his expression. "Benjamin?"

"Hope it's okay I came like this."

"Of course." Wes entered the room. "I'll take your coats."

Ben helped Lorabeth out of hers and shrugged off his own. Wes left momentarily and returned. "Oh. Sorry. Sit down. I'm a little flustered."

Ben gestured for Lorabeth to be seated on the sofa and he perched beside her.

"Is this your sister?" Wes asked.

"No. This is Lorabeth Holdridge, my...fiancée."

Lorabeth offered her hand and Wes shook it before sitting down across from them. "Congratulations. To both of you."

"Thank you," Lorabeth replied.

"This is awkward for all of us," Wes said.

Ben nodded.

Suzanne entered the room then. "I came to see if you

and your guests would like—" She halted when she recognized Ben.

"Join us," Ben said, and she took a chair. He introduced Lorabeth. "Lorabeth thought I needed to come hear you out," he began. "I was just madder'n all get-out that day you came to my place. Not in much of a mood to listen, I reckon."

"I'm glad you came," Wes said. "I understand."

They looked at each other.

"Your sister is a touchy subject apparently," Wes said. "I appreciate that you're protective of her."

Ben bristled. "She raised me. We took care of each other."

Wes nodded. "I don't know your situation or anything about what happened to your mother or Ellianna."

At the word *mother* Ben clenched his jaw.

"Ellianna was just a tiny little thing when I met her. No more than three or four."

"Where did you meet her?" Ben asked. "My…mother."

"In Florence at an Independence Day celebration. I thought she was a widow at first. Until I found out where she worked and learned she'd never been married."

Ben couldn't imagine his mother at a celebration in town. He'd never known her to drag herself farther than the saloon or the outhouse.

"I cared for your mother, Benjamin," Wes said.

Ben's body tensed. "Why feed me this *bullshit?*"

"Benjamin!" Lorabeth said from beside him and clenched his hand tightly. "Let the man talk."

He looked at her, at the encouragement and confidence in her eyes and took a deep breath. "Go on."

"Why would I lie to you? Why would I come find you at all if this wasn't so? I was just as shocked as you when Suzanne came back from your place that day and told me her suspicions. I didn't believe it until I saw you. After meeting you, I'm convinced I'm your father. I don't want anything from you except a chance to talk." His expression showed his earnestness. "Maybe a chance to know you."

With disbelief Ben asked, "And it took *twenty-four years*?"

"Please. Let me explain."

The sick feeling in his belly right now couldn't even compare to the nights of hunger and cold that had been his wretched life. Ben raked shaky fingers through his hair and surveyed the room without seeing anything except that filthy shack. He looked at Wes, and by this time his body was almost twitching with anger. "Tell me how that can fix all those years of me and my little brother and older sister goin' to bed with a belly so hungry it hurt. Tell me how talkin' can change Flynn and me havin' no one except a scared sister who cared if we lived or died."

All his resentment poured out in the words he couldn't stop now. "Flynn was so little. He should've had better. Some of the babies she had just—" Unable to sit any longer, he jumped to his feet and gestured. "*Disappeared.* Ellie knows what happened to them, but she won't tell me."

He was shaking now.

Lorabeth gasped. He couldn't stop. He wanted this man to know exactly what his lack of concern had caused.

"Ellie stole for us to eat. When our mother died, Flynn and I were sent to a foster home. We were starved and worked like animals. I nearly lost all my toes from sores and blisters." He looked at his shoes as though the pain was in the present.

Wes's eyes filled with tears and they ran down his cheeks uninhibited.

Suzanne sat with a stunned expression.

Lorabeth looked up at him, and she was trembling. He couldn't look at her any longer so he faced Wes.

"So go ahead," Ben ground out. "Explain all that so I can understand."

"I can't," Wes said in a ragged voice. "But, Ben, all those years aren't my fault, either. I didn't know about you. I can't change what happened, but you have to understand that I'd have taken care of you if I'd known."

Ben looked at Wes and felt as though a chunk of his heart was hanging out raw and bleeding. "No one ever cared about us."

"I care now," Wes said. "I cared about your mother, too, but she wouldn't let me help her. I tried."

Ben waited for something more. Something to make a difference in how he felt.

"I was twenty when I met her. I'd been riding herd with a drive and we shipped cows from there. She was working at the Junction Saloon in Florence. Just serving drinks and dancing, but she drank as many as she served. She was living in a room over one of the storefronts and she had a little girl. I started calling on her.

"She always drank, even during the day and no

matter the occasion. I tried to get her to leave the saloon and I offered to take her east when I went. She refused.

"I asked her to marry me, but she just laughed. I suspected I wasn't the only man keeping company with her. The drinking had such a hold on her that I got concerned for the girl. I suggested she give Elli-anna to someone to care for until she was better able. That just made her furious. She told me to never come back.

"I left on another drive and when I came back through this way, I couldn't find her. Nobody knew where she'd gone."

Ben looked him over with a critical eye. What would it benefit Wes to tell a story with no basis? He didn't have to expose himself as Ben's father. If he was telling the truth and really had cared about his mother and Ellie, he wasn't the selfish man Ben had imagined all those years. Ben would be forced to change his thinking.

"I know it doesn't change the past," Wes said, "but I'm sorry for how you came into the world and were treated. She was sick. I'd never seen a person who was controlled by a need for alcohol. Scared me so much I quit drinkin' myself."

Ben understood that. "Scares me so much I'm afraid to have my own kids for fear of bein' like her."

"You're nothing like her," Lorabeth insisted. "You can't even bear to see animals suffer, let alone children. You adore your nieces and nephews."

"Your childhood breaks my heart," Wes said as though he hadn't heard her. He sat head down, face in his hands. "If only I'd known."

Suzanne leaned toward her husband and placed her hand on his back. She rubbed it in a circle consolingly. "You had no way to know," she told him.

"I'm not the one who needs comforting," Wes said with a break in his voice.

Suzanne drew her hand back, but Wes caught it and held it. He raised his gaze to Ben's. "If only I'd found you back then, I'd have taken you both and made a family for you."

Ben read a thousand useless regrets. And he believed him.

Wes was a good man who'd had the misfortune to love a bad woman. Ben had no right blaming him for circumstances out of his control. He took a few steps away and stared at his reflection in the windowpane.

Ellie had told Ben that he couldn't live in the past, and she was right. Moving forward had worked for her. Lorabeth had told him he needed to forgive to be forgiven. "Really can't think of a reason why you'd lie about this," he said at last and turned back to the room. "Wouldn't profit you."

"It's the God's honest truth," Wes answered. After a minute he said, "Last year we moved from California to Kansas so I could work with the cattlemen. I'm an investor now. Suzanne and I have three children."

"I've seen 'em." Ben paused and glanced from husband to wife and back. "Will you tell 'em about me?"

"If it's all right with you I will. It's not because I hid you from them that they don't know. It's because I didn't know. Those are two different things. You'd have been part of this family if I'd had a say."

"You're not…ashamed of me?"

Wes's throat worked. "I could ask you the same question."

Ben thought it over a moment. He'd lived with shame his whole life, but a father who really cared about him wasn't embarrassing, was he? He glanced at Lorabeth, and she smiled encouragement through glistening tears. He wasn't ashamed of Wes.

"Guess I upset your life by moving here. It will be all right if you don't want to explain who I am to people," Wes told him. "We should probably agree. I'm going to tell my children. But if you don't want anyone else to know, then…maybe we can just be friends."

"I'm weary of hidin' my past," Ben told him. "I'm not ashamed, and I don't want to make up a story."

"Good." Wes looked relieved. "It's gonna be awkward for a while. We don't really know each other. But I want to know you. I don't even know how you became a veterinarian."

"Ellie's husband loaned me the money."

"The other Dr. Chaney?"

"First decent man I ever met. His father is another."

Silence enveloped the room.

"I spent a lot of years hating," Ben said, opening another vein. "Hating all the men who used her. Hating the man I believed was my father."

"That's a lot of hate to let go," Lorabeth said. "You must feel light as a feather."

Gazing into her eyes, Ben looked inside himself and discovered she was right. A burden he'd carried a lifetime had been eased because he'd learned the truth. He glanced at Wes. "I don't think you need forgiveness, but I'm lettin' go of the resentment."

"Thank you," Wes answered.

Suzanne left and returned a few minutes later with a tray of tea and served them. Their conversation eased into the easy give-and-take of people getting to know each other. Eventually Ben thanked Suzanne for tea and mentioned it was time for them to go.

The Evanses followed them out the door and stood on their porch. Wes put his arm around his wife.

Ben observed the gesture and realized he was happy for them. Grateful that Wes had found a good woman to be his wife. Waving, he guided Lorabeth to the buggy. She leaned and whispered in Ben's ear.

He hesitated. Turned back and looked at Wes. Her suggestion made Wes's warning about this transition more clear. But he didn't care what people thought. "Lorabeth and I would like you to come to our wedding next week."

The band played "Cockles and Mussels" for the fourth time, and when Ben raised his eyebrow, Ellie explained that Lillith kept requesting the comic song. He didn't much care what they played, because he wasn't listening half the time. He was processing what had taken place that day and thinking about what was yet to come.

"I want you to meet the Evanses now," he told his sister.

Ellie had been astonished when she'd learned that Ben had asked them to the wedding. Her feelings about Wes Evans were confusing. He was nothing to her.

Ben took hold of her arms. "It's gonna be all right, Ellie."

She nodded, digesting the change slowly. She'd seen them at the ceremony earlier, but they hadn't had an opportunity to meet until now. "I'm glad you've found him, Ben," she said. "I really am. And I'm happy you—and him—and his family are working all this out so amicably."

"Are you embarrassed about this?" he asked.

"No. We're not explaining every detail to the wedding guests and all of Newton. Even if we did, Caleb wouldn't care."

He leaned to kiss her cheek. Ellie watched her brother cross the room, seeing that skinny boy who was her champion, the boy who had been ready to die for her, who had killed a man to protect her. She was happy for him.

Wes Evans was handsome and pleasant, resembling Benjamin in a startling way, down to the manner in which he spoke and the turn of his lips when he smiled. Suzanne was charming and pretty, complimenting Ellie on her fine-looking children.

Fourteen-year-old Ginny and sixteen-year-old Booth had the same fair hair and blue eyes as Ben and their father. Twelve-year-old Clara was dark-haired and dark-eyed like her mother.

Nate and Simon immediately took Booth into their company, and Nate produced a bag of marbles.

"Is there enough light for them to do that outdoors?" Ellie asked.

"Nate snagged a lantern on his way," Ben answered.

"You're the same age as our niece, Lucy," Ellie told Ginny.

"I don't know her," the girl said.

"She goes to school in Florence," Ellie explained. "But I'm sure you two will have something to talk about."

"I'll go introduce them," Lorabeth said, taking Ginny's hand.

Suzanne and Clara left to find a hair ribbon Clara had dropped, leaving Ben and Ellie alone with Wes.

"It's probably gonna seem awkward for a while," Wes said to Ellie.

"Nothing will ever excuse my mother or what she did to us," she said to him. "There are things you don't know." The touch of anger that surfaced surprised her. "Just the fact that you ever had anything to do with her makes it hard for me. I'm not an unforgiving person, but..."

"We're all trying our best with the situation we have," he answered. "I can tell you're a fine person. I'm glad your life turned out the way it did."

None of what had happened to them was this man's fault, she reminded herself.

"You've met Caleb already?" Ben asked Wes.

"Oh, yeah. Booth manages to smash or cut something at least every other month. I'm sure you know about that with all your boys," he said to Ellie.

She agreed with a smile.

"Well, let's go find him," Ben said and placed his hand on Wes's shoulder as they walked away.

Ellie was struck anew by how much Ben resembled the man. Their hair, the broad shoulders, and now the way they walked. She was happy for her brother, she truly was.

And she tried not to feel hurt that he had found a father and a whole new family.

Chapter Seventeen

Ben's nervousness grew as the evening passed. It hadn't helped that when Luke Swenson had offered Ben a beer and he'd refused, Deputy Doyle had jokingly remarked that Ben was keeping a clear head for the night ahead.

Caleb had been standing among the small gathering of men. He'd given Ben a slap on the shoulder and led him away from the others. Next to Ellie, Caleb was the only one who even partially understood the strict standards Ben had set for himself and the reasons why. They stood side by side at the edge of the dance floor.

"Don't let 'em get to you," Caleb said.

Ben searched for Lorabeth in the crowd.

"She's your wife now, and making love to your wife is a good thing. Nothing like what you saw as a boy, Ben. Nothing like it."

"I know." At that second, Flynn's fiddle screeched, sounding like a young girl's screams, and his heart pounded faster. "In my head, I know it."

"The way she feels about you is all over her face," his brother-in-law told him. "Just love her back."

Ben studied the crowd and found her.

Lorabeth was the most beautiful woman Ben had ever laid eyes upon. In her ivory pearl-studded dress, she took his breath away. Her father had performed the ceremony and they'd taken their vows only hours ago. They'd been deluged with guests and gifts and cake ever since. When he looked at her across the social hall, he still couldn't believe she was his wife.

She made her way around clusters of guests until she reached him. "Dance with me again," she said, her eyes glowing, her cheeks pink with excitement.

He took her hand and followed her onto the dance floor, into the midst of friends and family who flowed aside and made a place for the bride and groom.

Apparently Flynn had noticed the crowd parting, and immediately the music changed to a slower more appropriately romantic tune. Ben took her in his arms.

"Are you happy?" he asked as they swayed to the music.

"Isn't mine the happiest face here?" she answered with a question of her own.

He had to agree. She was absolutely glowing. He didn't want to do anything to disappoint her. Not today. Not tonight. Not ever.

He'd made those vows and made them solemnly. This pure and innocent woman had chosen him, and it was his duty to honor her.

Just love her back. Was he capable of the kind of love she deserved?

He'd started out wanting to protect her, but now he

was involved. His head was involved, his body…his heart. He wasn't feelin' much like a protector. Hurting her would kill him.

"Caleb and Denzil have loaded all the gifts into the back of your buggy," Ellie told them a few minutes later. "You can pull it into your carriage house until you have time tomorrow or the next day to unload it."

"Sure," Ben replied.

His sister gave him a smile. "It's a custom for the bride and groom to leave early."

Ben glanced at Lorabeth. "You're right. We should go."

Ellie laid a hand on the sleeve of his black coat. "Don't be surprised if some of your friends pay you a late-night visit."

Ben had never participated, but he'd heard the young people talking about the pranks they played on newly-weds. "You didn't give 'em a key to my house or anything, did you?"

Ellie looked insulted and slapped his arm. "Of course not."

"Just makin' sure."

He and Lorabeth exchanged a look and she gave him an uncertain smile. He'd put off leaving as long as he could. With a backward glance at his sister, he found their coats.

Whispers and catcalls followed them to the door, so he hurried her along. Once they were in the buggy, she took his hand. Her fingers were cold. They both knew what was on the other's mind, but they hadn't discussed it. He wouldn't have known the first thing to say.

"We got lovely gifts," she said.

"Yep."

"I especially like the clock from your—from the Evanses."

She was every bit as nervous as he, of course. More so, because she was the woman, the one admonished to submit to her husband.

"I'd never deliberately hurt you, Lorabeth. You believe that, don't you?"

"Of course I do. You didn't need to tell me."

He stopped alongside the back porch. "I'll stoke the stove before I put up the horse, so you can have warm water."

Once he had a fire going, he pumped a kettle of water and set it on a burner. "You have some time now while I handle chores."

She nodded.

Ben wiped down the animal, got him a bucket of water, then stood in the carriage house watching the bay twitch its ears and munch oats.

He had no idea how long it would take Lorabeth to prepare for bed. He was probably doing things all wrong and should have gone upstairs with her.

Minutes later he climbed the stairs and entered the bedroom to discover his thoughts were right. She was standing in the circle of golden light created by the lamp on her dresser, still wearing the gown she'd worn all day.

"My dress buttons up the back," she told him.

So it did. He crossed the room and she turned her back to him. Several buttons at the top were undone and several at the bottom, but the center of the row remained fastened.

He fumbled with the tiny pearls until the back of the

garment parted. Beneath it she wore delicate satin garments edged with lace and pastel blue ribbon. She let the front fall forward, and he saw then how stiff and heavy the beading had been.

"I'm itching," she said, pulling her arms free and rubbing them, reaching for her shoulders. She made an attempt to scratch her back.

"I could rub in some glycerin for you," he offered.

Her expression was relieved and embarrassed at the same time. "I had no idea this dress would get so uncomfortable."

"I wasn't wearing it, but I'd have to say it was worth it, seein' you in it, I mean."

She stepped out of the dress and Ben reached to pick it up. The weight surprised him. "You must feel like a horse free of saddle and blankets," he said with a grin.

She placed a hand on her hip and said teasingly, "I don't think I've ever been compared to a *horse* before."

Seeing her in her underwear must've scrambled his brain. "Sorry."

She laughed. "Guess I'd better get used to animal comparisons since I'm married to a vet."

The familiarity of her acceptance touched him. He laid the dress across the cedar chest that sat under one of the windows. "You'll take care of it later, I suppose."

She moved to the dressing table he'd bought for her. She was slim and shapely in her delicate drawers and chemise, not as hesitant to face him as he might have imagined. But then what did she have to be ashamed of? She was beautiful. She was perfect. She was pure. And it was her wedding night.

He felt a muscle near his eye jump.

Lorabeth returned to him with a jar, twisted off the lid and offered it.

Ben took the glass container from her and dipped his fingertips. She turned her back and raised her hair away from her neck and shoulders, and his mouth went dry.

He smeared the cool substance across her irritated pink skin. Beneath his fingers every place he touched was smooth and soft.

"That feels so good," she said.

Once her neck and shoulders were soothed, he worked the glycerin into her arms. They were slender and delicate like the rest of her. A gentle rise and fall beat at the base of her throat above the pearls she wore. He applied a cool dab to the pulse point.

She looked at him, her tawny eyes trusting. "What am I supposed to do, Benjamin?"

He wished he knew. He didn't have a reply.

"Do you know what to do?"

It was his job to follow through with this act, to consummate their marriage and fulfill his obligation. The responsibility of being a husband weighed heavily on his conscience. "In theory."

He desired Lorabeth. He was drawn to her like a honeybee to a sweet, sweet flower. But he didn't want to ruin what they had by allowing lust to taint this moment.

She was a virgin, pure and untouched. He was a virgin, too, but he wasn't pure by any means. He knew how to respect and honor his wife, but he was a man with carnal desires. If he frightened her or if she looked at him in disgust, he wouldn't be able to live with himself.

"I like it when you kiss me," she said, her tone suggesting he do so now.

"Lorabeth." He glanced at the jar he held and set it aside. "It doesn't have to be tonight," he told her to assure her he had no intentions of rushing this. "If you're uncomfortable…"

"Tonight or tomorrow night or a week from now, it will still be the first time," she said logically. "And waiting might just make us more tense."

Ben removed his topcoat and hung it on the back of a straight chair, then unfastened his tie and collar. Her gaze never left his movements.

He was the husband. Just love her back, Caleb had said. Love her as Christ loved the church, her father had reminded him. He'd observed that love was the element that made all the difference.

His hesitation became perfectly clear. Crystal, sparkling clear. These feelings of protectiveness, the worry of disappointing her, the fear of shaming himself…had all arisen from the fact that he loved this woman.

Loved her beyond reason or practicality or circumstances or responsibility.

A loud clattering sounded from outside, metallic banging, shouts and whistles. Lorabeth pressed her hand to her breast. "Whatever…?"

Benjamin sighed. "The shivaree."

"The what?"

"It's a mock serenade done for newlyweds as a prank." After turning down the wick until the lamp was extinguished, he moved to the window, where he pulled the new drapes to the sides and tugged open the window. Clattering and banging accompanied an off-key rendition of "Beautiful Dreamer."

Benjamin waved at the singers. "It's the whole gang," he said. "Parker, Zeta, Hobie, Ida. Carrie and Damian are with them, too."

He closed the window and turned back. The pranksters tired of their singing quickly and moved on. "They're gone."

It had taken a few minutes for his eyes to adjust to the darkness.

Lorabeth remained where she'd been, her satin undergarments glowing white in the moonlight that streamed through the windowpanes.

Ben removed his shoes and socks, then his shirt. Stepping close to her, he ran his fingertips down the soft pale skin of her arms until he reached her wrists. He took both hands and brought the backs of her fingers to his lips.

She trembled in his touch. He wrapped his arms around her and held her against the thud of his heart, feeling her soft breasts against his chest. "*Please* don't be afraid of me."

"I'm not."

He tangled his hands in her hair and removed the combs and pins that had held honey-colored ringlets in place all day.

When he combed his fingers against her scalp, she groaned. The mere sound of her pleasure brought his body to ardent life.

He leaned forward to kiss her, learning again her exquisite taste and textures. She pressed into him and raised one palm to his bare chest.

Her touch on his skin sent a hundred signals from his nerve endings to his brain and body. She tested his flesh with the tips of her fingers. When he moved his head to change the angle of the kiss, she flattened her palm and breathed a sweet sigh against his mouth.

Ben raised a hand to cup her cheek, feathered a caress down her neck until he touched the warm pearls. He broke the kiss to lower his face to her neck.

Tilting her head aside, she accommodated his kisses under her ear, along the column of her throat. After fumbling for the clasp, Ben removed the necklace and slipped it into the pocket of his trousers.

Lorabeth raised a hand to pluck earbobs from each ear and hand them to him. He dropped them into the pocket with the necklace.

Lorabeth's skin tingled and she burned from inside. Growing warmth spread through her limbs. Each place Benjamin touched her fueled the intensity of this growing need to have more. His hands were slightly rough, a contrast she quickly learned to appreciate. His touches were gentle and inquisitive, thoroughly inflaming in a way she hadn't imagined.

Her first tentative exploration of his chest had amazed and enthralled her. His body was broad, hard-muscled, and his skin held a spicy scent that tantalized her senses until her head swam.

She delved into his hair, finding it thick and silky, liking the shape of his head, the turn of his ear, the rasp of his jaw.

"I can shave again," he said against her neck.

"No," she answered. She didn't want to interrupt what was happening between them. "Not now."

"My chin doesn't scratch?"

"No." She wanted to hold on to him. Benjamin kissed her again, and she reveled in the tender caress of his lips, the inconceivable way he made her feel special and wanted.

She remembered the night he'd touched her breast through her clothing and the way she'd wanted the touch to never end.

She stepped back slightly, and he instantly released her. "Are you all right?"

She nodded and reached for the lace on her neckline to untie the satin ribbon with a little tug. Eight tiny buttons fell under her determined fingers and she shrugged from her chemise.

She wanted to feel his bare chest against her. He stood as though rooted to the floor, not making a move to touch her. Her heart thrummed so hard, he had to have heard it. Maybe he was waiting for more...

She untied the drawstring, let her drawers slide down her hips, then stepped out of the puddle of satin. She stepped closer to discover his eyes were shut. "Are you disappointed?" she asked, hurt.

His eyes flew open. "No! You're beautiful. More beautiful than I imagined. You could never disappoint me."

He touched her breast then, a tentative caress that tested the fullness, then cupped her. With an open hand he stroked her nipple. Lorabeth felt the glorious sensation all through her body.

Her nervousness about what was to come was overridden by the thrill of this new experience. Fascination set her nerve endings ablaze. All-encompassing pleasure heightened her senses and kicked aside any hesitation or embarrassment. At last she was breaking out of her stifling mold.

She'd sat awake long nights imagining liberation, dreaming of a soul-reviving taste of life. She didn't intend to miss a minute of the experience by being timid. She'd vowed never to miss anything by holding back or being afraid of new experiences. Benjamin was fulfilling her dreams one by one and she meant to enjoy each step of the way.

She wanted to be the wife Benjamin needed. She never wanted him to regret choosing her. She had no idea what was going to happen or exactly how it would, but she knew they'd figure it out. Men and women had been doing this since the days of Adam.

She flattened her palms against his chest and raised her face for a kiss. He obliged her, skimming his hands down her sides and around to her back. He stroked the flesh of her buttocks and Lorabeth shuddered.

Ben lost himself to the sensations and textures and scents of his eager new wife. He hadn't expected her touches, though he had anticipated the feverish response of his body. He cautioned himself to go slowly, take his time, be respectful.

When she pressed against him, her soft breasts crushed to his chest, his head roared. Sensation took over reason. His head was filled with the scent of her hair and skin, his hands craved discovering all of her. His body thrummed with pent-up desire.

He urged her to the bed and they collapsed into its softness. Intuition took over and skill had nothing to do with what came next. Sheer instinct drove him. The ache of unfulfillment compelled him until fire consumed reason and caution.

Nothing existed except Lorabeth, warm and willing with no idea of the madness her explorative touches and throaty murmurs caused. He'd forgotten everything he'd promised himself.

Lorabeth gasped, the sound echoing, transforming into something piteous. The bed creaked beneath their movements, forcing his memory to recall another place, another time. Lorabeth cried his name in passion, but he heard pain and alarm.

She clung to his neck and wept, her body convulsing.

He hadn't been tender or respectful. He'd allowed lust to drive out all his good intentions. Sense returned and his world turned dark.

"Don't cry." His own voice was hoarse with self-disgust. "I'm sorry I scared you."

"I'm not scared," she told him.

He laid his cheek against hers. "Please don't cry."

"Okay, I'm sorry."

He rolled away from her, recognizing the cool sheen of sweat on his body, the harsh sound of his breathing.

"I hurt you." The knowledge tore a ragged crater in his heart. He turned to look at her, pale and beautiful in the moonlight. He peeled down the bedding and helped her underneath the covers. "I'm so sorry I hurt you, Lorabeth."

"Not so much," she said. "It's okay."

"It's not," he disagreed. "I told you I wouldn't hurt you, and I did."

She turned toward him and rested her hand along his cheek. "Only a little pain. Far more pleasure."

He wasn't listening to her assurances. Something he'd dreaded his whole life had taken over his will and his body, and he'd given himself over to it, like dry kindling touched by a match. He'd been lost to everything but the fire of wanting her.

He hated his weakness. "I'm just like those men I hated my whole life," he said aloud. "No better."

Lorabeth sat up, holding the sheet to her breasts. Her hair was gloriously tousled in the shadows. "You're nothing like those men," she insisted adamantly. "If you're like them, then you're saying I'm like your mother."

"Never," he denied, his heart pounding in slow agonizing thuds. Even breathing hurt when she spoke those words. "You're nothing like her. You're pure and innocent and perfect."

"Am I wicked then for wanting to do that with my husband?"

"No, Lorabeth."

"Then don't ever say that again. And don't think it. You're my husband, Benjamin. Husbands are supposed to take pleasure in their wives. Aren't they?"

He nodded. That was what Caleb had assured him.

"Say it," she told him. "You're a good and loving husband."

"I'm a…"

"Say it."

"I'm a good and loving husband."

"My wife loves me," she added.

She was so beautiful, it hurt to look at her. And she loved him. "You can't, Lorabeth. Still?"

"More," she told him and leaned to kiss him, caressing his cheek as she touched her lips to his.

He loved her, too. Loved her with all his heart. But the words wouldn't push past his lips. He needed to deserve her love. And he didn't.

Chapter Eighteen

Lorabeth lay awake for what seemed the entire night. The clock downstairs had only struck twice, however. She'd never slept more than a few hours a night, and usually sat up reading. She didn't want to disturb Benjamin. He was a fitful sleeper, turning his head, moving his limbs, occasionally muttering something incoherent. Right now he seemed to be sleeping peacefully, so she closed her eyes and tried to relax.

His soft, even breathing was a sound she cherished, though it was like a freight train rumbling past for all its oddity in her experience. Something magical had finally happened to her. She'd become a bride. And her husband was handsome and clever and not at all stuffy or pretentious. She adored him.

She lay on her side and studied his profile in the dim light. Her mind kept returning to the sights and sounds and sensations of their coupling earlier. Just thinking about it made her heart flutter. She'd tried to imagine, but her limited knowledge hadn't allowed her to even dream up the actuality of such an incredible act. How perfectly they were created! How clever of their Maker to plan such a wondrous thing.

Thank You, she breathed silently.

Her husband stirred beside her, rolled on his side to face her and his hand brushed her arm. She knew the moment the touch woke him. He drew away in surprise.

Lorabeth took his hand, locking her fingers through his. She loved the contact, reveled in the warmth and magnitude of his body beside hers. The wedding ring she'd bought for him was warm, and she loved the solid smooth feel of the gold on his finger.

"You're awake?" he asked, voice husky with sleep.

"Mmm-hmm."

"Was I snorin'?"

"No. Go back to sleep."

A few minutes later she could tell he'd done just that. The house was more familiar to him, the room one he'd used for some time. She would grow comfortable here, too.

She hadn't known what to say or do when he'd seemed so upset after their lovemaking. She'd assured him he hadn't hurt her. His regret tortured her. He'd seen too much during his formative years and knew only the dark side of a man's nature.

Now that she knew—really *knew* what it was his mother had done for money—she tried to better understand his concerns. He'd known that act as something shameful, not as an expression of love between two people. She would help him understand the sanctity and purity within the bonds of marriage.

Lorabeth was on the edge of sleep, somewhere between exhaustion and blessed relief, when the mattress jerked and the bedcovers were tugged away as Benjamin sat straight up in bed. "No!"

"Benjamin?"

He raised a muscled arm and swiped his hand down his face. As he became more alert, he turned to find her propped on one elbow watching him.

"What is it?" she asked.

"Just a dream. Go back to sleep."

"What was the dream about?"

He adjusted his pillow and rested back against it. "Don't remember."

"That's probably good."

"Yeah."

"Benjamin?"

"What?"

"I never shared a bed with anyone before. I think I'm going to like it."

"Not if I don't let you get any sleep."

"I'm not much of a sleeper. Did I ever mention that?"

"Don't think so."

"Well, I'm not. I do a lot of reading late at night."

"Why's that?"

"Don't know. Maybe because night is the only time I have a chance to do something just for me."

After a minute he said, "Not anymore. You can read in the day if you like."

She closed her eyes and listened to a soft patter against the roof. "It's raining. I love to hear the rain at night."

"I saved a present for you," he said.

"You did?" She was wide awake again. "Another present? You bought me a dressing table and mirror, what more could I need?"

"We arranged for you to have several days away from my sister's," he reminded her.

"She insisted."

"I'm taking a few days off, too," he told her.

She smiled in the darkness. "That will be nice."

He scratched his jaw. "We're gonna take a little trip."

Lorabeth raised up. "We are?"

"Yup."

"Where are we going?"

"How does Denver sound?"

"Colorado? All the way to Colorado? Oh, my goodness!" She would never sleep now! "On the train?"

"Yup."

"Where will we stay?"

"Plenty of hotels there. It'll be our wedding trip."

"Maybe I am asleep," she said. "But if I am I sure don't want to wake up."

"You look awake to me," he replied. "Go to sleep now. In the morning we'll shop for anything you need before we leave. Tomorrow you can pack, and the following day we'll head out."

She leaned over, rested a hand on his chest and brushed a kiss against his cheek. "Thank you."

"Sleep now," he said. And with that he rolled to his other side, adjusting the covers and finding a comfortable position.

Lorabeth settled back on her side of the bed and focused on calming herself. It wouldn't do to look haggard and tired in the morning. She needed to discipline herself to rest. Her life just kept getting better.

Lorabeth loved the train ride. They had berths in a sleeping car and spent one night crammed into bunk-style beds one above the other as the locomotive chugged and swayed and cinders hit the window glass on the curves.

They ate in the dining car, mostly sandwiches and fruit, but each meal was an experience to cherish. She visited with other passengers, and Ben taught her to play gin rummy with a deck of cards he produced from the pocket of his topcoat. She'd beaten him three hands in a row when the conductor called their stop.

Lorabeth was almost sorry to see their train adventure end, but there was still more ahead. Denver was a bustling city filled with new sights and sounds. Their hotel was modest, but clean and adequate. Lorabeth anticipated their time together after the train ride, eager to be alone and to recreate the night of their wedding.

Benjamin provided her with privacy while she dressed and bathed, but as he had the second night of their marriage, he made no move to kiss or touch her. She sat in the chair with a lamp burning low beside her and read a book of poetry he'd purchased for her. His restless sleep concerned her as from time to time he'd mumble or his body would jerk.

Once, when he groaned and sat up, she crept onto the mattress behind him and eased him back down, threading his golden hair away from his face and pressing her cheek to the back of one shoulder. She imagined reasons to explain his lack of interest: travel had been tiring; perhaps relations weren't acceptable when they were away from home; he hadn't enjoyed that night together as much as she.

The last possibility made her chest ache. In the recesses of her heart she'd known this time had been waiting for her. That Benjamin Chaney had been destined for her. She would let nothing spoil her newfound happiness.

Instead of being overly concerned with Benjamin's seeming disinterest in lovemaking, Lorabeth enjoyed herself in the stores where they shopped for clothing and accessories for the house, in the restaurants where he introduced her to new foods and especially during an evening at the theater.

He bought her gifts and asked her preferences about everything. Benjamin went out of his way to see to her daily needs and give her all the experiences she'd dreamed of. She worked to douse nagging doubts that plagued her about the lack of intimacy since their wedding night. Perhaps this was all normal. Perhaps men needed time between experiences. Perhaps there was more she should be doing.

Maybe she simply didn't know how to please him or encourage him.

Denying himself what he wanted was wearing on Ben's composure. The least little smile or touch from his new wife had him grinding his teeth in frustration. He'd thought the trip would help, that they'd be too busy and distracted for the physical issue to be a concern temporarily. But he hadn't planned on the days and nights with little separation and without the buffer of him going to work.

He admired Lorabeth's lack of inhibition and appreciated her childlike joy over every little thing. He learned she liked to get up early to see the sunrise. She didn't mind getting wet when it rained, and she preferred walking to taking cabs. The things he was growing to love about her, like spontaneity and passion, were the same things he feared in himself.

On their last night in Denver they shared dinner in a restaurant and then attended the performance of an orchestra at the opera house.

"Wouldn't Flynn have enjoyed that?" she asked, linking her arm through Ben's as they walked from their cab to the hotel door.

"You think so?"

"I do. All those violins playing in harmony was incredible." She smiled up at him. "You knew I'd enjoy that, didn't you?"

"You enjoy everything, Lorabeth."

He climbed the stairs beside her and turned the key in the door that led into their room. "I'll find a newspaper down in the lobby while you're gettin' ready for bed."

As he had every night, he departed, leaving her to enter the room alone. Polite was good, but how would they ever get comfortable with each other if he kept being so standoffish? Benjamin had entered the room and turned down the lamps each night without so much as a glance at her.

Opening the armoire, she took out yet another delicately embroidered and trimmed nightgown that she and Ellie and Sophie had painstakingly worked on for her trousseau and that Benjamin hadn't seen.

During the day he was attentive and he had showered her with gifts and concern. But at night she might not have been there for all he noticed. She washed and changed into the gown. The fabric was cool and satiny against her skin, unlike the plain cotton and woolsey she'd worn all her life.

Undressing her hair, she stacked the pins and ran her brush from scalp to ends. She hadn't worn a braid since she'd been married. Her gaze fell to the wedding band on her finger and she turned her hand, watching the light catch the gold.

The key turned in the door, and she met Benjamin before he could take more than a few steps into the room. The fabric of the gown swished around her ankles as she moved. She stopped before him. "It's our last night in Denver."

He kept his attention on her face and replied, "We'll come back another time."

"The maid brought hot water only a little while ago. It will still be warm for you."

"I washed in the bathing chamber at the end of the hall."

As he had each night. And each morning.

She stood between Benjamin and the lamp. He removed his black topcoat and hung it in the armoire. After busying himself with his tie until it came away, he removed his shirt.

With both lamps burning, she had her first opportunity to look at him. His skin was tanned and his chest broad and firm.

"When do you go without your shirt in the sun?" she asked.

"Cuttin' grass, puttin' up hay."

She took a step closer and noted raised marks on one shoulder that were lighter in color. "How did you get those scars?"

He glanced at his shoulder. "Long time ago. Doesn't matter."

"Matters to me."

He looked aside and then back at her. "Heath."

She frowned, thinking. "Wasn't that the name of the foster family that took in you and Flynn?"

"Yup."

"You don't mean by accident, either. The man whipped you?"

"I took care of myself. And then Ellie and Caleb came for us."

"What about Flynn?" she asked in horror. "He could've only been—"

"Heath didn't hurt 'im. I saw to that."

She studied the face of this proud kind man who'd endured cruel treatment yet grown into a loving and protective adult. Understanding dawned on her. "You took his beatings, too, didn't you?"

"I was older. Stronger." He moved to step around her then, but she placed her hand on his arm, preventing him from evading her.

"Any other scars?" she asked, holding his arm and moving around him. The muscle and sinew of his back was defined by the shadows, a sight so stunning it took Lorabeth's breath away. She'd seen pictures of Greek and Roman statues, but pictures of cold marble couldn't compare to Benjamin's strong male body in the flesh. Here and there a faded scar marred the perfection of his skin. She couldn't resist placing her hand on his shoulder and running her palm over the planes and across his shoulder blades.

Her blood pounded in her veins, and boldly she stepped right up behind him, wrapping both arms around his waist and pressing her lips to the center of his back. He smelled so good she wanted to cry with the pleasure. Ironed linen and spice and man.

Benjamin took her wrists in his gentle grasp and caressed the delicate insides with his thumbs.

"Benjamin," she whispered.

He turned and folded her against him. She pressed her cheek to his warm skin and he ran his hands over her back, down her sides, to her bottom and pressed her against him.

He wanted her. The certain knowledge buoyed her spirits and produced a lilting song of joy in her heart.

"I love you," she assured him. "I love the man you are. I'll love whoever you want to be."

She thought she loved him because she didn't know enough to jade her romantic notions. He covered her mouth with his, silencing her. With open mouths they tasted and explored as tension built and heat rose. Breathing became difficult. Thinking became impossible.

Benjamin raised his head and played his lips over hers in slow damp strokes, pausing at each corner to press a firm kiss, halting a hair's breadth away to taunt her with his absence.

She wrapped an arm around his neck and took the kisses she wanted. Her head swam with delight and promise. Pleasure rose and possessed.

Moments later they sprawled on the bed, bodies sliding and straining in a rhythm as natural as breathing. Stars burst behind Lorabeth's eyelids. Benjamin spoke her name and a tremor shook his body. Remarkable longed-for sensations flooded through her and she clung to him.

There was no yesterday and no tomorrow in his arms. Only this moment, this night.

He released her to sit on the edge of the bed. "Do you want to read?"

She wanted him to hold her. "No."

He got up and turned down the lamps, affording her a view she appreciated before the room went dark. Returning to the bed, he lay beside her, close enough to touch, but distancing himself in silence.

He had liked it, she knew he had. He would realize it soon. Realize how perfect they were together.

Chapter Nineteen

Lorabeth's confidence faltered in the weeks that followed. Benjamin's demeanor was decidedly cooler once they returned to Newton and settled into their daily routines.

She helped Ellie three mornings a week, and the other two mornings she still went to her father's home and did the wash and cleaned house. That left her afternoons for her own home, and often hours into the night after Benjamin had fallen asleep.

One day, after noon, she returned to the house to find him seated on the porch. The day was chilly, and it was obvious he'd been waiting for her.

"Hi," she said. "Did you come home for lunch?"

He nodded. "And to bring you somethin'. This wasn't your day at Ellie's, where were you?"

She had never revealed the fact that she was still doing her father's chores, but she couldn't lie. Her husband had asked her directly. "I was at my father's."

"Oh." He looked surprised. "I didn't know you

visited him during the week." He picked up a blanket-draped crate from beside the floor and she held the door open for him to enter first.

He set the crate down inside the foyer and removed his coat. Lorabeth did the same and hung it on the coat tree. "Benjamin."

He looked at her.

"I go to my father's two mornings a week to take care of the domestic chores."

He seemed to absorb that. "How long have you been doin' that?"

"When I only worked for Ellie during the week, I did it all on the weekend, but once I moved into the Chaney house, I used those two mornings off to tend to my other duties."

"I said you could work or not, whatever pleases you, Lorabeth, but I don't think it's right for you to continue the chores that were yours when you lived at home. Your sister doesn't do it."

"My father doesn't have a wife."

"I sympathize with that, but you have your own home now. You can't work every wakin' moment to do it all. He's the preacher and a widow. I'm thinking the church ladies could organize themselves to help."

Lorabeth knew he was right. She'd been entrenched in providing those household services alone for so long that she'd come to think of it as her duty. "You're right. In fact I'll make the arrangements myself. There's a laundry on Fifth Street. If he can't take his dirty wash and pick it up himself, one of the ladies can manage that task. I'll set up an account for him."

He nodded his pleasure at her decision.

"Now what did you bring home?"

Ben turned and removed the blanket from the top of the crate to lift out the mostly gold and black calico cat she'd dubbed Mittens.

"He's letting you hold him!"

"Yep. I worked on it ever since you met 'im."

"Think he'll let me?"

"Dunno."

"Hello, Mittens," she said to the tomcat. He'd gained weight and his fur had filled in over bare spots, though he still bore scars on his ears and nose. "Do you think we can be friends?"

Slowly, she reached to pet his head. He squirmed and meowed until Benjamin released him. Mittens stood a moment, his green eyes surveying the surroundings and coming back to blink at her in disdain. Then he moved to inspect the baseboards and the thick navy and cream carpet runner. He sat and blinked. "Meow!"

"Did you bring him home for a pet?" she asked Benjamin.

"Thought you'd like him around the house. You take over feeding and looking after him and he'll come around."

"Are you planning to spoil me for a lifetime?" she asked teasingly.

He looked away momentarily, then back, but he wasn't wearing a smile. "Just wanna see you happy."

She stepped forward to take his hand. "*You* make me happy, Benjamin."

Their eyes met and a fire flickered in the depths of

his ice-blue ones. He dropped his gaze to her lips. For a moment her heart dared to lift in anticipation of the desire she thought she sensed. His hand twitched in hers. And then he looked away, removing his hand from her touch. "Have you eaten lunch?"

He walked back toward the kitchen and she followed, fighting disappointment. "Not yet."

Mittens meowed and trailed behind them.

Benjamin took bread from the cupboard and cut four slices, then found ham she'd left in the icebox. He set the crock of butter out.

Lorabeth watched him with her heart heavy and aching. She could be a good wife if only he'd let her. He'd been holding back from her ever since their last night in Denver. Oh, he bought her presents and arranged schedules and events to make her life easier. He'd taken her to dinner at the Arcade twice. Yesterday he'd brought her another Swiss chocolate bar, and he'd been working with the cat for weeks to bring her a pet.

All the kind gestures and generosity in the world wouldn't replace what she truly wanted. What she needed. Couldn't he hear her heart crying out for him?

Please, Benjamin. She wanted him to love her. She wanted that one flesh that she'd dearly hoped was hers. Lorabeth was a butterfly that had hatched inside a jar. Every day she beat her wings against the sides where freedom was clearly visible. Benjamin held the power to free her.

The following day Lorabeth had the first conversation with her father wherein she felt like an adult in control of her own life. Taking charge was liberating. While the first snow of the season fell on Newton, she made arrangements at the laundry and with several of the women of the church who were only too glad to take turns caring for the parsonage.

She planned for another church member to spell her at the piano on Sunday mornings so she could sit with her husband every other week. In the weeks that followed, they had her father and Simon over for supper twice.

She inquired if Benjamin would like to have the Evanses over for Sunday dinner, and the afternoon went splendidly. Now that he knew his father would have had a relationship with him if he'd known of Benjamin's existence, he was obviously reevaluating beliefs about men and about himself that he'd held all his life. Lorabeth was determined to be patient and supportive.

The following morning she spent helping her sister-in-law organize Christmas dinner.

"Suzanne Evans is a very nice lady," she told Ellie. "She was quite active in politics when they lived in California."

"What did you fix for dinner?" Ellie asked.

"One of the farmers gave Benjamin a couple of turkeys," she answered. "I stuffed one and made baked yams."

"I'm sure it was nice." Ellie didn't say anything more. Madeline had begun to fuss in her cradle near the fireplace, and she swept her up. She wore an expression Lorabeth hadn't seen before.

"Knowing how Wes feels about him is helping Benjamin," Lorabeth told her.

Ellie sat in the kitchen rocking chair and opened the placket in the front of her dress for Madeline to nurse. "It's good for him," she agreed.

"It's helped his self-worth to know his father isn't the reprobate Benjamin imagined all these years," Lorabeth told her.

Ellie nodded but didn't meet Lorabeth's gaze.

Lorabeth placed a slip of paper in the recipe book to hold her spot and moved to sit on the hearth facing Ellie. "You close up whenever the subject of the Evanses comes up."

Tears came to Ellie's eyes and she looked to the side, blinking them back.

"What is it?" Lorabeth asked. "You can tell me."

"It's completely selfish and I'm probably just tired. I've been crying a lot lately. For no good reason." She looked down at Madeline and finally at Lorabeth.

"Ben and Flynn have always been like my own children," she said. "I don't know if you can understand that."

"I think I can. You took care of them."

"I don't think I'm jealous, but maybe I am. Flynn has Caleb and thinks of him as his own father. I don't think it matters a bit to Flynn that he isn't. Maybe down deep I resent the fact that Ben has a real father. And *I* don't." Her eyes revealed a measure of pain Lorabeth hadn't expected. "I feel like I'm losing him, and I know that's silly."

Lorabeth got down on her knees in front of Ellie and took her free hand. "It's not silly at all. Like you said, Benjamin is like your own child. You raised him and loved him and did everything you could to give him a good life. Then I came along and at the same time Wes showed up. I'm sure most parents feel a sense of loss when their child gets married. Your child got married and added more members to his family all at the same time."

Ellie tilted her head in acknowledgment.

"And, Ellie, I can't reassure you enough that from everything I know about Benjamin—which admittedly isn't a vast amount—that he appreciates and holds you in high esteem. I confess I didn't know how I would ever hold a candle to your sainthood in his eyes, but I've settled in with the fact that we're not vying for his affections. It's the same with you and Wes. You both love Benjamin, and he loves you both in different ways. Both good."

Ellie smiled and a little laugh burst through her tears. "Are you always so wise?"

"Heavens, no. I can be a complete dolt when facing matters of importance." She released Ellie's hand and sat back on her heels.

Ellie swiped at the last tears on her cheeks. "Like what?"

Lorabeth's face warmed with humiliation. Could she talk about this with Benjamin's sister? She would feel disloyal to her husband if she did, so she softened her concerns. "I just worry that Benjamin regards me more highly than I deserve."

"I doubt that. You're perfect for him, Lorabeth. Just like you've always been the perfect helper for me."

"Yes," she replied without feeling.

She was just perfect.

Ellie raised Madeline over her shoulder and patted her back. Instead of burping, the infant emitted a gurgling sound and all the milk she'd just consumed shot over Ellie's shoulder and the back of the rocker.

Lorabeth stood up too quickly to grab toweling. She caught her balance and helped wipe Ellie's dress and the baby.

Dr. Chaney appeared with a wrinkled shirt in his hand at that moment. "Ellie, can you— Oh."

"I'm going to go change," Ellie told him and handed him the baby. "She'll want to eat again since she just lost it all."

Caleb balanced Madeline on one arm. "I have a meeting in a hour. I need to iron this shirt."

Lorabeth took the garment from him. "You hold her a minute and I'll do it." She took the shirt and set the iron on the stove to heat. The wave of dizziness she'd experienced had passed, and she unfolded the ironing board and steadied herself against it. A moment later, bile rose in her throat and she tore out the back door to the outhouse and lost her breakfast.

Returning on shaky legs, she washed her face at the kitchen sink and patted her skin with a damp towel. "Madeline and I must have caught the same thing. Is she okay? Does she have a fever?"

He looked at Lorabeth thoughtfully. "She's perfectly fine." Dr. Chaney kissed the baby's head. "She just had an air bubble. I doubt you're sick, either."

"I just lost my breakfast. Ugh," she said at the reminder.

"How have you been feeling lately? Tired?"

"Well, kind of. But I never get a lot of sleep."

"Do smells bother you?"

She looked at him in surprise. "Now that you mention it."

"Lorabeth? Have you had your menses since you and Benjamin were married?" he asked. "Are your breasts sore or swollen?"

Shocked at his personal questions, she blushed hot and looked away, grabbing the shirt and spreading it over the ironing board. Her head swam.

"I *am* a doctor," he said kindly. "I ask those kinds of questions all the time. And I've seen those exact same symptoms each time Ellie has been expecting."

Slowly she raised her head and stared at him. *Expecting?*

A rush of delight washed over her in the seconds that followed. If God had seen His way to bless her with a baby so quickly, her marriage must be pleasing in His sight.

Her happiness dimmed as quickly as it had come. "Benjamin is hesitant to have children. Afraid he'll be a rotten father."

"That's out of the question."

"Not to him."

"I know," he answered.

"Don't say anything."

"I won't."

"Not even to Ellie. Not yet. I need some time to tell him."

"All right. Make an appointment and come for an examination."

She grabbed the handle of the iron and pressed Dr.

Chaney's shirt. She wasn't going to imagine that a baby would endear Benjamin to her. He hadn't touched her in weeks.

New fears and doubts crowded in. Every time she was around Caleb and Ellie she couldn't help but compare her marriage to theirs. Each time they exchanged a smile or Caleb rested his hand at Ellie's waist, Lorabeth's heart sank a little more.

She'd had so many hopes and dreams, and happiness didn't seem unattainable for her in-laws. Would she end up being as lonely as her mother had been?

And what would happen when a baby came along? Benjamin would never be a cold and distant father—he was open and loving with his nieces and nephews. Clearly, she was the one he held at arm's length. Something must be wrong with her.

She wanted this marriage so badly, she'd been determined to make it work. She wasn't going to give up already. She refused to settle for the life her mother had. She would not wither up and die before her time.

And she had a sweet secret, one she intended to cherish for a time.

Chapter Twenty

Benjamin bathed and changed clothes after a day in the barns. That day he'd taken the wagon to the railroad station and picked up supplies that had arrived. He tied a small crate containing something special he'd ordered for Lorabeth to the back of his saddle and rode Titus home.

He put up the ranger in the carriage house and found himself whistling as he approached the back door. The windows were steamed over, and warm moist air laden with the scent of savory beef assailed him when he entered.

She turned from the stove with a smile. "I saw you ride up."

He set the crate at the end of the table.

She glanced at it.

"It's for you," he said. "Open it."

She got an ice pick and sliced open the edge. Delving through layers of shredded newsprint and tissue, she discovered a ruby glass water pitcher and tumblers. She unwrapped the set and placed them on the table. Wild roses and gold trim decorated the sides.

"It's blown glass," he told her. "Hand painted, and that's real gold on the edges."

"It's a lovely set," she told him, but her voice didn't hold much enthusiasm. Hadn't she liked his gift? "They'll look elegant in the china closet you bought last week. Thank you."

"Can I help you with anything?"

She turned back to the stove. "No. I made a stew and biscuits. Simple fare."

"I love stew."

"We'll sit in here if that's all right. The dining room seems too big and formal for just the two of us."

"I like it in here," he agreed.

The table was already set with two place settings at one end, and he took a seat.

Lorabeth spooned rich dark beef and vegetables over split biscuits and set their plates on the table.

Ben had assumed the duty of saying a blessing before their meals because that's what Caleb had always done, and he knew Lorabeth was accustomed to her father's leading as well. He gave thanks for their health and their food and picked up his fork.

Lorabeth's plate was half as full as his, and she ate slowly. He told her about his day, and she shared hers. Her face was becomingly flushed from the heat of the kitchen, and she'd done something different with her hair, fashioning it in a knot on the back of her head.

"You look real pretty tonight."

"Thank you."

They finished eating, and he helped her do the dishes. "Want to read in the study for a while?" he asked.

"I'd like that."

He laid a fire and she settled on the settee with the book she'd been reading the night before. She was beautiful, his wife. He loved her beyond reason. He found himself watching her more than reading his book.

She noticed and set aside her story. "Since the china closet was delivered I've been thinking I'd like to paint the dining room. Perhaps wallpaper above the wainscot."

"Just pick out the colors and paper, and I'll find someone to do the work," he told her.

"Oh. All right. Ellie can help me select them. I think I'll go wash the water pitcher and glasses and put them away."

Ben got up to follow. "I'll help."

He added kindling to the fire, pumped fresh water and set the kettle on the stove. After picking up the packing material, he carried the crate out to the burn barrel at the back property line and returned.

Lorabeth had finished washing and drying the pieces and he carried the tumblers to the dining room for her.

She placed the set on display in the cabinet where only a few items graced the shelves.

"Thought the cabinet looked empty," he said.

Back in the kitchen she took the wet dish towels and hung them on a short line she'd strung behind the stove. It already held the towels from their supper dishes.

"It'll be bitter cold soon," he told her. "No reason for you to do the laundry on the back porch and hang it outside over the winter. We can take it out."

"I've been doing laundry once a week every winter for as long as I can remember," she answered. "But if

that's what you'd like…" She stared off into nothing-
ness for a moment.

Mittens meowed in his loud feline manner, drawing
their attention. He'd entered the kitchen and stood with
his curving tail swinging over his back.

Lorabeth got a white ironstone cup from the cupboard
and filled it halfway with cream from the icebox.

She knelt and placed it on the floor but remained
beside it. "Here you go, pretty boy."

The cat looked from the cup to her and blinked
haughtily.

"Come on. You like cream. It's right here."

The cat sat back on its haunches with a superior glare
for each of them.

"I'm not going anywhere," she said, her voice holding a surprising edge. "If you want this, you're going to
have to come get it."

And then she plopped down on the smooth wooden
floor he'd spent hours sanding and varnishing as though
she was going to wait out the cat's aloof resistance.

"You all right, Lorabeth?" he asked.

"I'm fine. I'm tired of him avoiding me. I'm a perfectly
nice person, and he knows it. He's just being stubborn."

"He's scared."

"Of what? Do I look frightening to you?" She turned
her gaze on him and an unanticipated fire lit those
tawny eyes.

"Other people have hurt 'im, starved 'im," he rea-
soned. "Other cats have picked on 'im. You don't know
what happened before he came here. He's not intention-
ally mistrusting."

"Well, I want him to let me close. I feed him, I change his sandbox. He needs to give me a chance. *I'm* not the one who hurt him."

"You're *mad*," he figured out at last.

"Yes."

"What's eatin' at you?"

"Nothing." But she stood and banked the fire in the stove with purposeful movements. "I'm going to bed. Join me if you wish."

And she swept past him.

Ben stared at the doorway through which she'd disappeared. Mittens stood up and padded over to the cup on the floor and lapped the cream.

"If I'd known you were gonna hurt her feelings I'd have dumped you back in that alley."

The cat looked up at him, swiped a pink tongue over its lips and went back to slurping up its treat.

Ben went after his wife. "Lorabeth, what in blazes is wrong with you?" he asked from the doorway.

She'd seated herself at her dressing table and was taking the pins from her knot of hair. "I guess I'm tired."

"Come to bed tonight instead of stayin' up reading," he told her.

"Is that what you'd like?"

He just looked at her. "I'm not tellin' you what to do, it was a suggestion."

She picked up her brush and ran it through her hair. "You could let me know what you'd like, since it obviously isn't me."

He took off his shirt and tossed it on the end of the bed. "What's that supposed to mean?"

She turned on the bench to face him. "Benjamin, do you think I'm wicked?"

His mouth opened before he spoke. "Of course not!"

She craved closeness, yearned to be the woman he wanted and needed. Her dreams seemed to be dissolving until she felt lonelier than she had in her father's house. "What's wrong with me that I can't be the woman you want?"

She got up and deliberately crossed the room to stand before him and place her palms against his bare chest.

His eyes smoldered, but he cast his glance over her shoulder.

"Have I been expecting too much?" she asked. "Is it too much to ask you to fill a place in my heart that you don't want? Have I set you up unfairly by expecting you to love me?"

Emotions crossed his face, among them panic, regret, fear. "I've tried to show you how I feel, Lorabeth. I thought you liked the things I bought for you."

She backed away to look him full in the face. "The gifts are all lovely. The dressing table, the books, the chocolate…the water glass set. Lovely. I'm not ungrateful. I'm not. But they're things. *Things!* I want you to give me your *heart!*"

Tears formed in her eyes, and the sight of her misery tore Ben's heart to shreds. He wanted to step forward and fold her into his arms. Her anger had surprised him, but her displeasure was a hundred times more effective at chipping away his defenses. Had his concern about his own doubts and fear been so selfish that he hadn't seen he was hurting *her?*

He'd been trying to be the best man he knew how. Could he fix this and still protect her?

There was a commotion out on the street, and Ben stepped to the window. Out front a carriage was stopped and an angry man was shouting. Ben unlocked and slid open the window.

"I said *move* you worthless hay-burnin' pile o' dung!" A whip cracked, and in the moonlight Ben made out a horse as it reared and tipped a carriage. "Move! H'yaw!"

This time the horse stood on its hind legs and the carriage toppled over, taking the horse down with it. The animal struggled to its feet and tried to leap forward, bound by the weight attached to the traces. The driver cracked the whip against the horse's neck and the animal screamed in fright.

"Stop that!" Ben shouted from the open window. "Stop!" He turned and ran out of the room.

"Benjamin! What's the matter?" Lorabeth followed, but he was faster and exited the front door well ahead of her, shooting along the path to the street.

Hesitantly she stood on the porch for a moment, watching in horror as a stranger whipped a horse that was tangled in the traces that held it to an overturned buggy.

"Stop, mister!" Ben shouted and the man turned toward Ben.

"Benjamin!" she shouted, running out to the curb.

Benjamin lunged toward the man. They grappled and fell to the ground with a chorus of groans. The man cursed a blue streak, and Benjamin determinedly grabbed the lash from his hands.

"That's enough!" he shouted, his outrage evident.

Being bigger and younger, he had the upper hand. Lorabeth watched him compose himself while the other man cursed and ranted from his spot on the ground. In one swift movement that caused her heart to leap, Benjamin grabbed the fellow, spun him around and tied his hands behind his back with the whip.

"I'm gonna see to the animal, and you're gonna lay right there. Got it?"

Ben spoke softly to the horse, letting it smell his hand before he tried to get close. The poor thing finally lay its head on the pavement in exhaustion.

Several of their neighbors had gathered on the street, and Ben gestured to one of the men. "Go for the marshal, will ya, Hanley?"

"Sure thing, Ben."

Two other men came and stood close enough to the stranger that he wasn't going to be getting up and fighting. "Damned piece o' meat cain't pull 'is own weight no more," he grumbled.

Benjamin looked at the horse's eyes and listened to its breathing. "This animal's sick."

Lorabeth joined him, her skirt forming a puddle around her as she knelt. "What will you do with the poor creature out here on the street like this?"

"I could try to get him into a wagon bed," he told her. "Take him out to the stables where I can treat him. He's not old and appears to be from good stock."

"I'll get my team and wagon," one of the men said from behind Lorabeth.

"I'm coming with you," Lorabeth called to him. "Let me grab clothing and lock the house." She turned.

"You don't have to…" he called, but she was dashing in through the front door.

Minutes later, dressed and carrying a bag, she watched from the curb with the other ladies as the men got the horse on its feet and into the back of the wagon.

"Can you ride back here with me, Jack?" Benjamin asked.

Determined not to be left behind, Lorabeth scrambled up to the seat beside the driver.

Once they arrived at the barns, the men assembled a ramp for the horse and led it down and inside. She went into the house, lit lanterns and made coffee, then brought each man a full cup. They drank and thanked her before leaving.

"Is there anything I can do to help you?" she asked Benjamin.

The horse was down again, and Ben was examining his head and ears. "Have you heated any water?"

"No, but I can."

"Not boiling. Just warm enough to dissolve a powder."

"All right." She hurried to the house to do his bidding and returned later with the teakettle.

Benjamin held a jar containing a white powder. He poured water into a bowl, then measured the white substance in and stirred. Finally he tested the temperature, let the liquid cool a bit, then used a huge glass dropper to dribble the medicine into the horse's mouth.

"Just look at his lips and gums," he grumbled angrily.

Lorabeth observed bleeding sores.

"I'd like to put a bit in that man's mouth and jerk him around by the reins until his temperament changes."

Benjamin's compassion for the animal touched Lorabeth. "Can you save him?"

"At this point I think it will depend on this boy's gumption to live," he replied.

Lorabeth tentatively stroked the animal's neck, and his skin quivered under her touch.

"Look at that," Ben pointed out. "He even has tender skin. A horseman should notice things like that about his own stock." Once he'd administered all the liquid from the bowl, he handed her the utensils. "If you'd wash those so I can use 'em later."

"Certainly."

He left and returned with a bottle and a clean rag. "Think you can hold his lips back while I dab this on those sores?"

"I think so."

The horse turned a cunning brown eye on her, but didn't fight their attentions.

"It's almost as though he knows you're helping him," she said.

"Horses are smart critters," he replied. "He knows I mean him no harm."

"Unlike cats," she observed.

He glanced at her, then continued with his task.

She watched him, grateful for a helping task. This was the first time she'd felt useful, the first time he'd seemed to need her for anything, and she was glad she'd insisted on accompanying him. Sometime later he covered his patient with blankets and sat back against the wall.

"You should go get some sleep," he told her.

"What about you?"

"I'll stay to make sure he rests through the night. I have more blankets and I'll bed down here."

"I can stay with you."

"No, you go be comfortable. Tomorrow I'll need to go into town to tend to my horse. You can stay with this one then."

"Okay." She gathered her skirts and stood, picking up the items he'd used. "Good night, then."

"Good night, Lorabeth."

They didn't discuss the argument they'd had. Things weren't exactly tense between them, but it was apparent that nothing had been resolved. Lorabeth visited Caleb at his office, and after an examination, he assured her that she and the baby were healthy. This should have been the time to tell her husband the news, but she hesitated in fear of his reaction.

The injured animal made a remarkable recovery in the week that followed, and Marshal Connor made the horse's owner sell it to Benjamin. The surly man left town on the train.

On Saturday night the Barlows held a holiday dance in their barn and invited the townspeople. Lorabeth had never visited one of the ranches before, so Benjamin drove her out early to show her the stables and the outbuildings. Charles and his wife were well-to-do and their home was evidence. Lorabeth helped the friendly woman carry food and drinks from the house to the enormous barn.

As the guests arrived, Lorabeth realized how full her world had grown since she'd known the Chaneys and fuller since her marriage to a respected and well-liked man with standing in Newton. Everyone welcomed and greeted her. Their acceptance delighted her.

Her in-laws arrived, and Lorabeth hugged the children and Ellie. She exchanged a look with Caleb. She wanted to tell Benjamin about the baby, but she was concerned over how to do that.

Ellie shifted Madeline on her shoulder and patted her back. "The Evanses are here."

Lorabeth turned to see Suzanne placing pies on the dessert table. "I hope she brought her raspberry pie."

"I was jealous of them, you know."

"Of the Evanses?"

Ellie nodded. "It took me a while to see that Benjamin wasn't being disloyal by getting to know his father. His feelings for me won't change. I'm truly happy for him. And for you."

Lorabeth took Ellie's hand. "I'm jealous of *you*," she confessed. "I'm jealous of your marriage to Caleb. And of course I'm jealous of you and Benjamin. His loyalty to you is unshakable. Benjamin depends on you. He...he *needs* you."

Ellie looked at her in surprise. "My brother worships the ground you walk on."

Lorabeth shook her head. "I know he cares for me. But he doesn't need me. I want to be—" preparing to speak these next words was as painful as opening a raw wound "—I want to be the air he breathes...the first thing he thinks of in the morning and the last at night...I want to be *needed*—like food or water."

"How can you not see what I see when I watch the

two of you together?" Ellie asked. "When I see the way he looks at you?"

"He doesn't…" Lorabeth's throat got tight, and her eyes filled with embarrassing tears. "This isn't the time or the place."

"Stay right there." Ellie turned and found her husband visiting with the Connors and Hollisters and handed Madeline to him. Returning to Lorabeth, she said, "Let's get our coats and go to the house for a minute of privacy. Pru won't mind if we sit in her kitchen."

Once inside, the stove gave off enough heat that they didn't need their coats, so they shed them. "Now tell me what has you so unhappy," Ellie said.

"I'm embarrassed to talk about it," Lorabeth answered hesitantly.

"Some things need to be said."

Lorabeth glanced around the room before looking at her hands and searching for the right words. "Benjamin doesn't…touch me. We've only been, you know, intimate like husband and wife twice since we were married, and that was weeks and weeks ago."

Ellie's expression was grim. Had Lorabeth revealed something too personal for a sister to know? Was Ellie shocked that Lorabeth would even care?

"Is that *normal*, Ellie? Because I don't know. If it is, then I must be a wicked person, because…" She couldn't even go on. Her face burned with shame.

Ellie took a deep breath and pulled out two wooden chairs to face each other. She gestured for Lorabeth to take one, then she sat. "Ben has no idea of what's normal and what isn't," she said. "Ben and I saw things in our childhood that no one—child or adult—should ever have seen. Children are impressionable, and what we witnessed was…well, it was sinful and disrespectful. Our mother entertained her 'clients' in the same room where we slept," she said. "I never knew whether to use the threadbare blanket for warmth or as a curtain to shield the view."

"I'm sorry, Ellie. You don't have to tell me this."

"Ben won't tell you. So I *do* have to. Ben won't tell you about something that happened to me that shaped his whole life. It's my secret to tell, so I'm going to."

Lorabeth was so intrigued that she couldn't deny her desire to possess this knowledge.

"When I was just a girl, maybe thirteen or fourteen, my mother took money to let a man have sex with me." She took a deep breath. "Ben stood outside, pounding on the carriage door trying to get in and help me."

Horror flooded Lorabeth. That this kind, generous woman had experienced such horror was inconceivable. And Benjamin had been there…and had been unable to help her. Unable to protect her.

Ellie leaned forward. "He was only eight years old, Lorabeth. Eight years old."

Tears stung Lorabeth's eyes. Her husband's concern about her well-being and his agony over the brief pain he'd caused her made perfect sense now. He'd been trying to protect her from something he knew as only bringing hurt and shame.

"He knows that what happened to me was not what takes place between a man and a wife," Ellie said. "Just like I knew it when Caleb and I were married. But he has to understand it in his heart—and experience love to truly understand."

"He has nightmares," Lorabeth said softly.

"I thought maybe he'd outgrown those."

Lorabeth shook her head.

"His helplessness ate him alive. He was angry and tortured for so long. He resented Caleb when we were first married…until he grew to understand Caleb's love for me—for all of us—and believed that Caleb meant me no harm."

"He's probably afraid of his own feelings toward me," she said perceptively. "He keeps himself held in such tight control all the time."

"You know my brother well," Ellie said.

"I thought his reluctance was because of me," she said. "Something wrong with me. I've been so selfish."

"There's nothing wrong with you. Let me tell you the rest."

"There's *more?*" Lorabeth asked.

Ellie went on. "When our mother died the boys went to a foster home."

"He told me about the Heaths."

"I got a job as a Harvey Girl, hoping to earn enough to get them back and take care of them. But I broke my arm and couldn't work. Caleb doctored me and asked me to take care of Nate. He was recently widowed. He taught me to trust. He taught me love and compassion, but it took a long time to break through. My past was a wall around my heart."

"Ellie, you're so brave and strong," she said.

"I wasn't then. But listen. One night the man who had

raped me lured away Caleb with a fake message and came to the house. He hit Benjamin, then tied him to a chair and abducted me. It was going to happen all over again."

"What happened then?"

"Somehow Benjamin got loose and came after me. There was a scuffle and…Ben got the man's gun away. He shot him."

"The man died?"

"Yes. Caleb explained to the law, and after questioning all of us, they ruled it was self-defense." Ellie's voice revealed deep emotion. "Ben risked his life for me. He saved me. But I think the fact that he was angry and scared enough to shoot a man—even protecting me—has colored his view of himself."

"I'm sure you're right."

"This was my story to tell you," Ellie said. "And now that you know, I hope you'll be able to help Ben."

"If love is what it takes, then I have plenty of that to offer."

Ellie leaned forward and hugged her.

Chapter Twenty-One

Lorabeth looked at her protector differently throughout the rest of the evening. He was the man she wanted to share the rest of her life with. He was everything she'd dreamed of and more. She'd vowed not to hold back and miss anything, and she was going to make good on that claim now.

The banjo player called ladies' choice for the upcoming dance, and Lorabeth found Benjamin and led the way through the crowd to the dance area.

Even without a word between them, awareness was as strong as ever. Halfway through the song, she said, "I'd like to go home now."

"Are you feeling poorly?"

"I feel fine. I just want to go home."

"All right." He guided her to the side of the room and left her while he found their coats, then they said their goodbyes to his family.

A light snow was falling as he drove the buggy toward town. He halted the horse near the back porch and assisted her down.

She accepted his help, knowing his need to do so. Inside she hurried up the stairs and into the bedroom where she laid kindling in the small heater and started a fire to take the chill from the air.

She had changed into a silver-blue gown by the time he came up the stairs to join her. Before he could reach the lamp, she stepped in front of him. "I'd like it if you left the lamps burning tonight."

He met her gaze assessingly, then agreed. "All right."

He untied his tie and removed his shirt. His boots and stockings came next.

Lorabeth turned her back and moved to sit on the bed. She got comfortable in the center.

"You want the wicks down low or left as they are?" he asked.

"They're fine as they are," she replied.

She could tell he was indecisive about what to do next. If he was coming to bed he'd have to remove his trousers.

"Benjamin?"

He turned his gaze on her, and his eyes shone vivid blue in the lantern light.

"I want a husband who isn't ashamed to want me."

He was careful to guard his expression, but she caught his initial wariness.

"I want to know all the secrets lovers share. Are you shocked?"

"I don't know."

"I want you to touch me the way a man touches his wife."

A muscle in his jaw worked. He held her gaze.

"And if someday you could find it in your heart to love me, I mean truly *love* me, I would be the happiest woman there ever was."

Finally he moved, kneeling on the bed and pushing her back against the pillows to lean over her. "I made a mistake," he said. "With all the presents."

"I liked them…"

"But they were a poor substitute. And I understand now. It's just…Lorabeth, you're so perfect, and I couldn't bear to hurt you or do anything to dishonor you."

"Benjamin."

"What?"

"Do you recall the tantrum I threw the other day in this very room?"

"You were angry with me. It was justified."

"Would a perfect woman lose her temper that way?"

"You were right."

"I'm not perfect, and I'm tired of trying to be perfect. I don't want to be on a pedestal where you can't touch me. I spent too many years living up to my father's standards to want to try to please another man the same way. Please don't expect perfection of me. I'm human— a flesh-and-blood woman, and I want to be treated like one. I want to feel like one. I want to make mistakes and find out the hard way. Is that so wrong?"

He leaned down to kiss her. "No," he said against her lips. "It's not wrong at all. I've been unfair to you."

She framed his face between her palms and studied the face she loved. "Don't hold back anymore," she begged him.

The flicker of pain that passed in his eyes told her it was time to lay it all out.

"I know," she told him.

He frowned. "Know what?"

"Everything. Ellie told me. She told me what happened to her. How you tried to help her when you were so young."

His face revealed surprise. Then concern.

"About what happened later when the same man came for her. And you—"

"I killed him," he finished for her. He leaned away and moved to a sitting position.

Lorabeth rose to face him. "You saved her. You risked your life for her."

"I'd do it again," he said.

"Of course you would. You would protect her at any cost. You would do the same for me. Wouldn't you?"

"What does that make me? I killed a man."

She reached to thread her fingers through his. His wedding band caught the light. "It makes you brave. And self-sacrificing."

"It scared me that I had that in me," he told her.

"You didn't shoot him out of anger, you shot him in desperation to save your sister—and yourself. You're not a killer," she told him. "You're a healer. You just did what you had to do. Now I know why you're so hard on yourself. You've set standards for yourself so high you couldn't possibly meet them. I know why you couldn't bear the thought of hurting me. I know why passion seems like a weakness to you.

"You're not responsible for the whole world, Benjamin. There was only one man who ever was, and He did the job well enough."

Ben had listened to every word with growing acceptance and incredulity. It hadn't been his place to tell about Ellie, and he would never have asked his sister to uncover these things. But she'd cared enough about him—and about Lorabeth—to reveal it all.

The amazing part now was that none of the shocking truths about his life had turned Lorabeth away. Not even his ignorance or blind stubbornness had changed her determination. She was incredible.

"I do love you, Lorabeth," he said at last. "I've loved you since we first met. I never let myself dream like you did. I've been afraid to trust. I was always afraid of bein' like the men I hated. Like the father I imagined. Since I met you—since I met Wes—I've had to change all my thinkin'. It hasn't been easy."

"You're a most determined man," she said. "I'm sure that once you've made up your mind to change, you'll do it."

He pulled her down alongside him. "And you're a determined woman."

She laid her hand on his warm skin and pressed a kiss to his chest.

He caught her hair around his wrist. "I want you, Lorabeth. In my heart I know you're willing and that lovemaking is a good thing. Sometimes my head doesn't quite catch up, so be patient with me."

He put all his feelings into the kiss he gave his delightfully impatient and impulsive wife. He was a fortunate man. In that moment he chose to trust her with his heart.

"There's something else," she said when he paused to trail kisses down her jawline to her neck.

"What is it?" he asked against her skin.

"It's about one of the gifts you gave me." She paused. "Remember that love never fails."

"I love you."

"We're going to have a baby."

His lips paused under her ear. Beneath her palm, his heart kicked into a gallop.

"When I first learned it, I knew God had blessed our marriage. All you have to do is love our children, Benjamin. Everything else will follow."

He raised his head to look at her.

"They won't be perfect," she told him. "And neither of us will be perfect parents. But we'll love them. And we'll give them all we never had and more."

"I believe you," he said, laying his palm along her cheek. He loved to look at her. Loved to touch her. He'd known there was something special about her from the moment they'd met, and now...now he understood that there was something special between them. They were good together. Meant for each other.

Trailing kisses from her lips and along her jaw, he enjoyed her quick intake of breath. He whispered words of love and promise against her ear and felt the shudder of pleasure that cascaded through her body.

"Is this all right?" he asked, slipping the gown from her shoulder and touching his lips to her silky skin.

"Definitely all right."

"What about this?"

"I love your hands on my skin like that."

"Like this?"

"Yes. And…oh…like that."

Ben kissed her with all the emotion and need he'd held back for a lifetime. Lorabeth framed his face with both hands and met every kiss with wholehearted abandon. How he loved this woman. He turned and took her hand, tenderly kissing each of her fingers, then the inside of her wrist. With slow deliberation, he worked his way up her arm, across her chest, bringing a flush to her skin. Her pulse throbbed at the base of her throat.

"No holding back, Lorabeth."

"No holding back," she agreed with a smile that told him his promises and actions pleased her.

Much later, after the fire in the stove had dwindled and the wicks in the lamps had burned low…after Ben had made Lorabeth feel like a real wife, he said to her, "I think there's just one thing you were wrong about."

She smiled sleepily. "What's that?"

"You *are* the perfect wife—for me."

* * * * *

THE ROYAL HOUSE OF NIROLI
Always passionate, always proud

The richest royal family in the world—united by blood
and passion, torn apart by deceit and desire

Nestled in the azure blue of the Mediterranean Sea, the
majestic island of Niroli has prospered for centuries. The
Fierezza men have worn the crown with passion and pride
since ancient times. But now, as the king's health declines,
and his two sons have been tragically killed, the crown is
in jeopardy.

The clock is ticking—a new heir must be found before
the king is forced to abdicate. By royal decree the interna-
tionally scattered members of the Fierezza family are
summoned to claim their destiny. But any person who
takes the throne must do so according to The Rules of the
Royal House of Niroli. Soon secrets and rivalries emerge
as the descendents of this ancient royal line vie for position
and power. Only a true Fierezza can become ruler—a
person dedicated to their country, their people…and their
eternal love!

Each month starting in July 2007,
Harlequin Presents is delighted to bring you
an exciting installment from
THE ROYAL HOUSE OF NIROLI,
in which you can follow the epic search
for the true Nirolian king.
Eight heirs, eight romances, eight fantastic stories!

Here's your chance to enjoy a sneak preview of the
first book delivered to you by royal decree…

FIVE minutes later she was standing immobile in front of the study's window, her original purpose of coming in forgotten, as she stared in shocked horror at the envelope she was holding. Waves of heat followed by icy chill surged through her body. She could hardly see the address now through her blurred vision, but the crest on its left-hand front corner stood out, its *royal* crest, followed by the address: *HRH Prince Marco of Niroli...*

She didn't hear Marco's key in the apartment door, she didn't even hear him calling out her name. Her shock was so great that nothing could penetrate it. It encased her in a kind of bubble, which only concentrated the torment of what she was suffering and branded it on her brain so that it could never be forgotten. It was only finally pierced by the sudden opening of the study door as Marco walked in.

"Welcome home, *Your Highness.* I suppose I ought to curtsy." She waited, praying that he would laugh and tell her that she had got it all wrong, that the envelope she was holding, addressing him as Prince Marco of Niroli, was some silly mistake. But like a tiny candle flame shivering vulnerably in the dark, her hope trembled fearfully. And then the look in Marco's eyes extinguished it as cruelly as a hand placed callously over a dying person's face to stem their last breath.

"Give that to me," he demanded, taking the envelope from her.

"It's too late, Marco," Emily told him brokenly. "I know the truth now…." She dug her teeth in her lower lip to try to force back her own pain.

"You had no right to go through my desk," Marco shot back at her furiously, full of loathing at being caught off-guard and forced into a position in which he was in the wrong, making him determined to find something he could accuse Emily of. "I trusted you…."

Emily could hardly believe what she was hearing. "No, you didn't trust me, Marco, and you didn't trust me because you knew that I couldn't trust you. And you knew that because you're a liar, and liars don't trust people because they know that they themselves cannot be trusted." She not only felt sick, she also felt as though she could hardly breathe. "You are Prince Marco of Niroli…. How could you not tell me who you are and still live with me as intimately as we have lived together?" she demanded brokenly.

"Stop being so ridiculously dramatic," Marco demanded fiercely. "You are making too much of the situation."

"*Too much?*" Emily almost screamed the words at him. "When were you going to tell me, Marco? Perhaps you just planned to walk away without telling me anything? After all, what do my feelings matter to you?"

"Of course they matter." Marco stopped her sharply.

"And it was in part to protect them, and you, that I decided not to inform you when my grandfather first announced that he intended to step down from the throne and hand it on to me."

"To protect me?" Emily nearly choked on her fury. "Hand on the throne? No wonder you told me when you first took me to bed that all you wanted was sex. You *knew* that was the only kind of relationship there could ever be between us! You *knew* that one day you would be Niroli's king. No doubt you are expected to marry a princess. Is she picked out for you already, your *royal* bride?"

* * * * *

Look for
THE FUTURE KING'S PREGNANT MISTRESS
by Penny Jordan in July 2007,
from Harlequin Presents,
available wherever books are sold.

HARLEQUIN®

Mediterranean
N I G H T S ™

---

*Experience the glamour and elegance of cruising the
high seas with a new 12-book series....*

MEDITERRANEAN NIGHTS

Coming in July 2007...

SCENT OF A WOMAN

by

Joanne Rock

When Danielle Chevalier is invited to an exclusive
conference aboard *Alexandra's Dream,* she knows it
will mean good things for her struggling fragrance
company. But her dreams get a setback when she
meets Adam Burns, a representative from a large
American conglomerate.

Danielle is charmed by the brusque American—
until she finds out he means to compete with her bid
for the opportunity that will save her family business!

HM38961

Silhouette®

Romantic SUSPENSE

Sparked by Danger, Fueled by Passion.

Mission: Impassioned

A brand-new miniseries begins with

My Spy

By *USA TODAY* bestselling author

Marie Ferrarella

She had to trust him with her life....
It was the most daring mission of Joshua Lazlo's
career: rescuing the prime minister of England's
daughter from a gang of cold-blooded kidnappers.
But nothing prepared the shadowy secret agent
for a fiery woman whose touch ignited something
far more dangerous.

My Spy

#1472

Available July 2007 wherever you buy books!

REQUEST YOUR FREE BOOKS!

Harlequin® Historical
Historical Romantic Adventure!

2 FREE NOVELS PLUS 2 FREE GIFTS!

YES! Please send me 2 FREE Harlequin® Historical novels and my 2 FREE gifts. After receiving them, if I don't wish to receive any more books, I can return the shipping statement marked "cancel." If I don't cancel, I will receive 6 brand-new novels every month and be billed just $4.69 per book in the U.S., or $5.24 per book in Canada, plus 25¢ shipping and handling per book and applicable taxes, if any*. That's a savings of close to 15% off the cover price! I understand that accepting the 2 free books and gifts places me under no obligation to buy anything. I can always return a shipment and cancel at any time. Even if I never buy another book from Harlequin, the two free books and gifts are mine to keep forever.

246 HDN EEWW 349 HDN EEW9

Name	(PLEASE PRINT)	
Address		Apt. #
City	State/Prov.	Zip/Postal Code

Signature (if under 18, a parent or guardian must sign)

Mail to the **Harlequin Reader Service®:**
IN U.S.A.: P.O. Box 1867, Buffalo, NY 14240-1867
IN CANADA: P.O. Box 609, Fort Erie, Ontario L2A 5X3

Not valid to current Harlequin Historical subscribers.

Want to try two free books from another line?
Call 1-800-873-8635 or visit www.morefreebooks.com.

* Terms and prices subject to change without notice. NY residents add applicable sales tax. Canadian residents will be charged applicable provincial taxes and GST. This offer is limited to one order per household. All orders subject to approval. Credit or debit balances in a customer's account(s) may be offset by any other outstanding balance owed by or to the customer. Please allow 4 to 6 weeks for delivery.

Your Privacy: Harlequin is committed to protecting your privacy. Our Privacy Policy is available online at www.eHarlequin.com or upon request from the Reader Service. From time to time we make our lists of customers available to reputable firms who may have a product or service of interest to you. If you would prefer we not share your name and address, please check here. ☐

HH07

SPECIAL EDITION™

**Look for six new
MONTANA MAVERICKS
stories, beginning in July with**

THE MAN WHO HAD EVERYTHING

by CHRISTINE RIMMER

When Grant Clifton decided to sell the
family ranch, he knew it would devastate
Stephanie Julen, the caretaker who'd always been
like a little sister to him. He wanted a new start,
but how could he tell her that she and her mother
would have to leave...especially now that he was
head over heels in love with her?

**MONTANA
MAVERICKS**

Dreaming big—and winning hearts—in Big Sky Country

COMING NEXT MONTH FROM

HARLEQUIN®
HISTORICAL

- **SEDUCTION OF AN ENGLISH BEAUTY**
  by **Miranda Jarrett**
  (Regency)
  No self-respecting Italian rakehell could ignore the lush beauty he
  spots on a hotel balcony, but no sweet English rose would succumb
  to passionate seduction…right?

- **THE STRANGER**
  by **Elizabeth Lane**
  (Western)
  Haunted by his past, he has never stopped wondering what
  happened to Laura. Will Caleb's secrets deny them a future
  together?

- **UNTAMED COWBOY**
  by **Pam Crooks**
  (Western)
  Riding the trail, Penn McClure only wants to satisfy his wild need
  for revenge—yet his heart may not escape unscathed!

- **THE ROMAN'S VIRGIN MISTRESS**
  by **Michelle Styles**
  (Roman)
  Beautiful Silvana Junia has a reputation for scandalous, outrageous
  behavior. Still, when she agrees to become Fortis's mistress, she
  has no idea of the consequences.…